DRAG KING DREAMS

Other books by Leslie Feinberg:

Stone Butch Blues

*Transgender Warriors: Making History
from Joan of Arc to Dennis Rodman*

Trans Liberation: Beyond Pink or Blue

DRAG KING DREAMS

Leslie Feinberg

CARROLL & GRAF PUBLISHERS
NEW YORK

Drag King Dreams

Carroll & Graf Publishers
An Imprint of Avalon Publishing Group, Inc.
245 West 17th Street, 11th Floor
New York, NY 10011

AVALON
publishing group incorporated

Alts vos iz eynzam, by Rokhl Korn, reprinted with the permission of Dr. Irene Kupferszmidt.
"Everything lonely has the color of my grief" in *Paper Roses, Selected Poems of Rachel Korn.*
English translation copyright 1985 by Seymour Levitan. Used by permission of the trans-
lator. "Around Lakes," by Abraham Sutzkever. *From Laughter Beneath the Forest*, KTAV Pub-
lishing House, Inc. Translated by Dr. Barnett Zumoff. Used by permission of the translator.
Blume Lempel [*Ikh heng tsvishn do un dortn*]—used by permission of Paul Lempel.

Library of Congress Cataloging-in-Publication Data is available.

ISBN-10: 0-78671-763-7
ISBN-13: 978-0-78671-763-7

9 8 7 6 5 4 3 2 1

Interior design by Maria Elias
Printed in the United States of America
Distributed by Publishers Group West

My heart brimming with love, I dedicate this to you, Minnie Bruce:

my partner on life's path,

my lover and friend,

my comrade.

"In the contradiction lies the hope."

—Bertholt Brecht

Acknowledgments

Thank you!

I'm very grateful to those who gave me feedback on all or parts of this novel, and to those who helped answer some nuts-and-bolts questions. Special thanks to Nic Billey, Deirdre Sinnott (Al Dente), Julius Dykes, Martha Grevatt, Ellis Guzman, Bev Hiestand, Dr. Josephine Ho (Center for the Study of Sexualities, National Central University, Taiwan), Michael Kramer, Chandra Talpade Mohanty, Anya Mukarji-Connolly, Milt Neidenberg, and Dean Spade (Sylvia Rivera Law Project).

I thank my literary agent, Laurie Liss, and the staff at Sterling, Lord and Literistic, for their steadfast support of me and of *Drag King Dreams*.

Thanks to my editor, Don Weise, and the whole crew at Carroll & Graf for their earnest commitment to this book, and for their labor that brought it to your hands.

My gratitude to warrior Pat Chin, who offered me enthusiastic encouragement for this novel before her death.

Heartfelt thanks to each and every reader of *Stone Butch Blues* who urged me to pen this next novel.

And Minnie Bruce, I wrote these chapters in the cold, predawn hours that you were teaching upstate and gave them to you like little gifts to unwrap when you'd return home to our tree house. I can still see you reading, curled up in the overstuffed chair in our kitchen, under the green, leafy reach of the "Dotty" plant. It was the first time I've ever watched someone reading my fiction, seeing with my own eyes what made you laugh or drew your tears. Thank you, my love.

1

"Who cares what anybody's got between their legs?" Vickie whispers in exasperation. I'm the choir she's preaching to, so I figure she doesn't really expect an answer.

My gaze is steely, fixed on the red-faced, blustering man who is pounding on the closed PATH train car doors. His confrontation with us has lasted throughout the train ride under the Hudson River into Jersey. It began as a headache. It has become a throbbing migraine.

Now Vickie and I are on the platform. The car door is closed, separating Vickie and me from the man wildly flailing to get at us, the uncaged beasts. His shouts are muffled. The rubber-rimmed plastic windows bounce with his every wallop. I can feel my own fists clench, bloodlessly tight, at my sides. My heart is pumping adrenaline.

"Quite a ride home," Vickie says. "Is it always like this at night?"

I'm immersed in the deep currents of this instant. "It's like this wherever I go." My throat tightens around the words.

The livid man tries to unzip his pants, rummaging between his legs to transform a penis into a weapon. But his zipper jams halfway and his hand is stuck. He's spitting hatred, fueled by fury. If Ruby were here she would lift up her miniskirt and waggle her bottom against the subway pane right in front of him.

I smile thinly, mockingly, and wiggle my little finger at him.

Vickie slaps my shoulder lightly, involuntarily. She is horrified. "You're gonna make him madder."

My laughter sounds shallow. "He can't get much madder than this."

The timbre of her voice drops. "Are you scared?"

I don't feel anything. I'm numb in this long wintry night. "I'm not scared of him. I'm scared of how many there are."

Vickie needs reassurance. This is not her terrain. She's an activist, not a street fighter.

"Together, we could take him." My tone is mechanical, bitter. "Besides, I don't think he really wants to get at us. If it were me and I wanted to get my hands on someone, I'd go out the door between the subway cars and be out on this platform before they could swallow their tongue."

Vickie pales. This does not reassure her.

We are watching the apoplectic man raging behind the transparent barrier of plastic. Inside the train car, late-night riders and early commuters gape at us. Across the tracks, the early rush-hour crowd gawks at the whole scene. Spectacle staring at spectacle.

"C'mon Max, let's go." Vickie tugs my coat sleeve. "We're just pissing him off more by standing here." I shake my head slowly from side to side. I won't turn my back until I'm sure the doors of the car will not reopen.

From the next car, the conductor slides a little window open and leans out before signaling "all clear" to the motorman, who in this case is a woman. The conductor sees everyone frozen, focused in one direction. He hesitates, squeezing further out the window to locate the ruckus. He tips his head toward the hollering from the next car and looks at me quizzically. He's friendly, the guy I give my newspaper to at the end of my ride most mornings. I lift my chin toward the problem and shake my head: Don't open the door. He nods ever so slightly and flashes me a weary smile. His diamond earring glints against his earlobe, a glittering star. I can see at a glance that Vickie doesn't catch any of this.

The conductor pulls himself back inside and slides the window shut. The train is slowly moving out from under the iron-beamed canopy of the Journal Square station. I smile and wave at the man who wants to kill us as he goes by, taunting him, knowing I may see him again.

My head aches as the tide of adrenaline starts to ebb. I'm tired, cranky. I've been up a long time, all night long. The only thing that feels real to me right now is the raw rock tunnel around us, a short alleyway through an urban mountain. Outcropped boulders, locked into place with bolts as big as my arm, gathered up in steel hairnets. I look out the end of the tunnel toward the glowing cobalt sky. "Almost dawn," I tell Vickie. "I've gotta get home. There'll be another train to Newark soon. I'll wait with you."

The platform across from us is crowded with those headed to New York. Their backs are to us, as they huddle and position themselves for the next train's arrival—too many people forced to compete for too few seats.

Vickie shakes her head as though she could dislodge the experience. "I couldn't go through this all the time," she sighs. "This is not the way I want to fight."

My anger flares like a match, the scent of sulfur in my nostrils. My tone is curt, resentful. "I don't have a choice."

I've struck a nerve. Vickie's eyes brim with pain, her voice cools. "It's not that simple, Max. You know that."

I chafe with irritation. "You can just go back to being Vic. I can't just change my clothes and go back to the day world and be a lawyer." I say each word carefully, like I'm teaching her. As I hear the words out loud, I'm sorry they're coming out of my mouth.

Vickie clenches her lips tight until they almost disappear. She adjusts her wig absentmindedly, by feel.

I wish the next train would hurry up and arrive. They don't run very often in these predawn hours. I lean forward on the platform and peer down the track to see if the signal lights are green. I dig my hands into the deep pockets of my pea coat, thick as a wool blanket, and stomp my boot heels on the platform to warm myself.

"You don't have to wait." Vickie's tenor is as icy as her breath. "I'm a big boy."

I make an effort to ease the tension between us. "Is Estelle gonna pick you up at the station and drive you home?"

Vickie leans forward to look for signs of a train. "No."

"No?"

She's visibly impatient. "No. I told her: Sleep in and don't worry about me. I'll be home for breakfast and get a few hours' sleep. I have to see clients all afternoon."

We stand next to each other, awkward.

"You live far from here?" she asks. Small talk.

"Nah, just a couple of blocks."

I hear the shriek of a whistle as the train to Newark roars out of the tunnel toward us. I can see a glimpse of the western Jersey sky lightening. That means to the east, across the Hudson River, the sun is inching up behind Wall Street. I'm anxious to get home before the day begins.

"Go," she suggests.

I look at my boots as I stamp them. "I'm sorry," I say. I mean it, but it sounds flat.

She nods, perfunctorily. "Go home, Max. Go to bed."

The train pulls up next to us, slowing down with a screech.

"You got your camera?" I think to ask.

She pats the big leather purse slung across her shoulder. We wave good-bye to each other, half-heartedly, as I turn away.

Relieved to be alone, I take the stairs, two at a time, up and out of the station into the frosty outdoors. The service road is still narrowed by post-9/11 barricades, its entryway watched over by a guard hunching over for warmth in the little wooden sentry station. The soldiers are gone now. No more teenagers in fatigues, automatic weapons slung over shoulders, clustered nervously around armored Humvees, ordered to search for an enemy in every face.

Now there're only the spiny-branched trees, dark silhouettes against the lavender rim of the sky. No birdsong. My every breath a cloud. My lungs ache, I cough, and my nose hairs bristle. The air itself could shatter into shards. There is safety in cold like this.

As I walk, I cast no shadow on the concrete. A pale sun begins its arc through streaks of salmon. Daylight is shortening the night. Frozen plumes of smoke and steam hover in the air—the breath of the city.

I pull the brim of my cap down low over my eyes and tug up my scarf to warm my ears. I can smell my body, my own eco-niche, reeking of other people's tobacco and stale beer. It's been a long time since I've felt the sun on my body, seen my own slender shadow trailing me—that small sliver of night I take wherever I go.

I'm on my block now, almost home. The traffic lights are still set to blink, yellow suns flashing: caution, caution.

2

"Max, wake up!" Ruby's voice roughly reaches down into the depths of my sleep and yanks me to the surface of consciousness.

I stare at the phone receiver in my hand as though it is a strange object, suddenly appearing out of my dream. "Star dust," I mumble into the phone, still half-asleep.

"What the hell are you talking about? Wake up, Max!"

I stir and try to explain, "We're all made of star dust. Really. It's true. I'm not kidding."

"Don't go all Discovery Channel on me," Ruby snaps. "Just tell me, is Vickie there with you?"

"What?" I rub my face with one hand to stimulate awareness.

"Vickie's not home yet. Is she there with you?"

I look around the sparse, dark landscape of my room. I've slept the day and evening away. The fresh candle I lit before I closed my eyes is sputtering low in a pooled bowl of liquid paraffin near my bed. I blow it out with a puff and watch wisps of smoke curl toward the ceiling.

"Max!" Ruby shouts.

I pull the phone away from my ear. "I hear you."

"Is she there?"

"No." I prop myself up on a bunched pillow. "What time is it?"

"When did you see her last?"

I try to think. "This morning. After we left the club. She took the train to Newark to catch the commuter. She was on her way home to Estelle."

"Well," the tension in Ruby's voice ratchets up, "Estelle waited up for her, but Vickie didn't come home. Estelle is worried sick. She's been calling you all afternoon, and I did too, but you didn't pick up."

"I don't remember hearing the phone ring. I'm sleeping." Maybe I am still sleeping; maybe I'm still dreaming. Slumber pulls me back gently toward its safety and I drift uncontrollably back into unconsciousness.

Ruby's tone jerks me back: "I was worried sick about you, too, sugar," she says, low and quiet. "Think, Max. Think. Did Vickie say anything about where she was going when she left you?"

This is not a dream. This is real. I concentrate. "She said she was going home to have breakfast with Estelle."

Ruby interrupts. "I've gotta get this other call; it's probably Estelle again. I'll see you at work tonight."

I don't know how long the receiver is dead in my hand before I hang it up. My stomach churns. The room is cold and dark. I sprint to the bathroom, shivering in cotton underwear, cursing the landlord as my pee steams into the toilet bowl.

Outside the trees are etched white against the evening. Snowflakes, little doilies, float past my window. The landscape has been transformed by a soft quilt of snow. I always forget how in just a matter of hours, moments sometimes, snow makes everything look so different.

* * *

The dressing room is in preperformance uproar: costume repair, ironing, makeup consultation, nervous banter. Ruby is the quiet eye of this hurricane. She sits, mascara in hand, staring into the mirror. When did she get so thin?

I come up behind her slowly, carefully, so as not to startle her, until she looks up and recognizes me in the mirror. I watch her reflection soften.

"Gimme a kiss, sugar," she commands. I brush the remaining snow off my coat, put my arms around her warmth and kiss the base of her neck, savoring the mingling fragrances: rose water, cocoa butter, Ruby. She shivers and holds my arms tight, tighter. Her whisper vibrates in my ear, "They found Vickie."

I pull away abruptly.

Ruby puts down her mascara and looks at me in the mirror. "They found her body. I don't know anything else."

My eyes connect with hers on the surface of the mercury lake. Ruby's chin trembles; she chews her lower lip. Long silence. Her breath is quick and shallow. Ruby shakes her head slowly from side to side. We have no words.

Mimi leans her head into the dressing room and barks at us all: "Time for the doors to open. Max, let's get moving."

I stand stock-still behind Ruby, facing her reflection in the mirror. "You'll tell me if you hear anything else, yes?" I ask anxiously. She nods and slowly raises a gold tube of lipstick toward her lips, but her hand doesn't complete its task as she stares into the silvery depths.

The bar outside the dressing room is a calm oasis. The doors won't officially open for another fifteen minutes. Deacon is at his piano, his fingers rushing like surf over the keyboard. He's running through everyone's musical routines, warming up. He stretches out his large, gentle hand to shake mine. His other hand continues to touch the ivories.

"How you doin', Mister Max?" Deacon's the only one in the world I'll let call me Mister. I used to chafe at it. It seemed strange coming from a man who had once confided to me, "I got a little bit a woman in me." But he grew up learning to call everyone Mister or Miz as a sign of respect. "And I just can't bring myself to call you Miz or ma'am," he explained to me.

Deacon's grip is tender but he won't let go until I give him a real answer. The room feels as though it's tilting. "I feel mad as a hatter, Deacon."

He nods, deep in thought, without missing a beat. "Well, sanity. It just might be overrated." Deacon smiles up at me wistfully. "We just got to hang on. Hang on by our fingernails." He knows about Vickie.

I check my watch: time to take my post at my battle station.

Thor is bringing up cartons of beer from the basement. He stops short when he sees me, bends over, and puts the boxes on the floor. I reach out to shake his hand, but he embraces me. "You okay, buddy?" he asks, thumping my back.

I don't know how to answer. "I'm in shock, Thor."

He nods his head and looks around the room. "I'm just a mess. Usually when something terrible happens, you know me, I'm ready to get out and organize a protest. But it's Vickie. She's so close. And we don't even know what happened. I don't know who to picket. I'm just full of grief, buddy, just like you."

Unlike Thor, I am suffocating in a quilt of guilt. I point to the stanchions standing like sentries in the corner of the bar near the front door. "I've gotta set up outside."

"Yeah, sure, buddy," he says, but he doesn't move.

Jasmine is watching us as she washes glasses behind the bar. She's new. I don't know her well enough to speak. I just wave, wordlessly, as I pass by.

I tilt the gleaming stanchions one at a time on their circular metal bases and roll them outside into place, forming a row next to the long line of people who are waiting impatiently in the snow to get into Club Chaos. I connect the metal posts with purple velvet ropes, turn up my coat collar against the freeze, dig out a pair of wool gloves, and pull them over the heels of my hands with my teeth as I survey the crowd.

I scan for early warning signs. Predators with razor blade eyes. Brooding, self-conflicted hulks who explode when alcohol and self-loathing mix. Eyes glazed with drug overflow.

Over the years too many people have walked out of this club with a stranger, gotten into a cab, a Lexus, a limousine, and disappeared from all but memory.

An image breaks the surface of the pool of my memory: Vickie standing on the PATH station platform; I see the train take her away.

I pick over the growing crowd, pointing to who may go inside to pay the price of admission. As the club fills, a cacophony of music and roaring cheers spills out each time the door opens. The performances have begun.

I spot three young people in line, nervously waiting to get into the club. Too young. I point to them and jerk my thumb like I'm hitchhiking. They look distraught, hesitate, walk toward me. "Mister, please let us in."

"Yeah, we gotta meet someone inside," one says.

"I'm sorry," I tell them. "The cops could shut us all down."

One of them sighs; the other stabs the air in front of my nose with a middle finger: "Fuck you!"

The third stands before me, distressed and visibly agitated. "Please mister, I've gotta get inside. I belong inside." It's true. Hair short and colorful. Visible flesh patterned with tattoos and piercings. A kaleidoscope of gender.

"I'm not 'mister' and I can't let you in." My tone leaves no wiggle room. "I know you belong, but there's other places you can go." I continue to talk as the young body writhes and twists in frustration. "Check out the group at The Center on Wednesday evening that Thor runs. Tell him Max sent you." The teenager nods—silent, resigned, grim—and walks away.

Vickie and I standing on the subway platform together—the man shouting at us in fury. But the train took the man away from us—I saw it happen. He saw us get off the train at Journal Square. He couldn't have known that Vickie would get on another train. Unless. Unless they ran into each other at the Newark station accidentally? I reel with culpability: Why did I goad him?

I feel a pat on my back and I wheel around, ready to hurt someone. But it's Thor. He looks harried and agitated. He points inside the club: "Max, it's Ruby. Something's wrong."

"Watch the door," I instruct him over my shoulder. I race into the bar, but it's packed so densely I can't get through. The front of the club is loud with talk and laughter and clinking glass. But in the back hall the music has died and everyone is frozen, staring at the unscripted scene on stage. Neon-color planets swirl silently, revolving around a mirrored moon.

I push my way slowly through the mass of bodies, parting the crowd with force and negotiation. As I get closer to the stage, I see Deacon kneeling over Ruby. He's got her half sitting up. By the time I'm close enough to the stage to shout, the other performers are lifting her body, arms and legs akimbo, carrying her toward the dressing room.

"No, take her toward the front door," I shout. But no one seems to hear me.

Mimi is frantically motioning to the performers left on stage to pick up the microphone. The show must go on! I despise Mimi, who values the night's revenue more than Ruby's life.

Ginger Vitus picks up the mike and forces a smile for the stunned audience. "We're Code Lavender tonight, my dears." She finds her stride. "That's right. We had to go to a higher level of security alert because Mister John Ashcroft called us personally to warn us that gender terrorists were plotting to come here tonight to subvert the binary." Thin laughter; a couple of people hoot and jeer at the mention of the Attorney General's name. Ginger motions to Deacon, who is scrambling to seat himself at the piano. Deacon plays the first chords of "Somewhere Over the Rainbow"—an anthem and a hymn.

I find Ruby lying on the dressing room floor, gasping and gulping for air. The people ministering to her move aside and let me squat beside her. I look up at the faces around us. "Give her some room. What happened to her? What happened?"

Someone in the crowd answers, "She went out onstage and she had just started to sing and then she dropped like a stone."

Ruby is gagging, invisible hands closing tight around her throat. I would give her my breath if I could. I don't know what to do. "Did somebody call an ambulance?" I cry out. "We've got to get her to the hospital right now!"

"I did," says Jasmine, as she pushes her way through to us and kneels down at Ruby's side. As she takes Ruby's wrist in her hand, I see her fingertips are resting on Ruby's pulse. "We have to hurry," Jasmine concludes.

Mimi directs her ire at Jasmine. "Who's out there watching the cash register?" Then she turns toward me, "And who's watching the door?" I see that both Thor and Deacon have abandoned their posts again, too, and are standing at the ready to help.

We all ignore Mimi. Jasmine looks around. "The ambulance crew can't get through that crowd out there. Is there a back way out of here?"

"Yes." I nod toward the door. "We could go out the back, through the side alley out to the front."

Jasmine looks at Ruby and glances over at the door, calculating distance and time. "Let's hurry."

"We need help," I shout. "Everybody out of the way. Thor, Deacon, come help."

Ruby grabs a fistful of the collar of my coat, almost pulling me over to whisper urgently, but she can't speak. "It's okay, honey," I reassure her. "Don't try to talk. It's okay."

She shakes her head with vehemence, tears of frustration in her eyes, puts her lips to my ear: "My gun!" She points toward the spot in front of the mirror where she'd been sitting. I reluctantly leave her for a moment, afraid she will die on this worn wooden floor before I can return.

I find her fabric sling bag and feel around, quickly but carefully, until I touch metal and leather. The revolver is holstered, waiting to be cinched as a leather garter back on Ruby's thigh after the show was over. I slip it into my deep side coat pocket as everyone else is turned toward Ruby.

I sidle my way back into the center of the circle around Ruby. "Everyone, get back. Let us through."

As the crowd parts, even Mimi gets out of our way. We lift Ruby until she is balancing on rubbery legs, an arm around each of our shoulders. As a group we maneuver through the hallway to the back exit, out into the narrow alleyway cluttered with tilting mountains of empty liquor boxes and garbage. I step carefully through slush, icy water seeping into my boots, my arms wrapped around Ruby.

As we carry Ruby out into the neon light of the street, people in line in front of the club recoil from us. "Where's the damn ambulance?" I shout.

I hear the siren scream.

A white St. Anthony's emergency vehicle pulls up alongside parked cars in front of the bar, its lights flashing and strobing. Its crew jumps out of the vehicle, the back doors fly open, a stretcher hits the street and pops up to waist level. They are reaching for Ruby. I'm struggling to hang onto her; they take her from my hands. I'm being separated from her.

"I'm going with," I tell the crew.

Jasmine steps up to the back doors of the ambulance, blocking my path. "I'll go," she declares. "They won't let you into the ER; you aren't a relative. Come in a couple of hours, after work."

"I want to go!" I demand.

Her expression tightens; she restates the logic coolly: "Only one of us can ride with her. I know some of the night shift. They'll let me stay with her."

I'm immobilized by fear of making a mistake. I don't know what to do. "Are you going be with her every minute?" I grasp Jasmine's shoulder. She tenses so visibly that I remove my hand quickly.

"Yes, Max." Her voice grates with urgency. "I know what to do." She climbs onto the back bumper and arms reach out to pull her inside as the driver guns the engine.

"Wait!" I yell, "She's HIV positive."

With a howl of its siren, the ambulance pulls away. Thor and Deacon and I stand helplessly in the slush, watching until it's out of sight. I'm breathless with fear. I've already lost Vickie. Have I just lost Ruby, too?

Thor puts his arm around my shoulder and pulls me tight against his body. "She'll be okay, buddy. She'll pull through this." He sounds as though he's trying to convince himself.

"She's always been a fighter," Deacon says.

"C'mon people, let's go." I hear Mimi behind us. "That's all we can do for Ruby right now. Now you've got a job to attend to, remember?"

I turn around expecting to see a crowd of people still gawking, but they've either slipped inside without paying or gone somewhere else to thaw out. I look at my watch. Another three hours before our shift ends.

"Where's Jasmine?" Mimi demands of us.

No one answers. I break the silence. "She went with Ruby to the hospital."

Mimi fumes, angrily brushing snow off her silk jacket. "She didn't ask me if she could go. She's new, she's AWOL—she's history."

Mimi spins on her heels to go back inside, but the three of us stay rooted in the snow. Thor shakes his head. "Let it go, Mimi. The rest of us are here to finish the shift."

"I can't do it," I murmur to Thor. "I can't just sit out here and pretend I'm not worried sick."

Thor changes tack. "We're all worried sick, Mimi. We can keep the bar going for a while. But a lot of people have already left the club. Scale back. Let Max leave in an hour and we'll do last call a little early."

Mimi faces the three of us, standing out on the sidewalk there in the deepening snow. She wheels around and storms back inside the club.

Deacon laughs hollowly. "That Miz Mimi's got a strange way of saying 'okay.' "

"Damn it," I curse. "How are we going to know what's going on at the hospital?

Thor thrusts his cell phone at me. "Here, take it. You be in charge of calling the hospital. Just keep us all filled in, okay, buddy?"

I hold the phone, comforted by its shape in my hand, by its function. The wind shifts and the air around us fills with snow. Thor lightly roughs up my hair with his fingertips, brushing off the snowflakes before they can melt.

I calm myself with the thought that this might all be a dream.

Walking into the foyer of St. Anthony's is stepping into another climate. Outside, the snow is squalling, dancing in the streetlamp light. The city is bedded down, quiet under a thick blanket in the dark. Inside the hospital it's hot and bright, noisy and frenzied.

Jasmine doesn't see me at first. She's listening intently to two night nurses who are waving their arms in animated gestures. Jasmine nods, slowly, and says something to each one. The one in lemon-yellow scrubs shakes Jasmine's hand. The teal-green one pats her on the shoulder.

Jasmine spots me and walks quickly toward me, hurrying me with a wave of her hand. "Let's go upstairs. She's already up in Critical Care."

"How is she?" I swallow my panic.

"Come," she answers. We squeeze into an elevator between a stretcher and three staff and ride in silence. With a "ping" the elevator doors open and Jasmine pulls me out into the hall with her. It's 4:00 AM, but the hallways of this city, its main arteries, are bright as noontime, clogged with double-parked equipment. The patient rooms, little neighborhood houses, face the thoroughfare. Each one appears dim as twilight.

Jasmine ushers me into a small staff lounge. Three nurses—pink, orange, and midnight blue—stop their eating and drinking to eye us. They consult each other wordlessly.

Orange speaks first. "Excuse me, are you visitors? You can't see a patient at this time of night. You'll have to come back in the morning."

Jasmine answers as she stares at the selections offered on the coffee and soup machine. "Judith Lieberman, from Admissions, authorized us to be here," she says. Her voice drops to an irritated murmur: "I left my purse at the club." I fumble in my jeans pockets for change and hand her quarters.

The nurses are conferring, sotto voce. Orange addresses Jasmine again. "Did you used to work here?"

Jasmine punches a button on the machine, a cup drops down at an angle. She mutters a little curse I can't translate but I understand, as drops of scalding water burble onto her hand while she tries to right the tilted cup. Her voice rises to meet the nurses. "Yes," she answers. "A long time ago."

They examine Jasmine closely, evaluating from a distance her dressiness—makeup, snug black dress, embroidered fabric shoes. I can see they judge her an outsider. Strange, she seems that way to me, too. But for a completely different reason—to me she seems like a daysider. She may be trans, but she's not queer, like we all are. To me she could change her clothes and go out into the day and just—live. That's what I thought about Vickie, I recall with an electric shock.

In my mind's eye I see Estelle, sitting like a sentry by her front window, watching the snow drift down, waiting for a life partner who will never come home. I glance at my watch. In an hour or two it will be light out and I can call Estelle.

I talk to Jasmine to hold the nurses at bay. "Deacon and Thor want you to call them as soon as you can, to tell them what's going on."

Jasmine's tone is businesslike. "I've already done that, while you were on your way over here."

I wander over to the staff bulletin board layered with postings. Skill-upgrade classes. A photo of a calico tabby with a note inked on its margin: "I need a good home!" A flyer announcing the locations of hospital union buses for a big "Stop the War Before It Begins" rally in D.C.

I walk to the large window expecting to see the city from above, from on high, but all I see is snow, illuminated here and there with flashes of red lights, glowing through the white blizzard. The nurses behind me are in an animated conversation about understaffing.

I can see Jasmine's reflection in the glass; I only want to know one thing. "Just tell me: Is Ruby gonna be okay?"

Jasmine offers a two-word response: "She's stabilized."

A chill runs down my spine. "Just tell me the truth. Tell me so I can understand."

Jasmine speaks slowly. "She has an AIDS-related pneumonia. Even without the trauma of finding out her friend was killed, she would have been overwhelmed by it eventually. She's on a respirator to help her breathe and to clear her lungs. They're pumping antibiotics and other meds into her."

"And?" I press.

"And, now she needs other tests and a doctor who can follow her and prescribe drugs to help manage the underlying condition."

The same question: "She'll be okay, right? I mean, it's her first AIDS-related infection. Lots of people get pneumonia and live, right?"

Jasmine looks at me so unwaveringly that I glance away. "There's better meds for treatment now," she replies.

"Ruby's a warrior," I say. Deacon gave me this mantra. My mind races: Where the hell is Ruby going get the money for all this? She won't be able to work, for a while at least. And where will she find a doctor who will respect her body and her life? I turn toward the door. "Where is she? I need to see her."

"Wait." Jasmine holds up her hand to stop me. "She's in room four-thirteen. If anyone tries to stop you, we have authorization. But before you go in, I need to tell you she's on a respirator."

"Yes." I shrug. "You told me."

"There's a tube in her throat." My stomach does a little somersault. "Sometimes when a patient fights the tube, in addition to sedating them they have to give them a medication that paralyzes them."

"What? It's reversible, right?"

"Yes, of course. But she'll look, well, frozen."

The room is faintly lit and quiet as a tomb. Just the rhythmic pump of mechanical breathing. I perch on the edge of the bed, feeling the coarse white sheets bunch under me. "Ruby, honey, it's me, Max. Can you hear me?"

She looks better than I thought she would, and worse. So thin and gaunt, but still so—Ruby. I kiss her forehead and lick my lips, tasting the medication in her sweat. The green graph on the monitor above our heads spikes and plummets. I stroke her wrist and hand below the IV line. "I think you can hear me. Holler if you can hear me."

Her lifeline on the monitor becomes ragged mountain ranges.

"Easy, easy." My voice drones, soft and low and constant. "You're probably saying: 'Don't go all Tupac on me.'"

My voice becomes a lifeline I throw her to hold on to. "I know this is so hard. For me, this might be the hardest day we've ever been through together in all our years. But you're a fighter, honey. You're gonna get through this. I'm in it with you. I always have been and I always will. I love you so much. Every step, we'll figure it out. We'll get through this together.

"And don't worry, we'll work out shifts—somebody will be here every minute. This will all pass. I swear it will. And then we'll rent a car and go to the beach on the Jersey shore at dawn, before anybody's there, and we'll feel the sun all warm on our bodies, and the waves will be cold as ice water and the surf will wash this all away."

I kiss her cheek again and feel warm wetness. I pull back a little, my face close to hers. Rivulets of tears are streaming down her face.

The door to the room flies open with a bang. A nurse in purple scrubs is standing, framed by light, in the doorway. "Who the blazes are you?" she demands. Her fists are planted on her hips. "How did you get in here?"

I can't remember the name that authorizes my presence. "I'm family," I say with such conviction that it is irrefutable. Purple nurse stares at me as though I'm a purple cow.

"I'm leaving," I say, hoping I haven't angered her so much that she'll take it out on Ruby.

Purple nurse strides to the monitor next to Ruby's bed and fiddles with it.

"He needs rest," she instructs. "You'll have to come back during visiting hours."

"She has got a lot of friends," I say each word slowly and firmly. But I'm off my turf. I rise slowly off the bed, bend over, and kiss Ruby's warm cheek. "I love you, honey, so much," I whisper in her ear. "I'll be back. One of us will be just a few feet away tonight until we can work out staying in your room with you. Don't worry. Just get well."

I turn to Purple nurse, trying to modulate my voice into steady calm. I want to understand Ruby's tears. I need to know if she's communicating with me. "Is she conscious that she's crying?" I ask, still putting extra spin on Ruby's pronoun.

Purple furrows her brow and touches Ruby's cheek. I notice, with relief, that her touch as a nurse is gentler and kinder than her tone with a late-night visitor. "It just means he—" she hesitates. "We'll check on this patient."

I stand and look at Ruby, a last glance, in the dim light. My fear suddenly centers on myself. What I'm thinking, but do not say out loud, is: Don't leave me here alone. Please come back to me.

"Do you have more change for the machine?" Jasmine putters around in the staff lounge. I reach into my coat pocket searching for quarters.

Jasmine looks alarmed. She moves closer to me. "Did you get rid of it?"

"What?" I ask.

She nods toward my coat pocket. "You didn't bring it with you, did you?"

I forgot I had Ruby's gun. I slip my hands deep into my coat pockets, feeling the cool metal in my right palm. I thought no one had seen me put Ruby's revolver in my pocket.

I move toward the window. Snow is falling straight down like white rain.

I turn to face Jasmine. A shiver ripples across my skin. "It was terrible to see Ruby like that. It's like she was dead."

Jasmine frowns. "But she is not."

"What do we do about everything?" I look around as though the answer crouches in a corner.

"About what?" Jasmine asks, her voice hoarse with exhaustion.

"What about the hospital bills? How much does all this cost? She doesn't have any insurance. Who has health insurance?"

Jasmine wanders over to the window near mine and looks out at the wintry storm on the other side of the pane. "I have to talk to the billing office." She glances at her watch. "And I've got to check to see who the patient advocate is here."

"We have to set up shifts to stay with her," I think out loud. "Deacon and Thor offered to take shifts. Other friends will, too. We all can take turns. But we need to work out a schedule."

Jasmine looks at me for a moment and turns back to the window. "I can stay this morning to get some things worked out."

The beginning of a plan. I suggest, "I could go home and sleep for a couple of hours and come back later to relieve you. I could pick up some of the things she'll need from her apartment. I don't have to work tonight. Will they let us stay overnight?"

Jasmine shrugs. "I don't know; I'll find out."

Outside the dawn is blooming, blossoming through the snow shower.

"I've gotta go." I exhale audibly, a rush of air. "It's morning. I've got to call Estelle." I pull Thor's cell phone out of my pocket.

Teal nurse walks into the lunchroom with a brown lunch bag in hand. "Sir, you can't use that in the hospital," she says, her voice flat with exhaustion, too. "You'll have to take it outside."

"Estelle." I speak her name out loud into the cell phone as though it is everything I mean. I'm sitting in the little vest-pocket park outside the hospital. Gotham appears to be a snow-white fairy tale, socked in by the storm. Daybreak; nothing is moving. Parked cars are almost buried, their brightly colored bodies sinking into a quicksand of whiteness.

I've scraped off part of a bench to sit on. Melting snow bleeds into my jeans. On the other end of the phone I hear her breathing in the quiet. I say her name more softly. "Estelle." Like a paragraph.

"Max," she replies. Just that.

I wait. Looking up at the sky through the vaulted branches, layered in fleece. Icy feathers falling on my nose. "Estelle. I don't know what to say. I don't have words."

"I know." Silence.

What do I say? I want to know more about Vickie's death. I want to know how Estelle is coping. But I'm afraid of sounding like television journalists thrusting their microphones into the face of grief.

"Are you alone?" I ask. "Do you want me to come over?"

Pause. "My sister's here." Her voice is level, leaden.

I wait. Chilled water leaks down my snow-covered legs.

"Max?"

"Yes?"

"Can you tell me anything?"

I don't know what I know. That moment yesterday morning feels so surreal that I don't know which wisps of memory might matter. "We were coming home from the club. Some drunk guy was hassling us on the way home. We got off at Journal Square. He stayed on the train to Newark. We waited for the next train. He couldn't have known that she was going to get on the next train. It didn't come until about, oh, I don't know. Just when the sky was getting lighter.

"I should have told somebody about the guy, I know. I'm so sorry. But I thought he was a coward. I didn't think it could have possibly been him. And he left. He was gone." I'm arguing with my own sense of guilt. Panic quickens my breath.

I hear Estelle's breath, an audible stream. She speaks haltingly, one word at a time. "It wasn't one person that did this to her. One person couldn't possibly have done what they did to her."

I forget where I am. I forget everything. I feel lost, with no mooring.
"Max."

I can't find my voice. I am the silence.

A sudden urgent need washes into her voice: "Max, how was she that
night? When you left her?"

Remorse floods me. I wanted to tell her that I was mean-spirited to
Vickie on the final morning of her life; that I didn't know it was going to be
the last time I ever saw her. I want Estelle to absolve me, but that's too selfish.

"We were flat-out tired. She was happy about the photos she'd taken
at the club. I remember she talked about coming home to you. She talked
about you with so much love, Estelle. So much love."

Estelle's voice splinters. "If I tell you something, Max, you won't tell
anyone else, ever?"

"Never."

"I've been angry at Vickie. I've actually been sitting here mad at
Vickie, hating her for taking my Vic away from me. Isn't that silly?" A dam
breaks and all her grief floods, rising waves of sobbing.

"Estelle," I say, like a poem. Like a song. "Estelle."

But she has hung up. The connection is broken.

It's daylight now, wan and gray. Nearby I hear the whine of tires spinning futilely in the snow, a whiff of burning rubber. The snow has tapered
off, and the wind gusts up from the East River.

I wonder where the birds have gone.

Ruby's chest rises and falls with a motorized wheeze. The ventilator
rhythmically pumps into her lungs what should be there, pumps out
what should not. Jasmine says that every once in a while they run a mild
electric shock though Ruby's body to tell if she's over- or undermed-
icated. It sounds like torture. And if Ruby is feeling pain or terror right
now, there's no way for her to tell us.

Thor gets up from a chair near her bed slowly, stretching, one groaning deep breath and then another. "Hey, buddy, I'm gonna go home and get some sleep. I'll call you in the morning and see how you're both doing." He pats my cheek.

I gently place the bag I've brought from her apartment on the edge of the hospital bed. Her brightly-colored cloth bag with polished wood hoop handles is bulging with things I've packed—a little bit of home away from home. I didn't know what to choose, so I scooped up toiletries, jars of pomades and creams, toothbrush and deodorant, razor and shaving gel. And I've brought her gold silk pajamas to slip into when she awakens from this pharmaceutically induced slumber. The giant stuffed parrot she keeps on her bed at home is wedged into the bag, too. I pull it out and place its plush softness near her skin.

I use my teeth to tear the tough plastic encasing a cheap portable CD player I bought yesterday on Fourteenth Street and slide batteries into its belly to bring it to life. I sort through the music I brought from her apartment and insert the *Miriam Makeba* CD. I turn the volume down very low, so as not to wake the man who's sleeping in the bed next to Ruby's, or to bring down the wrath of the evening staff. But as the sterile hospital room fills with the music of Makeba's voice, the neighboring patient peers around his curtain at the sound of the Xhosa "Clicking Song."

I take one of the washcloths I've brought to the bathroom and soak it in hot water. I come back and draw Ruby's curtain around her bed, leaving the two of us alone within the music. I snap the damp washcloth to cool it just a bit and then mold it tenderly around her face. I squirt some shaving gel on one palm and rub it between my hands until it swells into thick white foam, and then gently spread it on her cheeks and neck, her upper lip and chin.

Carefully I scrape away the shaving cream with the razor, examining her face as I do. It's so hard to see Ruby suspended in a moment of equipoise between life and death. The ventilator is weighing in on the side of life; so are the medications, and, knowing Ruby, so is every cell of her will. But her body appears lifeless, shrunken, and frail. This is the husk of my dearest friend. Only when her eyelids open after sleep will her power be revealed again.

I pat her face clean and dry with a towel and massage her cheeks with the familiar scent of her aftershave lotion.

I climb onto the bed and carefully lie down along the length of her body, lending her my warmth. "Ruby," I say softly, "I'm here with you. Please come back."

3

The PATH train is rumbling and lurching, fording the Hudson River from below its waters. I'm headed home from the hospital. Morning rush is almost over.

The person sitting across from me on the train has opened the newspaper like a screen. "Weapons of Mass Destruction!" the headline blares.

The door between the cars slides open and the friendly conductor steps in. It's been a couple of weeks since I saw him—the morning I lost Vickie. The train slows. He nods to me with a smile, inserts his key in its little hole in the control panel, and announces: "Grove Street station. Next stop Journal Square."

He sits down wearily on the seat across from me. "How you doin'?" He leans back and crosses his legs.

"Remember that night you saw me last?" I begin. "When there was a commotion on the train. Somebody was hassling me and my friend?"

He purses his lips and nods slowly.

"My friend never got home that night."

"Say what?" He leans forward.

"Killed."

His breath whistles low, like a far-off train. He knits his brow, "You think that guy did it?"

I shrug. "I don't know. It looked like more than one person. We'll probably never know for sure."

"You tell the police about that guy?"

I hesitate and then speak carefully, not knowing how he will react. "No. I try real hard to stay away from the cops, you know?" I don't say that I don't think the cops care about Vickie's life. I don't say that I wonder if it was cops who did it.

I look him in the eye. He understands.

I add, carefully, "But if any of these facts are important, I'd be grateful if somehow the information got to wherever it should go." I close my eyes and conjure up the man's image, seeing him raging to get at us. As I watch him in my mind's eye I describe him out loud: height, build, color of eyes and hair. "A bald spot here," I place my palm on my head like a yarmulke. I open my eyes, abruptly ending the séance.

The conductor mulls over the information, registering each fact with a short nod of his head.

"That's all I know," I conclude. "The way I see it, if the information is important, it doesn't matter where it comes from. And besides, this guy is trouble any way you spell it, so he's somebody you might want to keep an eye out for."

He looks at me so intently that my face heats up. I'm used to people staring, but not to being seen. Abruptly he stands. The train's whistle shrieks as the car speeds out of the tunnel. Muted gray light replaces bright fluorescent illumination. Rain beats on the windows and drums the metal around us.

We pull into the rock overhang of the station. The conductor repeats his ritual: insert key, slide open window, lean out, twist key.

I wait. He's still looking out the window. I step out of the car onto the platform. We face each other. He gives the visor of his cap a gentle tug. "Go home now," he says. "Get some rest."

The platform is crowded and everyone on it is soaked, umbrellas and coats shiny wet. The escalator is broken, again. And so is the elevator. Able-bodied human traffic fills the stairways. I make my way upstream like an intrepid salmon.

Outside, the city is enveloped in fog rising from melting snow and ice. I turn my collar up against the driving rain, but as soon as I step out from under the umbrella of the PATH station I am sopping wet, water running in rivulets down my body, soaking my underwear.

The streets are awash. Huge chunks of snow break off from curbside glaciers, floating past me like ice floes in the swollen rivers of the gutters. Puddles pool, some as big as lakes across the entire street; the wind brushes their surface, aging the skin of the water.

As I turn the corner and look toward my apartment, I stop in my tracks. I don't want to go home yet. Every morning I hurry home in the dark to that haven and try to get to sleep before the light comes up. But now it's morning, it's daytime, and I don't want to be inside, alone, isolated. I don't want this day to be the same. I don't want to just go home and go to sleep. I want to go somewhere. I want to do something different. But I don't know what.

When I was a child, I pored over photographs and maps in my geography book, excitedly telling my aunt Raisa how when I grew up I was going to row the length of the Amazon River, scale the heights of Mount Kilimanjaro. Now my little path leads from work to home. When did my world shrink so small?

I don't have a driver's license or passport, a credit card or bank account. I've never flown on an airplane; I've only looked up to see the clouds. I've never walked through a forest. The closest I've come to woods are the trees in Central Park. I've never seen the wildness of the ocean, just the little basin of beach at Coney Island.

"Never as a tourist," Aunt Raisa used to advise.

I argue with her now. "How else can I see the world?"

She is standing next to me on this windswept corner now, shaking her head.

My voice rises in childish frustration. "I'm always a tourist, wherever I go. Even in my own neighborhood. I'm always on the outside looking in. There's nowhere I can go that I belong."

I don't even know if I'm brave enough now to travel. If I were suddenly released from the house arrest that the world has sentenced me to, would I be too fearful to strike out in new directions?

I stand at the intersection of five corners, looking westward toward my apartment building—the well-worn path. Where would I go if I didn't go home? Right this moment? I can't make a decision; can't make my feet move. "I'm afraid," I whisper out loud. *"Ikh bin dershrokn."*

Raisa's voice warms me. "Akh, mayne leyb." Leyb—*I am still a lion in her eyes.* "What are you afraid of?"

"I'm afraid to be seen in the daylight, mume, *a stranger in a strange land."*

"Tayere, my dear." The music of her voice. "The people who do the work of the world every day, the world belongs to you all. Take it!"

I shake my head. *"I can't find my place. I'm so different. I've always been so different."*

"I'll tell you a secret, leybele," *she smoothes my hair. "Everyone is different."*

Raisa melts away like the snow, leaving me.

The people who pass by are bent over against the wind, running after airborne umbrellas or covering their heads with plastic bags or soggy newspapers, unaware of my presence. It feels like an opening, a doorway: this morning I could walk wherever I choose, an unseen visitor welcomed by invisibility.

I remember one night last fall, I rounded a corner near here and felt as though I'd stepped into another land—as close to the Ganges as I may ever be. The memory directs my feet northeast, in the opposite direction from my home.

I was so sick that night that I left work early. When I got off the train, it was after 11:00 PM—the back of the station was closed. When I came out the front, I saw police cars blocking the street entrance to the neighborhood nicknamed Little India. The whole neighborhood seemed to glow with unearthly light. As I drew a little closer to see what was happening, I heard music.

Thousands of people were dancing in the street in a huge half-mile circle, smaller circles spinning off within. Giant red tinsel stars with shimmering golden tails adorned the lampposts. Huge flood lights illuminated the streets, bright as daytime.

The crowd undulated to the metric of music: voices, sitar, and drums electrically amplified. I remember arms—twenty thousand moving in symmetrical sweeps, like the wings of birds, wheeling and turning in unison. The short dance sticks in their hands clicked together, flashing bursts of color in the surreal white light, as the drumbeat quickened.

I worked my way into the dense crowd that lined the sidewalks to watch and stayed half the night, until I got so cold and coughed so hard that I had to thread my way down the street into a restaurant crowded with families eating and watching the celebration.

"What is this?" I asked the man who brought me a menu I could not read.

"Navratri," he told me. "Nine days."

"Does this happen every year?"

"*First time here in America. In Gujarat it is very, very old.*" *He pointed to an altar in the street.* "*Shakti.*"

"*Shakti?*"

"*Goddess.*"

As I looked out the window, I noticed, with a jolt, swastikas. Different realm, I calmed myself, different meaning. Sacred red swastikas. Ancient symbols woven into garlands of yellow marigolds hanging in half circles from the eaves of the restaurant.

"*Tea?*" *I asked.*

"*Masala?*" *He replied.*

"*I'm sorry?*"

"*Spice tea?*"

"*Yes, please.*"

I nibbled on anise seeds until the tea arrived—sweet and milky, the bouquet of cardamom and cloves in its steam. I stood outside again, holding the cardboard cup of tea in my hands until it was as cold as I was, watching the dancers.

The music electrified my sinews and muscles. I wanted so much to step into this circle, to become part of it, but this was not my dance.

I watched women dancing differently than men; some old women dancing differently than some young; people in various forms of dress, moving their hands in distinct patterns. I saw a few onlookers raise their eyebrows discreetly whenever the same group of young men whirled past us in their own small circle, spinning in relation to each other with their own synchronized hand motions.

How would I dance, if this was my music?

And then I noticed one person who did not dance like the women or the men. She looked Roma, wearing a full colorful skirt and embroidered vest, her scarf billowing in the air above her as she whirled in distinct patterns of motion. Later, as I looked at those observing the dance from across the street,

I saw another person, dressed in a flowing sari not unlike those worn by women standing nearby, who I would have guessed was born male-bodied.

I wanted to create a path across the street to talk to both of them, but what would I say? In what language? What made me feel connected to them? Because I don't fit in my neighborhood? Because I assume they don't fit in theirs? Does that make us the same? Even similar? There's so much I don't know. Are they sacred in their culture, while I am profane in mine? I stood there on the curb, hands dug deep in empty pockets, no words on my lips, thinking: Once, long ago, we were all honored. Perhaps now what we share is the almost forgotten memory of ancient songs.

That night, when the music ended, the crowd began to dissolve and they both were gone. The street was growing deserted. It was 2:00 AM. Refrains of music still reverberated in my body, but I was alone, wide awake, wondering where to go except to home, and to sleep.

Now, as I turn the corner from Kennedy Avenue into Little India, I'm relaxing in the rain—I'm already as wet as I can possibly get. But I sink into disappointment. The street is deserted. It is past ten on Monday morning, but the stores and restaurants are shuttered.

Where the sidewalks are not shoveled yet, I walk in the street, looking at whatever I can see in store windows. Posters advertising Bollywood action flicks and romances. Ropes and hoops of gold, flowing colorful silk saris. Foods I've never tasted, described in an alphabet I can't read.

In the middle of the block, a man is bent over, hard at work. I can hear him hacking and chipping at the ice with the edge of his shovel. I walk onto the clean sidewalk and stop in front of a shop that is closed, but not shuttered, touching the glass with gloved fingertips. I peer into the store. It seems to sell everything under the sun, every nook and cranny filled. The front window is filled with divine statues, some large, some tiny. Most are of an elephant deity, seated or dancing, hewn from metal or from stone.

"That is Lord Ganesha." The man behind me has stopped chopping at the ice to see what I am looking at. "He is the lord of categories."

I wonder if it is a coincidence or with consciousness that this man has decided to explain this particular deity to me—I, who have so angered the earthly lords of categories.

"Categories are a problem for me," I say, enigmatic but not unfriendly. I look back inside at the pot-bellied Ganesha, ears big as palm leaves. On most of the statues his trunk coils to his right; a few curl to his left.

"Everything that can be counted or understood is a category," the man continues, as though we have been talking together for a long time. He leans on his shovel. His knit cap and down coat are soaked. "Lord Ganesha is very popular. He is the destroyer of all obstacles."

"Ah," I nod my head in understanding, "no wonder he is so popular."

The man takes off his watch cap and mops the rain water running down his face. "Unless of course you need an obstacle," he adds. "Then he places one in your path."

I smile at him. He smiles back at me.

"Thank you for explaining this to me."

He looks me in the eye, "I can see that you are on a journey." He pulls his cap back on his head and bends over to resume his task.

I walk the rest of the way back to Kennedy Boulevard in the middle of the street, stopping occasionally to let a car pass by.

On the other side of the street, the scent of incense wafts from the open Pakistani-Indian grocery. Fruits and vegetables spill out in stalls under an awning that sags from the weight of rainwater. Music plays from a tinny speaker. I stop to touch the bundles of tiny, tinted roses—pale greens, lavenders—antiqued by the cold.

A journey: Until he said it, I didn't think of my life that way. More as a struggle, one step at a time, to get past all the obstacles in my way. But then, maybe that's what journeys are.

I look around at the street I'm walking down. Here is my trip around the world. Casa Dante's restaurant. Irish soda bread in a bakery window. St. John's cleaners. China Buffet. Philippine parcel service—balikbayan boxes delivered door to door across an ocean.

Store after store guarantees safe delivery of my neighbors, their messages, or their money back to the people they grew up with. International phone cards, the promise of a loved one's voice in exchange for pennies.

As I pass a jewelry store, I see a young woman carefully placing a tray of glittering white gems on display in the window, next to a little yellowed card that boasts, "Our diamonds come direct from mines in Africa."

"Never as a tourist," Raisa warned. I see the sparkling stones glisten with the sweat of miners, rinsed in their blood.

The rain is gelatinous now, falling like slush in my hair. My teeth are chattering. I head toward home, past the courthouse and the twenty-four-hour bail bond agencies sprouted like mushrooms around it. Past teenagers of all nationalities crowded on sidewalks, milling in the rainstorm, joking and smoking, putting off going into the nearby high school until the last possible moment. Nearby, storeowners stand watch at their front doors, eyeing the teenagers circumspectly.

I am on my block now, my feet numb and raw. I am in my front hall, shaking off the sleet. I don't bother to check my mailbox, stuffed with junk mail. No one sends me letters.

Still quaking with cold, I climb the stairs. As I head up the stairway past each landing, I hear children's voices squealing with laughter; music from the Caribbean, the Middle East; I smell fresh ground coffee and the acrid aroma of the first morning joint lit by the woman who cares for her elderly father.

One more flight up on tired legs and I am on my floor now. My hand trembles as I fit the key into the lock; with a turn of the tumbler, I am home.

Light shines through my windows as the sun burns off the mist. I rub my scalp and orient myself. No work tonight. Day off. I have no idea what else to do with myself. I pick up the phone next to my bed and dial Ruby's hospital room. Deacon answers, fatigue deepening his baritone.

"How is she?"

He pauses. "She's just the same. You try to get some sleep now."

I can't sleep. Not yet. Outside, the city is bustling. Cars whiz by on the ribbon of highway that leads to the Holland Tunnel. Trucks and cars vie for turns on the streets below me; a fire truck wails nearby. Jackhammers tear up a sidewalk down the block.

I walk into the kitchen, but I'm too tired to eat. I wander into my little computer room, wall-to-wall with books and stacks of paper. I'm too sleepy to think.

I wander back into my living room. It looks unfamiliar in the day-time. My punching bag hangs from the ceiling in the center of the room. I hold the canvas body bag, patched with strips of duct tape, between the palms of my hands, but I don't want to hit anything or anyone right now.

I see my inner life projected onto the walls of my living room: odds and ends of Yiddish poetry, inked on the ivory-colored plaster. I need to add something for Vickie.

I find a sable-hair brush and squirt ink into a chipped porcelain coffee mug. Carefully, I kneel on the floor beside the wall and paint the plaster canvas: *Farvorlozte betler, farshtoysene printsn, fargesener shmeykhl, farshpetikt geveyn*—"Lost beggars, outcast princes, forgotten smiles, unwept tears"—

The phone rings in my bedroom, interrupting my work. I let the machine pick up the call. A computerized voice urges me to negotiate a second mortgage on my home.

I ink each character carefully: "who will bow and invite you in, all of you, when I'm gone?"

I stare at the tips of my fingers, streaked with the color of night.

4

"Fight!" Thor tells me breathlessly. "Hurry up, Max."

For a split second I'm frozen, like an ice sculpture of a bouncer, outside the front door of Club Chaos. The rims of my ears are aflame with cold; my fingers and toes are numb. It's a relief to be summoned inside.

The outer bar is virtually empty. But it's not hard to see where the fight has erupted at the far end of the dance floor. The magnet of confrontation has drawn onlookers like a ring of metal filings.

In the center, Goliath is holding David by the neck, slowly squeezing the life out of his body. The big man is beefy, broad, bulging under a vast expanse of plaid flannel shirt. He's been coming here for years—shows up regularly and then disappears for a spell. He rarely speaks, is quietly polite when he does. But now the gentle giant is wringing someone's neck with one hand and desperately reaching for something in his victim's grasp with another.

The red-faced person who is strangled in his grip is nattily under-dressed. I never saw him here before tonight. Earlier he had offered me a sawbuck to avoid standing in line outside the club. I had waved the dead president's face out of mine. Now the man's tassel-loafered feet are almost lifted off the ground.

I semicircle around the two to see what the dying man is struggling to keep an arm's distance away. It's a Canon camera, digital, expensive. A cell phone, its clam shell snapped in two, lies at his feet.

Now I get the picture.

Gingerly, tentatively, I place my hand on the flanneled shoulder. There's no reaction to my touch, no recoil. "I think I understand what happened," I murmur quietly near his ear. "I know how to fix this," I whisper. "Let me try. If it doesn't work out, you can do what you want to him."

Flannel glances in my direction, not meeting my eyes. I feel his shoulder soften perceptively under my palm.

"But if you kill him," I add, "everyone will find out you were here."

The big guy slowly opens his clenched hand until his quarry drops and gasps, massaging his throat with one hand and clasping the camera in the other. I reach down and yank away the camera. Canon is visibly outraged, but his voice has not returned and he still lacks the strength to lunge.

I turn the camera over, slide open a little panel on the bottom and pop out the memory card. I reach out my hand toward the circle of onlookers. "Somebody, give me a lighter." No response. I snap my fingers with urgency. "A cigarette lighter, c'mon, somebody," and hold up my open palm.

A lime-green Bic lighter appears in my hand.

Canon finds his voice: "What the fuck are you doing? Give me that!"

I drape the camera strap around my neck. I hold the memory card above the lighter's flame until the plastic that encases it slickens and melts and then drop the diskette into a whiskey glass half filled with ice. Memory pops, sizzles, and dies.

The giant is gentle again. He drops his gaze in the direction of my boots and nods—once, twice.

Canon stumbles to his feet. "You had no right," he begins to build hoarse momentum. "Give me back my camera!"

I take it from around my neck and hold it as far from him as I can, as though it's a baseball that I'm about to pitch. His face, which had almost regained its normal color, reddens again. "I'm calling the police on you," he gestures at the big guy, "and you," he points to me.

Mimi enters the circle to intervene. The warning look I flash her holds her at bay. This is what she pays me to do. I pick up one of the broken pieces of his cell phone and hand it to Canon: "Go ahead, call them." He bats it away.

My tone is quiet, full of menace. "You have no idea where you are," I advise him. "You broke our rule when you brought this camera in. You have no idea what we do to people who break the rules and bring trouble down on all of us. So you want to call the cops? Tell 'em you were here? Risk letting your job find out? Your wife?" I point to his wedding ring. "Or do you want to walk out of here with your little camera?"

Canon stares icily at me as he reaches for his camera. I pull it out of his reach for a moment, meeting his glare with a mirthless smile before handing it to him.

The moment Canon retreats and takes his leave, the circle around us begins to lose its shape and dissolve. Deacon drops some coins in the jukebox and continues to punch buttons even after the Staple Singers offer to take us to a place where nobody's crying, nobody's worried, nobody's lying to the races.

Thor pats me on the back. Mimi makes a beeline for me. "Get that big guy out of here, right now."

I wave her away with a tired hand. "Let him be, Mimi. For now just let everything be." She perseveres: "I called Netaji and told him to drive this guy home. And I'm telling you right now, I don't ever want to see that guy back in here again, do you hear me?"

I look at the big guy, sitting hunched over in a chair at a corner table, and shake my head slowly. "He won't come back. Not after this."

"Well, just make sure he doesn't." Mimi insists on having the last word before she stomps away.

The big guy stumbles to his feet. I go over and steady him with one hand. "You okay?" I ask.

He turns to me and begins to speak, his mouth twisting into something almost like a smile. As he opens his mouth, I suddenly realize it's not words that are going to come out. I try to dodge the gush of vomit, but I'm right in the line of fire and it's too late. The thick goo coats the front of my sweater, dripping onto my boots.

He bends over and heaves, again and again, as the pool of his shame widens at my feet. I've got him by the belt so that he doesn't fall. Thor tries to give me a hand, but he's slipping on the vomit. I pull the guy backward until he's sitting on the floor, and I calm him with my voice until I see that his body is no longer convulsing.

Mimi is shouting, but I can't hear what she's saying. I'm murmuring to the giant. Earlier, I reminded him that if he was arrested, everyone would know he had been here. Now I'm quietly administering the antidote to the poison. "You don't have to feel ashamed," I whisper, again and again. "There's just no words yet for what you're looking for here, that's all. But that doesn't make it bad."

Over the man's shoulder, I see Netaji. "Hello, my darling," Netaji says to me. "Oh my, our friend here has had a very bad night."

Netaji, who is bigger than I am and smaller than this guy, gives me a hand helping the big man lumber to his feet. "Come on, my darling," he says to the man. "Let's get you to your home."

I point to the guy's back pocket. "He has a wallet that may have his address in it. In case he passes out."

Jasmine hands Netaji two twenty-dollar bills and me a bar towel. I lightly mop the front of my sweater with the towel. Netaji hands one of the bills back to Jasmine. "Much too much. Thank you," he says.

Mimi explodes. "Please don't tell me that money is from the cash register."

"Okay," Jasmine replies.

Netaji and I walk on either side of the guy who is leaving this club, and all he comes here to find, for the last time. We steady his wobble, guiding him toward Netaji's livery cab parked in front. Netaji opens the door for him. But the guy turns to me, takes my hand in his two large hands and shakes it, nodding with downcast eyes, before getting in.

"How are you doing, Netaji?" I lean against his cab—a respite.

"I am very well," he smiles.

"Are the cops hassling you much?"

He maintains his smile. "Always. That is the life of the driver."

"How's it going with your passengers? Are they hassling you?"

Netaji leans inside the open window of his cab and pulls out a Mets baseball cap. He tugs it down low, till the brim is just above his eyes. I watch the fluid grace of his body solidify. "Hello, boss," he says in a new voice. He lifts the brim and winks at me.

"So they don't hassle you much?"

He shrugs and waves good-bye: "Mostly the Yankee fans."

As his cab pulls away, I'm left standing on the curb alone in the cold, the acrid smell of someone else's humiliation freezing on my sweater and boots. The bar is emptying out quickly. Show's over.

Back inside, Club Chaos is the opposite of its name—the calm after the storm. Onstage, Ginger Vitus is belting out a drunken rendition of "I Will Survive." Deacon is humoring her with a halfhearted accompaniment.

Mimi is complaining because someone stuck a couple of bright green antiwar stickers on the walls around the club, and according to her, somebody's got to scrape them off. "Max!" she barks.

"Not my job," I preempt her order.

I don't know how Mimi could notice something new on these dirty plaster walls, except that the neon-green disrupts the color-coded scheme. Thousands of *tshotshkes* hang from the walls and ceilings—little trucks and stuffed unicorns, hammers and spatulas, GI Joes and Barbies—all of them spray-painted powder blue or bright pink. I've worked here for so many years that the air, sour with vomit and alcohol, tobacco and sweat, smells almost comfortingly familiar. I pass right through the bar area, into the stairwell. By feel, I descend into the dank, chilly basement, where the air is not fouled by stale pleasure. My hand knows just where to reach up for the chain as I switch on the single lightbulb overhead.

I dust off the backpack I keep hanging on a nail in the concrete wall and rummage around for a clean T-shirt and deodorant. Carefully, I peel off the soggy, stinking sweater and T-shirt I'm wearing in one smooth motion. I turn on the faucet in the old sink. Its porcelain is almost worn away, revealing its geological layers. The faucet sputters with rusty water before a clean, cold stream flows. I splash my face and upper body with the icy water, shuddering with cold and with relief at feeling clean.

I pull off my boots and rinse off the splatters of vomit.

As I roll on deodorant and pull on the fresh T-shirt, I can feel how tense I am, how clenched. There's no time to get to the all-night gym to work out and get home before it's light. But I can work out down here. Everyone upstairs knows not to bother me when I'm in the basement.

I brush the cobwebs off the rolled-up yoga mat leaning against the wall and carefully unfurl it under an old pipe that runs across a corner of the room. I take off my socks and steady myself on the rubbery surface, bringing consciousness to my breathing until I feel anxiety evaporate like dew. Breathing slowly, I stop living in my brain and sink back down into the rest of my body.

I feel discomfort in my lower back, a nagging reminder of a violent tangle between soused bar patrons last week that I couldn't unravel with words.

Breath takes me lower, to a place where my own words—"You have nothing to be ashamed of"—struggle to be heard.

As if in a dream state, my hands reach for the pipe overhead. With a little leap, I grasp it. Tension floods out of me as my body hangs, elevated, gravity calling me back. I pull my weight upward, until my chin rests above the bar, and let myself descend. I travel this same circumscribed path, over and over. My back responds to the urging, warming up to its centrality in this motion. With closed eyelids, I leave the earth again and again, only to return.

I pull, once more, my arms trembling with effort to pull my weight upward, when a creak on the stairs shatters the moment. I drop to the floor, the soles of my bare feet recognizing the mat.

Jasmine descends, apologetic. "Mimi wants to see you. She wants to pay you and close up."

I have no idea how long I've been working out. My T-shirt is damp under the armpits, soggy down to my navel. Clean sweat. I feel awkward, standing in bare feet, half dressed and sodden. "I'll be up in a minute," I answer, annoyance rasping in my voice.

But she doesn't walk away, she comes closer. "Can I ask you something?"

"What?"

"Tonight," she asks hesitantly, "the fight. What would you have done if talking to him hadn't worked?"

I turn, a small involuntary smile on my lips. I feel myself showing off—a weakness. I thrust my arm forward into the space in front of her body, my fingers transformed into talons.

With lightning speed she blocks my arm's motion. For an instant we are locked, facing each other, connected at the wrist—claw to wingtip, eagle to crane. Jasmine fights to keep a little smile from curling her lips, a mirror to my moment of conceit.

Our weapons drop to our sides, becoming hands and arms again.

"I'll be up in a minute," I tell her.

Jasmine retreats back up the stairs. As I quickly dress, I turn off the overhead light with a jingle of the chain and climb the stairs. I am rehearsing what I'm going to say to Mimi.

The bar upstairs is like an empty movie set between scenes. The front door is closed and locked, the lights are off in the backstage area, the front bar dim. Jasmine is washing the last few glasses in slow motion.

Thor is sitting at the bar with Deacon, talking, laughing quietly. I sit down on a barstool near them, sapped by the shift.

"You want something?" Jasmine nods her head toward the bottles of booze, lined up in front of the mirrored wall like a legion of foot soldiers.

"A cup of black coffee, please." I point toward the coffee pot, boiled down on the hot plate to just a cup or two. Without a word, she sets up a white porcelain mug in front of me on the bar and pours the coffee.

"Thank you," I say, real gratitude in my voice.

Her voice sounds weary, too. "You want a shot of something in that?"

I cover the top of the cup with my hand. "No, thanks."

Mimi interrupts us by handing me a little wad of green paper money, folded in half. "What took you so long down there?" she asks. "I've got to get to the bank."

"Wait." I stop her before she can turn to walk away. "What about Ruby?"

Mimi raises one eyebrow. "What about her?"

"Are you gonna pay her anything while she's out?"

"I can't afford to pay people for not working." She tries to close the subject and walk away.

Jasmine, Deacon, Thor, and I all turn toward Mimi.

"She's worked for you for years," I argue. "You pay us cash off the books. So we can't get disability. We don't have health insurance. What the hell are we supposed to do when we're sick?"

Mimi sighs like a parent talking to a child. "You don't have to pay any taxes. So I would hope you all take advantage of being paid in cash to save a little for a rainy day. That's up to you, not me."

"You could pay her something while she's out of work. She's earned it!" As my voice begins to rise with frustration and fury, I can almost feel Deacon counsel me to bring it down just one notch. So I do. "Mimi, she's worked here a long time. She brings in a lot of business for you. She deserves disability pay. She's earned it ten times over."

Mimi shakes her head. "No can do. Receipts at the door are down. In fact, if Ruby wasn't out now, I might have to cut everyone's pay."

"Yeah," I scoff. "And when receipts are up do you give us a raise?" I don't bother to wait for a response. I swing around on my barstool and sip my coffee. The mug trembles in the face of my anger.

Mimi will not allow this public discussion to end on my note. "Max, I want to talk to you right now." I can see in the mirror behind the bar that she's beckoning toward the dance floor area.

Jasmine is furiously polishing a glass that is already sparkling.

"Take it easy, buddy," Thor advises.

Deacon pats me on the shoulder. "Max knows what to do."

Mimi is waiting for me on the shadowy dance floor. She hisses like a snake. "Don't you ever talk to me that way again in front of my employees, do you hear me, Rabinowitz?"

I don't speak—that's my answer.

She tries a different tack. "If it was up to me, I'd pay Ruby a little something for being out. But I'm not the owner. It's not up to me."

I shift my approach. "Then give me more hours so I can pitch in for her. I'm only working three nights a week."

She shakes her head. "I've got a bouncer on the other shifts. You've got the weekend shift, that's the big money maker."

"But I don't make tips as a bouncer. I don't make any more money if the club is empty or full. You said you might add another bartender at some point. So put me on the bar."

Out of the corner of my eye I can see that Deacon, Jasmine, and Thor have drifted as close as they dare to the dim dance floor to listen more closely.

"Give me a couple of shifts as a bartender to earn extra money."

Mimi's chortle sears my skin. "You? On the bar? Oh, Max, honey, that's never gonna happen."

"Why not?" I bellow.

"Sweetie, you're too mean. You're not a people person. You don't play well with others. That's what makes you a good bouncer. I hired you to be a pit bull. That's what you're good at."

Even in the poor light I can see her smile, cruelly, as she points toward the stage: "Now, if you want to get up there and sing and dance and take your clothes off, that would draw a crowd. I'd pay you for that."

Her words are a knee to my groin. I don't want her to see the pain of her blow, so I turn my back on her and walk away. Deacon and Thor and Jasmine amble back toward the bar. Jasmine pours the last splash of hot coffee into my mug. I sit down at the bar in defeat.

Jasmine reaches behind the back of the cash register for her purse and pulls out her wallet. She eyes the money in her hands carefully, then lays some $20 bills on the bar. "We can make our own disability fund," she says. "For now. Until we can figure out something else."

Deacon nods. He pulls a brightly colored cloth wallet from his front pocket. Dipping into it with thumb and index finger, he pulls out his money and puts it in the pile. Thor digs into his back pocket, pulls out a worn black leather wallet, and adds more to the kitty. I pull out the thin wad of cash in my pocket. Like the others, I quickly calculate how little I could live on this week and kick in the rest.

"That's a good start," Jasmine proclaims. "I'm on my way to the hospital to sit with Ruby. It's my shift. I'll work out a budget with her. We can figure out what she'll need till she's back on her feet."

Part of me is appreciative that Jasmine is taking over so many areas of responsibility with Ruby, and part of me resents it.

Deacon thumps the bar. "That's a mighty good plan," he says with finality. He stands up to leave. "I'd better get some sleep. I've got the pleasure of the afternoon shift with Miz Ruby." He leans over and whispers, close to my cheek, "Don't fret about what Mimi said before, Max. She doesn't know you. She's never seen your heart."

"Thanks, Deacon," I murmur. And then more loudly, "Any of you want to go for a quick breakfast before it gets light?"

Deacon waves goodbye.

Jasmine shakes her head.

Thor pulls a handful of bright green antiwar stickers out of his pocket. "Sorry, buddy. I've got work to do."

5

"Get me the hell out of here!" Ruby's voice rasps in her throat. It's bedlam in the hospital room.

Ruby is flailing at the tubes taped to her arms, trying to get out of bed, but she's weak. Deacon is trying to tuck the sheets around her to keep her in bed, but his soothing words are like gasoline on a crackling fire.

"Get out of my damn way. They're gonna kill me in here if I stay. Get the hell off me." Ruby rails against Deacon's gentle touch.

The male patient in the bed across from hers is staring; his visitors peer—timid, but electrified—at the unfolding scene. Magenta nurse is throwing her hands up in the air, announcing to the other patients and their visitors, "There's nothing we can do for him if he's going to act this way." And to make things worse, she adds to Ruby, "Sir, you can't leave until your doctor says you can."

Well, that does it. I shout at Magenta, but it's Ruby's voice that fills the room. "You better hope you can run faster than me!" Ruby tries again to get up and Magenta takes a step backward.

Ruby looks me in the eye. "Get me out of here. Now!"

I lift my palms like I'm serving breakfast on a tray. "Could somebody please tell me what's going on?"

Ruby still has me nailed in her glare. "Max, I'm only gonna say this one more time: Get me out of here. Right now."

I acquiesce. It's her decision.

Ruby is pulling on the tube that runs like an external artery near her breastbone. "Wait," I urge her. There's a box of alcohol wipes on the table next to Ruby's bed. I gently peel at the tape holding down the plastic catheter. Magenta nurse goes wild. "Sir, you cannot do that!"

I stand back. "Then you do it!" I raise my voice.

Ruby's voice drowns mine out. "The hell she will! That woman is not coming near me, do you hear me? She is gonna keep her damn hands off me."

I put my two cents in: "And stop calling her 'sir,' " I shout at her. "Or we'll start calling you 'mister.' " I continue working, tugging the tape with one hand, holding down the tube with the other.

Magenta nurse announces, "I'm going to get Security."

"You go right ahead, sugar. I'm gonna sue y'all," Ruby shouts. "And where was that damn Security when I needed them to protect me from you?" The door closes behind Magenta.

I admonish Ruby for writhing in rage while I'm trying to deal with removing the tube. "Hold still."

The door reopens and Azure nurse leans in. She sees what I'm doing and raises a hand: "Stop," she says, "let me do that."

"No!" I reply firmly.

"It's okay," Ruby tells me. "She's okay."

Azure nurse moves to my side. "It's all right," she says gently. "I'll do this." I yield to her, but I don't move away.

The nurse murmurs to Ruby, "Are you sure you want to do this?"

Ruby looks up at her, coughing a little, but calm. "If they were all like you, sugar, I'd stay right where I am. But I'd rather die at home than let some of these haters be the death of me here. You know what they did to me?"

Azure nurse chews her lip and nods. She slides out the tube and applies pressure with gauze. She squeezes Ruby's hand tightly. "I'm so sorry," she says. Ruby pats her hand. Azure unpeels a Band-Aid.

Now the door flies open again. This time it's Magenta nurse, who commands the armed rent-a-cop at her side: "Get them all out of here." The other visitors cling to the male patient in the nearby bed.

The battle lines are drawn. Azure nurse draws closer to us all. Magenta swings her arm as though the gesture alone could cast Azure off balance and aside. But no one moves.

Magenta points to the bed as though Ruby is not in it. "He is not your patient. You shouldn't even be in here."

Azure nurse is trembling but her voice is strong. "I'll take this up with you when the Chief Steward gets back on the floor. In the meantime, this patient has requested to go home and she's asked for my help."

Magenta steps forward with the security guard, her face reddening, her storm gathering. But in a countergesture, Azure nurse's arm arcs toward the door. Her voice is quavering, but her message is not: "You are out of line and you are not needed here. Now go and take Security with you." Not waiting for a response, Azure nurse draws the curtain around Ruby's bed. Magenta storms out the door, the security guard stumbling to catch up with her.

"Make sure no one comes in here," Azure commands me, and I obey.

Ruby's already wearing the gold pajama bottoms. Now that Ruby's unhooked from the catheter, Azure helps her slip off the hospital gown and put on the tops of her pajamas. The spangled outfit in which she arrived at the hospital seems to have disappeared. I would have brought something nice for Ruby to go home in, but who knew today would be the day?

The door opens again—this time it is Jasmine, who comes in with a knowing nod.

Jasmine and Azure put their heads together: a handful of prescriptions from the doctor in charge to get Ruby through until she can find another doctor; a promise to gather eyewitness accounts of abuse for the union steward.

The door half opens. It's Deacon, fumbling with the doorknob; he found a wheelchair and he's trying to get it through the doorway. Ruby is already stumbling to her feet. Azure and Jasmine help Ruby into the wheelchair. I stand as bouncer at the door. A small clique of nurses cluster near their station in the hallway, Magenta in the middle. Others nearby whisper to each other and shake their heads—for good reasons or for ill.

I step out of the doorway to let the wheelchair pass. We are mobile now. Magenta urges Beige nurse to step forward with a clipboard. "You have to sign this release before you leave," she says timorously.

Ruby waves it aside imperiously. "The hell I do!" and motions for her wheeled coach to proceed toward the elevator.

Jasmine grabs my shoulder as we walk. "Let's regroup for a minute. I'll get the prescriptions filled and come by the house. I'd like to take Ruby down to Chinatown to see my doctor. It'll help her breathing. But let's get Ruby home so she can rest. I'll talk to my doctor and see what she thinks is the best way to proceed. She'll know the best clinic. Can you get Ruby home?"

Ruby waves her arms to get my attention. "Are you with me here, Max?"

"Yeah." I pat her shoulder. "I'm here."

"Because." Ruby coughs. "You sure as hell were not here when I needed you."

As those angry words register, pain sizzles like electricity through my body. Deacon bows his head slightly; Jasmine looks in the opposite direction. Ruby stares straight ahead at the brushed steel of the closed elevator doors.

When the elevator arrives, it's half filled with a patient on a gurney, an attendant, two nurses, and a couple of visitor families. Deacon wheels Ruby inside and we all squeeze in around her wheelchair. I'm watching as the floor numbers above the door illuminate as we descend, trying to hold back hot tears. Someone strokes my arm, once, lightly—Deacon or Jasmine, I don't know which; I don't look at anyone.

That wasn't fair, what Ruby said. I'm furious. I can't be there every minute.

We go out through the reception area, past the giant crucifix on the wall. Deacon looks outside the glass wall as though he can see into our future. "We will not have an easy time getting a cab out there."

Jasmine stares at the cell phone in her hand as though it were going to ring with the answer.

Deacon points to the phone: "You could call Netaji. He may still be driving now. He'll come."

Jasmine hands him the phone. Deacon turns it over in his hands, opens it up slowly, punches in the numbers. He turns away from us, phone clamped to one ear, index finger damming up the other. Ruby is slumping in the wheelchair. This whole process is taking so long.

I know Jasmine is trying to say something to me silently with her eyes, but I won't look at her. I'm just trying to hold myself together until I can get off by myself, calm down, and lick my wound.

Deacon snaps the clamshell shut with a nod of confidence, "Netaji's at Forty-third and First. He'll be along soon." Deacon hands the phone back to Jasmine and takes over at the helm of Ruby's wheelchair. We all head outside, rolling toward the curb of the busy avenue.

A cold March wind slices through our clothing the moment we step

outdoors. I unbutton my pea coat to cover up Ruby, but Jasmine opens
up a folded blanket and tucks it in around Ruby's body.

"If we could catch a cab," I suggest, "maybe we should take it and call
Netaji to let him know." No one answers me.

Cabs with illuminated "available" lights pass us, one after another, like
we're not there. I walk a couple of paces ahead and hail a cab. The driver
pulls over. I hold him there with a gesture and wave to Deacon and Ruby.
The driver looks back in the rear view mirror and accelerates away. He
pulls up twenty feet ahead to pick up a young white woman and her elderly mother. I run toward the cab, cursing.

I turn around and see Deacon helping Ruby into Netaji's cab. Netaji
gets out of the driver's seat and kisses each of us on the cheek. "Hello my
darlings," he says. "Don't worry about a thing. I will get Ruby home safely.
Come on, everyone get into my chariot."

Ruby is settled in the backseat, and Deacon climbs in beside her. Jasmine kisses Netaji good-bye and tells me, "I'm going to get the meds. Are
you going to be all right?"

"Yeah, sure," I reply, my voice sticky with bitterness.

She tugs on my coat. "Try not to take it personally."

"Sure." My smile twists wryly.

Jasmine leans forward, kisses my cheek lightly, and walks away. The
wind blows cold on my face, chilling the wetness her lips have left behind.
The city is covered by a bright blue bowl patterned with fish-scale tufts of
cloud—a mackerel sky.

Ruby is back. I've missed her so. And I forgot, in the short time she
was away, how thorny love is.

Ruby staggers around her apartment, touching everything with a light
brush of her fingertips, as though she's seeing each object for the first time.

It took a lot of exertion for her to get up the stairs to the top floor. I thought Deacon and I could kind of carry her upstairs with her arms around our shoulders and our arms around her waist. But the tenement stairwell was too narrow. She had to sit down on the steps and go up, butt first, one at a time. She's still panting and coughing, but she doesn't want to lie down. Deacon and I are in the kitchen, worried, each keeping half an eye on her.

Deacon points to the photo gallery on Ruby's refrigerator door—magnetized memories. "When was this taken, Mister Max?" he asks.

I squint at the photo: Ruby and I standing in front of a banner at a protest. Each of us has one arm raised in a clenched fist and the other arm around each other. "Mmm." I examine the photo for clues. "It was around '73. Right after the Wounded Knee takeover, I think."

Deacon nods slowly, "Uh-huh. You two been friends a long time." He studies the photo. I know what he's trying to do, but he can't fix it.

Still nursing resentment, I call in to Ruby, "Deacon will stay here with you today." I know I'm sulking, saying I'm leaving now when Ruby's just gotten home, but I really do want to get out of here and be alone, too.

Ruby answers from far off in her own feelings, "No, you stay."

Deacon chuckles, his hands fingering folded Nigerian print fabric on Ruby's kitchen table—a project interrupted. An old *McCall's* magazine lies atop the folds of cloth: Designs by Bayyinah. Deacon leafs through the magazine. "She'd look so fine in this," he holds up a photo, but I'm looking at Ruby, who is staring at the little carved onyx giraffe I gave her for her birthday many years ago.

Deacon nudges me. "You think she'd like it if I sewed this for her?"

My shoulders shrug involuntarily. "Ask her. She hates to sew, anyway."

Deacon goes back to poring over the magazine. "This is something I could do for her." He scoops up the material and the magazine and hurries excitedly toward Ruby. She holds his arm as he whispers in her ear. She smiles, nodding emphatically. He kisses her face. Ruby leans her forehead briefly against his shoulder. Deacon clutches the fabric closer with one hand, waves to me with the other, and departs.

Now Ruby and I are alone. I sit, stiff as a board, on a kitchen chair. I can see her sink heavily onto her yielding couch.

"You mad at me?" she asks quietly.

"Yeah," I say, but there's less steam in my tone than I expected.

Ruby doesn't make a sound. She asks, gently, "Would you bring me a glass of water, sugar?"

A bit dour, I let the water run cold before I fill the glass and then take it to her.

She reaches for the glass and looks at me, her eyes filling with tears, but all she says is, "Thanks." She drinks a couple of sips and puts the glass down on the floor near her feet.

Slowly, wearily, Ruby digs around in the big cloth bag stuffed hurriedly with all that was hers in that hospital room. She pulls out the CD with the Nina Simone mix, gesturing for me to play it on her stereo. I pop it in and that earthy voice floods the room with pain and pleasure. "Wild as the Wind," Simone's contralto takes each note any possible way it could go.

So Ruby and I sit like that, our own silence accompanied by music. And then the next cut comes on—"Mississippi Goddamn!"—and I understand what Ruby's trying to tell me.

"You want to talk about it? About what happened at the hospital?" I inquire gently.

She makes a face and turns toward the wavelengths of the song. "I should've known they wanted me dead when they marched into my room with those torches and pitchforks."

"What?" I sit bolt upright, until I see her laugh, and now we're both laughing. All the while, the pounding rage of the music is saying everything.

I sigh, "We never should have put Ginger on a shift. She's got a beautiful heart, but she's not sober enough to deal with crises."

"Well," Ruby exclaims, "the girl's a mess. But she does have a fine heart." Ruby pats the space on the couch closest to her. I move a couple of inches closer, but she puts her arm around me and pulls me against her body. I'm wishing I could say how angry I am in life as beautifully and as powerfully as Nina Simone.

Ruby catches my neck in the crook of her elbow and pulls my face against hers. Her cheeks are warm and damp. The antiseptic scent of the hospital still lingers on her skin.

"I'm sorry," she says. "That was mean."

"I'm sorry, too," I reply, as my own eyes brim with unexpressed regrets and fears. "I wish I could've been there when you needed me."

A little laugh begins in her throat but becomes a rattling cough. "I know it wasn't your fault. Sometimes whatever happens waits till the people who can deal with it leave."

We sit together, surrounded by the music. My mind travels, against my conscious will, to the past we share. "Ruby, you remember when you shot that guy in the foot?" It wasn't funny, but I chuckle at the memory now.

"Oh Lord, yes." Ruby leans her head back against the couch. Her voice softens against a hard memory. "That boy was killin' you."

"I was doing alright until I tripped over the leg of one of his friends." I sound a little defensive. "The next thing I knew he was banging my head on the boardwalk. There were those big nails sticking up. I knew there was one by my head. He was trying to bring my head right down on it."

I recall with a shudder what one of those nails did to Ruby's thigh. Ruby sees me looking at her thigh and she covers that old wound with her hand. "Oh yes, I remember," she says. "He was gonna kill you."

"They all wanted to kill us."

Ruby purses her lips. "They all wanted to mess with us. But he wanted to kill us. He was the lead dog. The others ran with their tails between their damn legs when I pulled out my gun. But the one on you, he just stared at my gun. If I hadn't of shot him, he wouldn't of stopped."

I squeeze her hand. "Thank you."

"You're welcome. Where's my gun now?"

"Don't worry, I stuck it in the tool box under your sink."

She pats my thigh.

I laugh. "That guy's probably selling used cars now, telling everyone he's limping 'cause of an old war wound."

Ruby swats my thigh. "I've told you, take my other gun and keep it with you. There's too many fools out there. They got no right to take your life."

I shake my head. "I'm afraid I'd pull it out every time someone gets in my face."

Ruby sighs, "No you wouldn't. You're too smart. You got discipline."

"I'm not saying I won't take you up on it. Just not now." I feel all riled up inside, thinking about that old fight at Coney Island, thinking about those onlookers who cheered as we went down.

Ruby looks agitated, too. "Are you staying here with me, tonight?"

"Sure," I nod, slapping the couch. "Jasmine will be by soon with your medicine. And we'll all go with you to Jasmine's doctor tomorrow morning. Netaji's going to drive us there and wait and bring us all back."

Ruby covers her face with her hands. "I'm tired."

I sigh. "I know."

"I've always been able to take care of myself. Always."

"You're still taking care of yourself," I whisper. "Everybody just needs a little help when they're sick."

She tugs with her teeth at the plastic hospital ID bracelet still around her wrist, but it doesn't tear. I bring back a pair of scissors from the kitchen and snip it off. She rubs her wrist as if freed from a handcuff. "I hate all this," she tells me. But I already know that. Her voice rises, more like an accusation than a question: "What if it was you!"

I lean my head back against the couch. "I'd hate it, just like you."

She lays her head against the couch and turns her face toward mine. "Remember the promise we made in that jail cell?"

I smile wanly. "We made that promise more than once. But I realized today that all we can do is help each other get through hard times. We can't stop the hard times from happening. At least I can't."

The sound of new chords of music are the harbinger that Simone is about to sing "Strange Fruit." When I was young, I couldn't hear this song without curling up like a bug on the floor in anguish, my fists pressed against my face.

"Listen, tayere," *Raisa whispers in my ear. "Don't be afraid of the truth. Be afraid of the lies."*

I look up, expecting to see Raisa. But it's Vickie, sitting in Ruby's over-stuffed chair under the poster of Josephine Baker. I'm not surprised. Vickie lifts her camera and snaps a photo of Ruby and me, sitting here on the couch listening to truth.

Simone's voice runs through my body like a river of grief.

Ruby looks around the living room and says, out of the blue, "We outlived our life expectancy as drag people, you and me."

I think maybe she sees Vickie, too.

Ruby leans in the corner of the elevator, letting the metal walls help hold her up. Deacon and Jasmine are on either side of her. As the elevator door opens, a powerful aroma of herbs seems to lift us all.

A sign directs us down the hall to Dr. Wang's office. "Take your time, no hurry," Jasmine and Deacon urge Ruby. It's such exertion for her, I don't know if she hears them. Slowly, slowly, we make our way down the narrow corridors until we get to a door with a hand-lettered sign in Chinese and English: "Herbal medicine."

Inside, an old woman stands straight as a sentry behind a counter. She's in front of an oak wall of drawers, each labeled with hand-lettered ideographs. It looks like a Dewey decimal system for herbs, to me. Jasmine nods to the woman, who in response extends her hand toward a row of wooden chairs lined up against the wall. I assume she is Dr. Wang, but she resumes her stance as sentinel.

There are people ahead of us in the row of chairs. Two older Chinese men who glance at us and go back to their conversation. A young Black woman concentrating on a magazine. A Latino man rocking a sweaty child on his lap. A middle-aged white woman who catches my eye and smiles at me eagerly.

I look at the items in the glass case in front of us. Small bulbs of ginseng resembling little nongendered people with arms and legs and heads are propped up against bright red and orange boxes of elixirs. Pills bottled in amber or green glass. Dried sea horses. Packaged snake skin.

At the other end of the waiting area, rose-colored fabric is strung up as a curtain. A younger woman comes out from behind it with a sheet of paper that she hands to the older woman behind the counter.

The younger woman notices Jasmine, saying: *Nín hǎo ma.* As I watch her take in everything about Ruby in a single glance, I think: this is Dr. Wang. I want Dr. Wang to save Ruby. I stayed up most of the morning online, cruising the information superhighway to find everything I could about Chinese medicinal herbs and acupuncture.

Dr. Wang assesses the line of people waiting to see her. She looks at Ruby and Jasmine and lifts her arm toward the rose curtain. "Please," she says. "Come in."

Ruby struggles to her feet. Dr. Wang widens her frame of vision to include me. "All of you, please, come in."

Dr. Wang disappears behind the fabric. Those who have been waiting in line to see the doctor drop their eyes discreetly as we pass, only stealing glances.

Behind the curtain is more office space, just big enough for a desk and a wooden chair. A photo of a white crane on the wall behind the doctor. A silver bowl on the windowsill, heaped with a little pyramid of slightly shriveled oranges. A calendar on the wall, crimson red and bright with golden fish and shiny coins.

Jasmine sits next to Ruby on a wooden chair. Deacon and I stand behind them both. Dr. Wang nods to Ruby with a small smile, taking the large-boned wrist in her hand. Ruby sits up as straight as she can, looking very nervous and very proud. Dr. Wang holds Ruby's gaze as her fingers find what they are looking for in the weary wrist—the waves of life slapping the shores as they rush through the body. The doctor's fingertips are moving, barely perceptibly, pressing in a kind of rhythm—the cadence of pulses in relation to each other—as though she is recalling the memory of playing a flute. Does she hear the melody of Ruby's life?

What does the doctor listen for, and what does she see? Fire crackling in the iris? Wind whistling along the bones like the keening of a train along iron rails? Water pooling in the lungs? Groaning wood? Earth still cultivatable?

With the other hand the doctor writes in a notebook. Dr. Wang is inking characters with her pen from north to south, like delicate icicles or bits of hanging moss. Under each bit of writing, Dr. Wang inks a number—a value? Quantity? Potency?

Ruby looks up at Dr. Wang from time to time, shyly, smiles and looks down at the edge of the desk again.

The doctor twists to reach up for an old, battered cherrywood box—very long and narrow—on the shelf behind her. She pulls a stethoscope and blood pressure cuff out of it. I am startled by my own assumption that whatever was in the box would be extraordinary, and strange to me.

Dr. Wang smiles at Ruby—a bigger smile this time. I'm waiting for good news, but there is no news at all. The doctor makes rows and rows of characters on another piece of paper and hands it to Jasmine. They speak a few words to each other in the melody of their own language and nod.

Dr. Wang presses Ruby's hands in hers and nods vigorously. Ruby smiles uncertainly, looking from the doctor's face to Jasmine's for answers.

Dr. Wang says simply, "This will help you, for breathing, for strength, for energy."

Jasmine tells us that with Dr. Wang's help, Ruby has an appointment later in the week at an AIDS clinic. I'm hopeful.

Deacon goes downstairs to call Netaji to pick us all up. Jasmine, Ruby, and I go to the waiting area to sit.

Dr. Wang ushers the parent with a child to come behind the curtain— a social pact of privacy.

The older woman behind the counter examines Dr. Wang's written instructions, setting about her task. She is the pharmacist of flowers and leaves, bark and root. Now I see—behind and under every chair—the whole office is filled with bags bulging with twigs and buds, the harvest of spring fields and autumn woodlands. The pharmacist remembers where each drawer is with a precise turn and reach. With a handful or a pour or a pinch, she places all the ingredients on a square of butcher paper.

Jasmine sits on one side of Ruby, their hands entwined. I sit on the other side of Ruby. She nudges me. "When's the last time you saw a doctor?"

"You mean a stealth visit to the ER?"

"No, like a checkup."

I shake my head. "I don't know, when I was a kid, I guess. You?" I throw the question back to her.

She mulls it over and shakes her head. "A long time. Then I went to one clinic just one damn time and I found out I had got the virus." Ruby looks around the room and nudges me again. "You think this is gonna help?"

"Sure," I say, a little quickly. "This is thousands of years of knowledge."

Ruby slaps at me with a weary hand, "Don't go all infomercial on me now."

Jasmine, who hadn't appeared to be listening, leans forward and smiles—just a little one—in my direction. It's the first time she's ever smiled at me.

6

"You heard about Club Pi?" Jasmine hunches forward on the bar, chewing on her lower lip.

Thor leans back on his barstool and shakes his head. I'm watching an old butch at the end of the bar droop slowly forward into her beer mug.

"It's a new club. They're going to have some drag shows. Club Pi is going to draw business away from Club Chaos." Jasmine is fretting. "I'm afraid Mimi won't hire Ruby back." Now Jasmine has my complete attention. "I know the new manager at Club Pi. He used to manage The Grapevine years ago."

"The Grapevine," I laugh wryly. "Now there's a blast from the past."

"Yes," Jasmine addresses the memory with a faded smile.

My eyebrows knit in concentration, "I don't remember ever seeing you at The Grapevine in those days."

Jasmine's reverie shatters. She stands upright, her tone abrupt. "I was a different person then."

Thor looks from Jasmine's uncomfortable face to mine.

"Well." I shrug. "I would have thought I'd remember you anyway."

Jasmine clips her words. "You mean you think you'd remember an Asian in that club?"

I try to picture Jasmine in another persona. Short hair, maybe. Different clothes. It wouldn't change much. She burns with an uncommon beauty, inside and out—emerald fire.

I'm at a loss for words. "I'd remember you, I think."

Jasmine turns to wash glasses. Thor slowly sinks toward the bar, resting his head on folded arms.

"I've gotta go." I stand up gingerly, stretching the aching stiffness from my body.

"Hey buddy, you're off tonight." Thor sits back up in slow motion. "What you gonna do for fun?"

I can't think of an answer. "My modem died. I'll stop by and see if my friend Heshie has an old one. He'll probably let me test drive one of his virtual reality gizmos. They're like futuristic amusement park rides. That's fun."

I laugh out loud. "For as long as I've know Heshie, he's been trying to perfect some wild flying machine. He's obsessed with that toy. I think Heshie's channeling Orville Wright." I add more respectfully, "Or maybe he's a Michelangelo."

I flag a cab in the dark and direct the driver uptown and west, toward the Hudson River. I know the river's icy winter crust is breaking up now. I can almost hear the floes clinking against each other like wind chimes—tinkle of metal, hollow clack of bamboo—as the strong currents of the river drag them toward the sea.

We are nearing the old factory building where Heshie spends most of his time prototyping futuristic games. Warehouses loom over near-deserted streets. Here and there, scantily clad bodies gyrate and thrust their pelvises in the direction of any car that slows as it passes. Sexual labor on the auction block. Some are just kids—children in platform heels.

"Stop over there." I point to a building.

"You sure, pal?" the cabbie asks.

I reach forward and hand him a sawbuck. "Keep the change."

Heshie's alto voice is recognizable, even when it crackles from the metal speaker by the door. "I'm buzzing you in," he says.

But the homeless man inside the warehouse hallway has already opened the door for me. *Raisa whispers in my ear, "He's a* luftmentsh, ley-bele; *he has nothing to live on but air."* I scrounge around in my pocket for a dollar, but he waves it away with great dignity and goes back to his corrugated cardboard mat in the corner of the stairwell.

The elevator is locked this time of night. I take the slab marble stairs up to the eleventh floor. At each landing in the wrought-iron stairwell, the pale blue light of dawn filters through windows frosted with soot.

I stop on the ninth floor, huffing and puffing. The hallway of this building is so old and filthy. It must have been beautiful when it was brand-new, back in its Deco day.

As I rest on a step, I imagine its scaffolding, erect on a bare patch of land, still a skeleton. Mohawk ironworkers, sky walkers far from home, sit on its ribs, their legs dangling in space, watching the sun rise over the climax forest of the city. Now the building is in its decline.

I take a deep breath and climb the last in the series of flights. Heshie's waiting for me, looking at me blearily over his bifocals. I dig my hand in my jacket pocket and pull out the carcass of a dead modem. "I need one just like this," I implore. "This is my passport."

Heshie motions me to follow him into the immense loft. The floor is wood, polished with layers of grime and grit. Resting here and there on its surface are metal pods, shells, harnesses—contraptions. He stops to rest beside a hollow metal husk, draped with wires, suspended by cables from a frame, arms extending from its sides. He runs his hand lovingly over the bolts and bulges of welded seams.

I touch the cold shell: "Invented a new virtual dream?"

Heshie's annoyed. "It may be virtual, Rabinowitz, but it's still reality." He walks to his desk piled high with printouts and sits down wearily, ablaze in fluorescent light.

"I like virtual reality," I say, looking around. "When I blow up in one of your machine worlds, I can still go on playing."

"Oh, respawning." He rummages around—first in a drawer, then in an overflowing tool case—and finally pulls out a used modem and extends it toward me. "That's a different kind of dream." He's talking to me but now he's looking at his computer monitor, the most familiar face in his life.

"Heshie." I point to his worn, faded "The truth is out there" T-shirt. "I'm surprised that any self-respecting techno-geek is still wearing that shirt."

Heshie fixes me in a steely gaze. Maybe he doesn't like the word "geek." Maybe I've insulted him.

"How long have you known me, Rabinowitz?"

I can't remember not knowing Heshie.

His tone is less sarcastic than I expect: "Have you ever known me to be trendy?" My laughter makes him lean back in his chair and smile.

I remember the conversation with Jasmine about the new club opening soon—Club Pi—threatening to draw customers from Chaos.

"Hey, Hesh, can I ask you something?"

He pushes his glasses up the slope of his nose. "What?"

"What is Pi?"

Heshie's whole body relaxes. A Cheshire grin. "Like hearing an old lover's name." He pecks at his computer keyboard and waits for the sound of his printer spitting out what he's asked for. We don't talk; the printer just keeps churning out pages, as he polishes his glasses with the tail of his T-shirt. I don't speak; Heshie hates to be rushed. He draws a circle in the air with his index finger. "See that circle?" With his finger, he cuts the circle in half. "That's the riddle," he says.

"I need a little more than that, Hesh."

He's irritated that I've interrupted his reverie. "If you divide this," he redraws the circle in the air between us, "by this," he cleaves it in half again, "the numbers after the decimal just go on and on and on. That's Pi."

"That's it?" I'm disappointed.

He smiles. "Oh, that's just the beginning. Pi is like Scheherazade, telling a story that doesn't ever seem to end."

"Why is that a big deal?"

He nods toward the printer that's still churning out pages. The printout is folding itself into one continuous paper sky with endless flocks of gray geese flying in formation from horizon to horizon. "We've been looking for the answer for thousands of years, but we haven't found it yet. After we reached the first thirty million numbers after the decimal, there was still no end in sight. It seems to be an infinite relationship. That makes some people more sure there is a god and others more certain that there's not."

I look at the numbers, trying to see a pattern. "Maybe we're missing the forest for the trees?" I murmur.

Heshie becomes more animated. "Once you go into those woods, nothing is ever the same."

"Is the trail marked?"

"Only the first fifty-one billion trees."

The printer is still clacking and spewing. "Are you printing out all fifty-one billion numbers?" I ask. "That'll use up a lot of forest."

Heshie shakes his head. "I'm giving you the gift of the first thirty million numbers. But you're still just holding a question, not an answer.

"Pi," he says softly, "is a poem to infinity."

7

I feel like a circus bear on a bicycle. Commuters waiting for their trains study me in the early morning light as I pace back and forth on the Newark train platform. Some gape, some glare.

The trains screech and sigh into the station, looking like mythic serpents—glassy eyes, brightly lit nostrils.

I wait for Estelle's little commuter train, full of dread. I like Estelle. She's real with me. But in every memory I have of Estelle she is hanging on to me, grabbing my arm, squeezing my hand. Her need to touch, to connect physically, has always been so great that she seems not to notice the discomfort she is clutching.

I don't want to be handled today. I don't want to feel the pain in her body. I don't want to feel the heat of my own.

But now it is Estelle's train rushing past me, a blunt-nosed aluminum garden snake that squeals to a stop. People emerge from the train, first in a trickle, then in a flow. I stand on tiptoe looking for her. Oddly, when I spot her, I flood with relief. Among strangers, here is a familiar face that lights up with recognition, someone who is glad to know me.

"Max." Estelle stands in front of me as people stream around us. Grief has made her reticent to hug. I open my arms. "Oh, Max." She gives my consenting body a short, tight hug.

We stand in awkward silence for a moment. Estelle looks over my shoulder, and then around at the station. "Thank you for meeting me here, Max."

"I wanted to see you," I say, realizing that is true, too.

Her eyes are red-rimmed. She's gaunt and pale under her makeup. Estelle and I both face the escalator that takes us down into the main Newark terminal. Estelle takes a deep breath. "I have to do this, Max. I haven't been able to face coming to this station since," her voice trails off.

I take a deep breath. "Me neither."

"Let's go inside, Max." Estelle is shivering. "We can do this together, can't we?" Without answering, we both move toward the escalator and ride down its steep slope without speaking.

We step out into the crowded corridor of the terminal as though we are forensic experts surveying a crime scene. But there's no clue to Vickie's death here; just life, all around us. The halls are packed with rushing people. Long lines appear at fast-food counters and then melt away. A few homeless people cling close to the walls.

Pairs of police swagger down the hall, puff-chested like roosters.

In a small oasis from the chaos, a group of Deaf teenagers are engaged in lively storytelling, animating not just their hands and arms but their whole bodies.

In a nearby corner, light-skinned women are bent over businessmen's shoes, their noses close to the fragrant, scuffed leather as they polish and buff for a couple of bucks. A Black woman in coveralls is mopping up a spill near the water fountain. Her countenance claims she's not paying attention to anything except the puddle. But I watch her notice everything around her from under her cap brim.

"I need a cup of something hot," Estelle announces, tugging on me gently. We make our way across the thoroughfare of human traffic as though we are crossing a freeway. She guides me like a parent, a smidgeon of my jacket between her fingertips, toward the smell of roasted coffee beans.

"How about you, Max?" she asks as we arrive at a counter with no line. "What about hot chocolate?"

I shake my head, "I've been up all night," I explain. "I need leaded, not unleaded." I turn to the man who works the stand. "Coffee—light and sweet—and one hot chocolate." He glowers at both of us. Estelle doesn't look away. This isn't the first time she's been condemned for the crime of being in public with the likes of me.

He prepares our drinks quickly, with the efficiency of someone who is always busy. He places them on the counter in front of us. I pull out my wallet and hand him dollar bills. I put out my hand, palm up, for the change. He places the coins on the countertop out of my reach, instead, and with a smirk of satisfaction at having registered his disgust, folds his arms across his chest.

Estelle takes the two cups from the counter and gives them to me. She reaches for the change and, with a shuffleboard sweep, sends the change flying behind the counter. "Oh, I'm so sorry," she says, holding out her palm for the change.

He glowers as he bends over, but when he straightens up with the money in his hands, and Estelle looks him dead in the eye, he deflates, chastened.

"Estelle, I've missed you," I laugh. And it's true.

Her smile trembles. "I've missed you too, Max."

We travel with a current of commuters toward the main terminal. I gesture with my cup toward space on well-worn wooden pews marked "Ticketed Passengers Only." As we sit down, Estelle slowly takes a panoramic look around the main hall. We are surrounded by polished marble—sand-colored stone walls, speckled salmon floors. It's a secular cathedral, a monument to journey.

Above our heads, a huge rolodex of arrival and departure information flips updates on comings and goings.

"How are you doing, Estelle?" I ask.

"Oh," she says, almost absentmindedly, "it's getting so there are moments in a day that are a little better."

Estelle surveys the room, studying the crowd of people hurrying past us. She looks up at the huge frosted-glass orbs that hang from the ceiling. They are girdled with ironwork bands in the shape of zodiac signs—fixed constellations of fate. "Do you believe in fate, Max?"

"No," I shake my head.

"You're secular, Max, aren't you?"

"Yes," I nod.

"Vic and I have always been *veltlehkers*, too." Estelle sighs out loud. "Oh Max, how I wish I had met her here that morning."

I wish I had come this far with Vickie, too. It might not have changed the outcome. But at least I could have fought alongside her.

"It's strange," Estelle continues. "I feel like Death arranged to meet her here that morning, alone. And if I had interrupted that appointment, she'd be with me here today. That sounds so silly out loud."

"I understand."

Estelle looks startled and relieved. "Do you really? I'm so glad. I can't tell anymore if I'm sane or not." She looks around. "I envy these people. They're all going somewhere. And with such a sense of purpose. I haven't been able to face coming to this train station, and I thought that was what was keeping me from the world. I thought: I can't stay stuck out where I am. I have to get into the city to see people. But now I'm here and I realize—I have no place to go."

"You came here to meet me," I remind her.

She smiles and pats my hand perfunctorily. "Of course."

A cop has us fixed in his sight, like a radar gun. I try to avoid locking eyes with police. I shift my body toward Estelle, away from him. She is frowning at the cop—I look over in time to see him glance away uneasily.

"Max, how do you deal with it all the time?" she asks.

I shrug. "No choice."

"I'm sorry," she says quickly. "I don't mean to pry."

I sip my cooling coffee. "Of course it bothers me. Every time I turn around it's getting in the way of me living. I glare back, I ignore it, I fight, I don't fight. I just get through it. What else can I do?" I don't want to go further than that. But I add, "They're all staring at you, too, for being with me."

"I know," she smiles wistfully. "But would I be insensitive if I admitted to you that it's almost a comfort? Since Vickie died, people pass without noticing me. If they do, they think I'm just a nice lady." Her body quivers with revulsion. "Everyone I come into contact with now only seems to have one gender and they don't even think about it."

I laugh quietly. "Yeah, nobody thinks they have an accent."

"Now that they're staring at me for being with you, I know I'm back with the people I want to be with. Do you understand, Max?" Estelle's voice rises in desperation. "And I don't know where to go. I don't know how to get there anymore. I can't find that world without Vickie."

"There are cross-dresser clubs and conventions," I remind her.

Her voice tightens with irritation. "I know that, Max. Vickie and I have traveled that circuit for many years. The trouble is, I can't find my place there without Vickie."

She takes a sip of hot chocolate and places the cup beside her on the bench. "The last day of the conventions, I'd see all those men, those beautiful human beings, looking so forlorn at the end. The first day they're vulnerable and shy in their ball gowns, looking so lovely and so dear. Then on the last day they're back in their trucker caps and trousers. All that's left is just a little trace of bright red nail polish those last few hours. It breaks my heart to see them going home to a divorce or going home alone. My heart just aches for them.

"But there's no room in my heart for another now," she says with finality. "You have to give your all to someone who is being their all. I just can't. I'm having enough trouble taking care of my own heart right now.

"Oh, I have friends," she scoffs at some invisible conversant, "I'll make friends. I might even live long enough to flirt again. But there'll never be anyone in my life like Vickie. She was a magnificent human being. And that's what she saw in me. She saw what no one else ever did before. I don't know if anyone will ever see that in me again. Really see me. See who I am. You know what I mean, don't you, Max?"

"Yes, Estelle. Of course I do."

She cocks her head and looks at me. "You don't have anyone like that in your life, do you Max?"

"No," I answer, looking straight ahead.

She nods slowly. "Do you wish you did? Oh, what am I saying. Of course you do."

Her assumption annoys me. "No, I don't want a partner. I have enough trouble taking care of my own life. And I don't want anything else in my life that anyone can take away from me."

I don't even realize the impact of my words until I see Estelle reel. I reach out toward her. "Estelle," I say, "I'm so sorry."

"No," she leans forward, elbows on her knees as though she may throw up. "No, it's what you feel. You have a right to feel that way. I guess I'm just surprised. I guess I just assume that everyone wants what I had with Vic, with Vickie."

My hand hovers above her hunched back, but I don't touch her. I'm not sure what to do. Above us, mechanized letters and numbers shuffle like cards, tumbling into new relationships to ask: Where are you going? Where have you been?

Estelle sits upright, takes a lungful of air, and lets it out slowly. "Max, can we go outside?"

We rise slowly. I toss my coffee cup in the trash can and rub the parts of my body that were pressed against the unyielding grain of the wood. The morning rush has slowed to a trickle. Once we pass through the doors that lead to downtown Newark, we are outside on a bright, cool morning.

"Oh dear," Estelle says. "Too many buildings for me. It makes me feel claustrophobic. You should come by the house some time, Max," she offers. "Sit out in the back yard. It's so quiet and so beautiful. I haven't planted anything this spring. It's been raining so much. I just let the perennials come up. Instead of everything being very neat and mani-cured, it's growing quite wild back there. I think I like that better, at least for now." Estelle puts her arm around my waist. "You will come out some day, won't you, Max?"

"Yes," I say.

"You can just mat down the grass and sit under the trees and feel the wind blowing. It's so much lovelier. It's like meditation just to sit there. It's such a comfort," she says, her voice traveling farther from me. "There's such screaming in my ears."

She watches cab drivers negotiating fares. "I know I have to start plan-ning the memorial. I just can't do it yet."

"You have time," I say.

"Yes," she laughs bitterly. "I do have time—lots of it. But," her tone shifts, "I'm afraid that once the memorial is over the last traces of Vickie will disappear. But then I worry that if I don't organize it, everyone who loved her will forget her."

I rest my hand on her shoulder. "None of us will ever forget Vickie."

She turns to me and smiles, anxiously. "That's true, isn't it?"

"Take your time, Estelle. You'll know when the time is right. And then we'll all help you."

Estelle stops, lost in contemplation or emotion. She lifts up one hand and touches a crabapple branch bent low with pink blossoms. "It's nice to see something so beautiful growing in the middle of all this concrete and pavement, isn't it, Max." It's a statement, not a question. She turns toward me, "Do you ever get out of the city into nature?"

I raise my arms out wide, "This is nature."

She laughs. "Where do you see nature here, Max?"

I look up at the buildings towering over us, reflections of clouds drifting in their blue glass faces. Her gaze follows mine.

"That is beautiful," she says, turning her eyes toward the sky.

"This landscape is beautiful to me," I say. "It's our beehive. Our anthill."

Estelle smiles tolerantly. "But it's concrete and steel."

I shrug. "It's all about sticking atoms together." I point with my toe at the pigeons pecking at the concrete sidewalk. "These birds lived high up in the cliffs of Africa." I look up at the skyscrapers. "Now they've made a home for themselves here in these rock faces. This is the only ecosystem I've ever known," I say, to myself really. "It's where I live, nocturnally."

Estelle squints up at the buildings. "Do you get out in the daytime very often?"

I shake my head. "Not much."

Estelle sorts through her words slowly. "May I ask you something I've wondered about?"

I suck in my breath and nod.

"Vickie once told me you said there you had two rules for survival: don't let your face get marked in a fight and don't get arrested. I don't understand, Max, isn't the city more dangerous at night? Or is it that people can't see you in the night?"

I tolerate her question, shake my head. "People can always see you—day or night. It's just that the rules are different at night. I know how to work those rules." I know she doesn't understand, really, so I add, "And I love the night, Estelle. I love the darkness."

Behind her smile, she studies my face carefully. "Tell me, Max, how are you doing?"

I laugh a little, uncomfortable. "Hanging in there, I guess."

Estelle nods, but she looks disappointed. I've blown off her question.

I look up at the skyscrapers again. "It's amazing these buildings don't collapse. They're under so much pressure."

The sound of realness in my voice, of something honest, raises Estelle's gaze to my face. I point to the top of the tallest building. "There's the downward pull of gravity. It spills down in a cascade from top to bottom.

"The wind is an incredible force from all sides—fluid flowing past a solid object. The wind strums the building. And the building has its own hum. If they harmonize, the waves of vibrations start to widen, like the bridges you see bucking like broncos in a storm on the Weather Channel.

"And then sometimes the ground shakes."

Estelle bends her head down in listening mode: "Earthquakes?"

"Yes. The plates of rock move with this sudden release of tension and send waves of motion. So the foundation is very important. There're two models of design: flexible or rigid."

Estelle looks up at me, covering her eyes with her hand as a shield from the sunlight. "Which works best?"

"I don't know," I laugh, "I'm still trying to figure that out. Depends on the terrain, I guess."

Estelle looks up at the silvery glass buildings stretching toward the sky. "They don't fall down very often though, do they?" She amends that quickly, "I mean, of their own accord? That's reassuring."

I let out a deep breath of air. "Well, apparently almost every single building that's ever been destroyed has been lost in a very simple way: They were abandoned. They disintegrated." I look up at the buildings soaring above me. "Stonemasons say a building starts to fall as soon as you put the last brick in place."

Estelle touches my arm, very gently, without clutching.

8

I climb the well-worn stairs of my tenement building, past the missing teeth of the banister's smile. It's the end of the night—late for me. Early for everyone else—aroma of coffee and bacon in the air. I hear different music on each floor, like taking a trip around the world in five flights.

I turn my key in the lock, open my door to safety and solace, and lock it behind me with a sigh of relief. I'm too exhausted to eat. I just want to sleep. But as I remove my coat I can smell my shift at the bar on my clothes and my body. I watch myself perform rituals of order: remove coins from my pockets, put them in a coffee can on my dresser; take off my clothes, stuff them in a plastic grocery bag inside the hamper; line up my boots next to each other under the dresser.

I dash through the cold apartment to the bathroom, close the door and turn on the shower, letting the steam rise in clouds in the small, chilled room. I look at my face in the mirror, but I can only see my reflection through the fog of steam. My doppelgänger appears to be trying to tell me something; I can't make out the message.

I step into the shower and feel my rigid, robotic body soften into skin and supple muscle. I lean my hands against the chipped porcelain tiles and let the water run over my scalp, my eyes closed behind the waterfall. I wash off the grime, physical and emotional, one layer at a time. I swish droplets in my mouth and spit out the grit of the things I haven't said into the water swirling down the drain.

I turn off the faucet reluctantly, step out onto the rug in the warm room feeling cleaner, lighter, fresher. A sound nags at my ears like a whirring insect. I towel dry and prepare myself to bolt back into the coldness and bury myself in the yielding futon and quilts. But as the bathroom door opens, the sound grows louder—the fire alarm in the hallway.

I pull on a fresh T-shirt and a pair of jeans and move quickly toward my living room door. The closer I get to it, the louder the alarm's call grows. As I crack open the door, the urgency of the alarm and the bitter stench of smoke scares me. In a moment of panic I wonder what I should take with me. There's no time to disconnect my computer and monitor. There's nothing of value on the hard drive worth trying to download. It's just an access road to the information highway.

The only thing in my home of value that matters to me is what is on the walls: inked poetry, maps bristling with colored pins, painted images.

I carefully step out into the hall on bare feet. I recall the man on the third floor whom I've sometimes seen with a young woman who is scarred and blind.

The music behind his closed door has traveled from the Middle East to this hallway. I rap my knuckles on his door. No answer. I knock again, hard and insistent. The music lowers. "Who is there?" he asks. The alarm bell is demanding attention. He opens the door and peeks out looking for the source of the sound before he seems to notice me.

"Smoke." I point with my index finger as though it were a cat sitting on the banister. He looks back inside, appraising decisions.

"I'll run downstairs and see what's going on," I tell him, hearing my own voice sputter with the oil and water mix of exhaustion and adrenaline. My hands are quivering; my feet are cold. "I'll come back up and let you know."

He nods, looking over my shoulder distractedly. "Yes, yes. Thank you."

I run down the stairs into a thicker smell of smoke. Alma, custodian of the building, is standing with her back to the fire alarm, holding a neighbor at bay. "It's no problem. No more fire," she assures. "Don't call the fire department," she adds, protecting the landlord.

Too late. The sound of fire engines outside the door. Firefighters, heavy and huge in boots and slickers, hard hats and masks, tromp into the hall, hefting axes in their hands. The narrow hallway is too small for all of us. I am the one who squeezes by, stepping outside onto the front stoop.

I look up at the brick face of the building: no flames, no scorch; just smoke billowing from an open basement window. I go back inside. The hallway is empty now. Loud talk from the basement—demanding male voices, placating female voice.

I sprint back up the stairs to the third floor. He is waiting, anxious for my report.

"I think it's okay," I tell him. "It's probably the furnace again. The fire truck is here. I'll keep you posted."

"Wait," he shakes his head, "I'll go with you. My sister is asleep. Let me see what is going on before I wake her."

"Should I stay with her while you go?"

"No." He shakes his head. "You are very kind."

We walk downstairs quickly, in awkward, apprehensive silence. We listen to the firefighters, their loud voices and laughter and heavy-booted stomp receding. They are headed out of the building, out of the dim first-floor hallway into the bright day.

Alma is waiting for us at the base of the stairwell.

My neighbor speaks to her before I can. "Señora del Tierra, what is happening?"

She waves our collective concern away with her hand and then wipes it on her skirt. "*No te preocupes.* The landlord says the new part for the furnace will come soon."

Smoke burns the back of my throat. I beckon toward the door and my neighbor follows me. In the foyer, he points to the single hand-printed word on the label over his mailbox: Ashrawi.

There is no name over my mailbox. My metal box is straining with the bulge of mail addressed to "Occupant."

"Rabinowitz," I tell him. I gesture toward myself. "Max."

He extends his hand to me. "Hatem," he says. "Hatem Ashrawi."

We step outside into the daylight together. The cold concrete reminds me I'm not wearing any shoes. I feel embarrassed to be outside half dressed. But no one is paying any attention to me. Firefighters sweep small groups of onlookers away from the truck and fumble with hoses lying limp and flat on the street.

I scan the crowd. I assume that those whose feet are also bare live in my building or the one next door. The others live in nearby tall tenements or the shingled houses that lean in their shadows. All the faces are those of strangers—dayside people. One man glares at me, smoldering with malice.

"C'mon, my friend," Hatem says. "You have been very good to me. Please, let me buy you a cup of coffee, yes?"

Unexpected kindness. I do not want to be rude to this person. He speaks to me with such formality that it feels like respect. I nod once. "Thank you."

He points to the deli on the corner; it's usually closed when I'm awake.

As we pass the flinty-eyed man, he spits at Hatem's feet and then wipes a little saliva from his chin with the back of his hand. Hatem is beckoning me to follow him, acting as though he doesn't notice. Everyone notices.

Hatem looks down at my shoeless feet and nods toward the glob of spittle. "Be careful, my friend." I step gingerly on the cold asphalt and pebbly concrete sidewalk. Hatem walks slowly beside me, wordlessly.

As we open the door to the deli, a bell jingles, announcing our arrival. The man behind the counter greets Hatem with a broad smile: "*Salam aleichem.*"

Hatem walks around the counter to embrace him: "*Aleichem salam*, Mohammad." They hug each other briefly, thumping each other's backs.

"How is your sister? What is happening over there?" Mohammad asks Hatem.

Hatem waves away concern. "Everything is good."

They both turn to me. Hatem extends his arm. "This is my neighbor, Max Rabinowitz. He helped me this morning. He is a good man."

Hatem's friend leans across the counter and takes both my hands in his. "If you are a friend of Dr. Ashrawi, you are a friend of mine."

The bell over the door jingles again. An old woman comes in, walking with great difficulty. Mohammad greets her like a friend, too. "Good morning, Missus Maloney. How is your grandbaby? What can I do for you?"

She fishes in her purse, clutched tight to her chest, for a crumpled dollar bill and looks over his head. "Good morning, Moe." She begins to speak in numbers, a language they are both fluent in. He punches the digits into a machine and hands her a ticket; she hands him the crumpled bill. The lottery: tax on her dreams.

We all watch as she walks, slowly, toward the door. Mohammad turns to us both again. "What can I get you both? What would you like? I just made a nice pot of coffee, would you like a cup? Please!"

I smile. "Thank you."

"Your name is Max," he repeats, "yes?"

I nod.

He pauses. "Rabinowitz, yes?"

My neck muscles tense. "Yes."

He nods slowly. "I see you some days," he says, pointing out the window. "You come down the street before the light, when I'm opening up the gate to my store. Sometimes I wave to you, but you don't see."

I have seen him opening his store, but I never saw him notice me.

He turns and pours hot coffee, steam rising from three cardboard cups. "Light and sweet," he says, placing the cups on the counter and pushing two toward us.

Hatem looks at me: "Did you want milk and sugar?"

Mohammad is chagrined. "I'm sorry, my friend. Here, I pour it out. Tell me how you want it."

I reach for the cup. "No, that's good. That's very good."

He pulls the cup back: "Are you sure? It's no big deal. Really! I throw it out."

"No," I laugh. "It's good. Thank you."

Mohammad lights an unfiltered cigarette. He offers the pack to both of us. Hatem says no with emphatic good humor. Right now the old familiar habit is calling my name like a siren song. I lash myself to my own mast and reluctantly decline his offer. I sip the sweet coffee and milk, letting it warm me.

Mohammad points to the television on the stool behind the counter. It's tuned to CNN. "Maybe it starts tomorrow," he says quietly to Hatem, who stares at the screen. An anchor person announces that all U.S. personnel are being ordered to leave Kuwait. The looming war is so imminent it pounds in my skull.

"It's a terrible thing," I say.

They both look at me, and then at each other.

I gesture at the television. "It's a crime, what they're going to do."

Hatem speaks: "Yes. Many people will die."

"Blood for oil," I say flatly. Both men sip their coffee with great concentration. We all watch the images flicker on the screen—GIs kissing loved ones good-bye, hefting government-issued gear over their shoulders, one last glance.

A map appears on the screen as a journalist's voice, crackling over satellite transmission, says that based on chatter overheard by the Pentagon, the government in Tel Aviv is preparing for the war. The sliver of land on the map is easily recognizable. I say its name out loud: "Palestine."

Both men look up at each other, and then at me. I am suddenly self-conscious, and I feel it in my feet. "I'd better go," I say. "I work at night. I haven't slept yet." I point to my feet, as though they explain everything.

Mohammad looks down at my bare toes and looks up at Hatem in horror. "He has no shoes!" He directs his worry back toward me. "You will cut your feet. Take my shoes."

"No." I wave his gesture away. "Thank you, I'm okay."

"No, please. You'll take my shoes and bring them back later. I'm always here." He crushes out his cigarette and begins to remove a polished black shoe.

I shake my head and hold up flat palms to stop him. "No, no!" I say firmly. "But thank you. You've been very kind." I tap my empty coffee cup and dig in my pocket for a dollar.

Now he holds up both his palms. "No," he says firmly. "No. You are our guest." Hatem nods. The more respectful they are to me, the more embarrassed I feel. On the spot, pinned down by human generosity.

I awkwardly leave the empty cup on the counter and nod at the door. "Thank you both," I say.

Hatem shakes my hand. "Thank you for helping me and my sister."

Mohammad leans across the counter and takes my hand in his calloused grip. "You are welcome here any time, my friend."

I believe he means it. "Thank you," I reply, trying to think of something real to say. "Thank you for welcoming a stranger."

Mohammad claps one hand to his chest as he continues to hold my grip firmly. "Ah, my friend, we are cousins."

I wave good-bye to them both and step outside into the light. The sun is warm. Across the street, a small group of neighbors remain, gossiping about the nonevent of the fire. The man who spat at Hatem is standing with a younger version of himself in front of my front stoop. I pause for just an instant, standing on cold pavement, wondering if I should go back to the store. I only hesitate for a split second, but a little smile bends his tight lips—in a millisecond I have lost a round.

We stare at each other as I diagonally cross the pavement. He mocks me with a glance at my feet. I continue to make eye contact, a bond of loathing. His son moves to the bottom of the apartment building steps, blocking my path with his body, his father at his shoulder. I stride past them and clip the younger with my shoulder, throwing him off balance with my momentum.

I win a round.

9

I awaken with a start, shivering and sweaty under the quilt. Next door, my neighbor's television is turned up full blast. The president's voice booms in my bedroom.

The ring of my phone makes me shout with alarm. I'm surprised to hear Heshie's voice.

"Hey, there, Rabinowitz. How the hell are you?"

It's Heshie's voice, but he sounds like he's reeling. "Hesh, are you okay? Are you drunk?"

"Of course I'm drunk, Rabinowitz. And if you were a real Jew, you would be, too."

It must be Purim.

"It's a *shande* that you're not," he scolds.

It's not a matter of shame, merely a lost opportunity, from his viewpoint. "A *shod*," I adjust. "Hesh, you old *shicker*, where are you?"

"Working on a new machine, where else?" His throat tightens around his voice: "Are you listening to him on TV?"

I hear the president's voice, loud. I can't make out the words, but I get the message.

"War." Heshie's voice becomes stern. "It's your duty to get drunk."

"I think it's just the opposite, Hesh. Anyway, maybe I'd better be the designated Jew who makes sure you don't get too drunk to get home."

"Mmmm," he murmurs to himself. "I've got a cot here. I'll sleep right here with my machines."

We sit in silence. The drums of war are pounding on my bedroom wall.

"Hey, Rabinowitz." He says my name softly. "Are you okay?"

"Me?" I laugh. "I'm sober."

"No, I mean are you really okay?" Now I know Hesh is really drunk. He's talking to me as gently and caringly as he would to one of his computers. "Sometimes I'm afraid the world is too much for you."

I don't want him to suddenly be real with me. "Hey, thanks a lot!" I deflect my own unease.

But he persists. "Then where would I be? You're my *landsman*. You're my *mishpokhe*." He is dragging me some place that I don't want to go. "We had some good times as kids when you came to stay with my family, you remember?"

He means when my mother was so sick, but he's not saying that.

I survey the topography of my childhood. "No, I don't recall any good times from being a child."

"You don't remember any fun we all had?"

I shake my head as though he can see me. "I don't remember fun. I remember when your parents made me go to Hebrew school with you and a couple of the older kids kicked the crap out of me afterward."

"You see!" he says. "That's why you hate religion."

"I don't hate what you believe in, Hesh. I just don't believe in it."

He cajoles. "At least celebrate the holidays."

"Naw, Hesh, for me it's a package deal."

"But," he digs in to argue, "What about the ethics of being a Jew, Rabinowitz?"

"Mine or Theodor Herzl's? Yours or Henry Kissinger's?"

"You don't believe in anything, do you?" His voice heats with anger. "How can you call yourself a Jew?"

Here we go. He's drunk so I pull my punch. "When you start gentile-baiting me, it's time for this Jew to hang up."

He's already shifted to a contemplative mood. "You're not a Jew like I'm a Jew."

"Well, that's true, Hesh. So what? There's lots of ways to be a Jew. I grew up in the 'coops,' Hesh. The Jewish Bronx was almost all secular, you know that. You grew up on the Lower East Side. In your neighborhood, I was the odd one out. In mine, you would have been. Anyway, listen, my friend, any argument that's been going on for more than a hundred years can wait till morning. Get some sleep."

Quiet on the other end of the line. I think maybe he's fallen asleep. "Hesh?"

Pause. "Yeah?"

"I remember the time we came over when you all sat *shiva* for your father." I hear the impact of my words in the dead silence on the other end of the phone. It hit me in the gut when he alluded to my mother's illness. Maybe I shouldn't have just dropped his father's death into the conversation like that.

"It had meaning for me, Heshie, to sit with you all and share our grief. You know my friend Vickie got killed. Just before that big snow came. And when the snow melted, it was like she never was here; like she never *was*. I want to rip my clothes and cover up all the mirrors and sit with everyone else who knew her and sob and wail and talk and laugh until I know I'll never lose her again."

Suddenly my bedroom feels too shadowy. I grope for matches and light the little candle beside me for comfort. In the flickering light, the drawings I've painted on my bedroom walls and ceiling comfort me with their familiarity. I forget I'm still on the phone until Heshie speaks.

"I'm sorry about your friend."

I inhale deeply and let the air out slowly through my lips. "I did something terrible. Something I'm ashamed of. And I can't fix it." There is no response on the other end of the phone line. I think about what I said to Vickie before she died. I can't remember the words.

Heshie speaks. "What? What did you do?"

I think back to the instant on the PATH train platform. "I told her we were different. It was true. But I said something that made it seem like her way was just a game, just a change of clothing. Like her life was so easy and so simple; not like mine. Then she got killed."

We share the quiet for a long time. I'm talking to myself when I continue. "There'll be a memorial soon. I don't know what the hell I'm gonna say."

Hesh sounds a little more sober when he speaks. "*Nu?* You can't make it right?"

"How?" my voice grates with irritation. "There's only one person who could forgive me, and she's dead. But I can't stand up there and talk about her like everything was fine between us and not admit that I lashed out at her, that I hurt her just before she died. Do you understand? I put her identity down, just before she got killed for it. What does that say about me?"

I'm sorry I asked the last question out loud. It was rhetorical and I don't want Hesh to answer. But he does. "My father used to tell me: a human being is just human."

"There's no forgiveness on this one. I've just gotta find a way to live with the fact that I've got some streaks in me that I really don't like."

"Everybody does," he replies, lost in his own inebriated thoughts.

"Yeah," I mutter, "but I don't have to live with theirs."

"Hey, Rabinowitz, why are you telling me this? Do you want me to forgive you? I would, you know."

Heshie's compassion makes me laugh softly, awkwardly. "I don't know why I told you, Hesh. I guess I think you don't care as much about people as you do computers. You don't expect much from us, so I guess I figure you're less disappointed in us when we fuck up. I guess I hoped you wouldn't think less of me."

Hesh's voice is gentler than I've ever heard it before. "I do care about you. The funny thing is, Rabinowitz, sometimes I like you best when you fuck up." His words begin to slur: "Garbage in, garbage out."

My anger triggers. "What the hell are you talking about?"

"Everyone always tells me it was their computer that screwed up. I like people who admit it was user error."

We laugh, together.

"Hey," he says, "you've got broadband! I called Comcast. I told them you were a freelance programmer at the company I work for. They're gonna call you to set up a time to come over to your place and install it."

"What?" I panic at the thought of strangers in my apartment. ·

"No more dial-up modem," he reassures me. "Now you'll be able to video stream in real time."

I calm down at the thought that I could cruise the information highway with a V-8 engine instead of a horse-drawn carriage. "Thanks, Hesh. Now get some sleep. Trust me, you're drunk enough that you can't tell the difference between 'cursed be Haman' and 'blessed be Mordecai.'"

"That's the problem," he says. "I keep watching CNN and no matter how much wine I've got in my belly, I still know the president is evil."

"Go to sleep, my friend. And call me tomorrow when you're nursing a secular hangover."

"Do you even believe in God?"

"G'night, Hesh!"

I blow out the candle with a puff, get up and lumber into my office, and switch on the little portable television on the top shelf of my computer desk. In the darkness, I flip the channels. Every station is recapping the Commander in Chief's forty-eight-hour warning that Goliath is about to wage a defensive war against David. The CEO in the Oval Office says to the Iraqi people: "The moment of your liberation is at hand."

With a click of the remote, his image shrinks to a small speck of light and then disappears. My body feels icy; I wish my aunt Raisa would come to stand beside me.

It's Purim—when nothing is as it seems. In my mind's eye, I see Heshie and his brother gorgeously cross-dressed at the Purim spiel; Heshie in his flowing white beard and his brother as Queen Esther.

Purim—when miracles seem possible. I still remember, though, what Heshie's mother advised me in their kitchen: "*Hof oyf nisim noz farloz*—hope for miracles—*zikh nit oyf a nes*—but don't rely on one." I figured she was preparing me for my mother's death. I'm longing for comfort now, in any form. I wish I had a Purim *hamentashn*, prune paste, with sips of Mohammad's sweet, light coffee. I peer outside the window. Mohammad's store is closed. In the apartment above his store, the ethereal light of television shimmers on the walls.

Outside my window, the Purim moon climbs high in the sky, round and radiant.

I go back to my bedroom and sprawl on my futon. I reach for matches near my bedside and relight the stub of wax in its congealed puddle. Its primordial flame comforts me—ancestral fire. I am warm here inside my own cave. I've painted my walls and ceiling—my legacy to the next generation of tenants: Paleolithic animals in cloven flight flicker past in candlelight; black coal streaks, earth brown, dark amber, warm mustard, robin's egg blue, blood red. No predators, just the race for survival.

Human handprints on the ceiling, from the cool cave walls of Pech Merle, wordless, intimate message sent from a long-forgotten communal past: from the touch of our hands to yours, we exist, we existed.

I feel anxious, disturbed. I roll over and sink slowly into sleep, trying to release the disturbing dream of reality.

"Leyb," *Raisa's voice nudges me in the darkness of my bedroom, trying to keep me from sleep.* "*Always remember,* mayne tayere: *If you don't fight against the war, the war will still come to find you.*"

I can't remember the last time Thor was angry with me, but he's mad now. He isn't shouting on the other end of the phone line. His voice is taut. "The bombs are going to drop tomorrow, buddy. The next day students are gonna walk out of classrooms—even high school students. Kids who have to answer to their principals and teachers and parents. People are gonna walk off their jobs or refuse to go to work. They've got kids and orthodontist bills, they're in debt for their house or their car. People all over the country are saying there's gonna be no business as usual the day after the bombs start dropping."

I correct him, "If the bombs drop."

He corrects me. "When the bombs fall, Max. So now you tell me. Are you really going to go in to work the night after?"

"Thor, I can't afford to lose this job. Not until Ruby can get back to work."

"Oh, fuck that," Thor loses his cool. "Don't put this on Ruby."

I raise my voice, but it's not filled with anger, the way Thor's is. "This is real, Thor. This is her life on the line. She can't work right now."

Thor's plea sounds more like a demand. "I'll give you the night's pay. We'll all pitch in to make up the money. Ruby won't lose anything. But you can't come in to work the shift after the invasion starts. Don't you understand?"

Why doesn't he get what I'm trying to explain to him? "You don't understand. It's not just about a night's pay, although that's not *bubkes*. I can't screw up this job. I can't get fired right now. Don't you understand, Thor? Where am I gonna find another job? Tell me that! I promised Ruby that she didn't have to worry. That we'd find the money. I can't put this job in jeopardy."

Thor is silent.

"Thor," I implore.

His annoyed exhalation is amplified as it travels along the phone line. "There's a day-after protest in Times Square at five PM. Are you at least gonna be there?"

10

I toss and turn in my bed, twisted up in the sheets.

"*Get up,* leybele!" *Aunt Raisa commands me.*

"*I don't want to get up," I tell her. "I just can't."*

"Az me muz, ken men—*when you must,* tayere, *you can."*

"*It's so hard," I whine. "Why does everything have to be so hard?"*

Raisa dressing me for school as my mother lay dying in her bed. Me dreading torment in school corridors, cafeteria, and gym locker room. "Please don't make me go to school! Please!"

She tugs on my dress, tears sparkling in her eyes. "Az men zitst in der heym—*if you sit in your house—*tserayst men nit keyn shtivl—*you won't wear out your shoes."*

"*I don't care about my shoes!" Cheap patent leather, cracking where my foot bends.*

She pulls my small body into her soft flesh. "Be brave. Me darf zany

shtark vi ayzn, *strong like iron. Don't hide from the world,* mayne leybele.
What you don't like about the world you must change."

"*I can't.*" *I flounce.* "*I can't.*"

She holds my shoulders and shakes me gently so that I will awaken to her
words: "Az me vil, ken men iberkern di gantse velt." *How on earth does she*
think I can turn over the whole world?

I open my eyes. Gray light filters through my bedroom curtains. I get
up and pull the curtains apart—as much of the world as I am ready to
allow inside. The sky is overcast. I'm numb and hungry.

I close my eyes and see my mother, scrambling to serve breakfast in the
hours long before dawn. She's always in a rush to arrive at work before the
sewing begins in order to stitch together the grievances of all who work
there. She serves up wisdom like she serves up the food: in a hurry. She
knows she is going to die soon; I do not.

"*Are you listening?*" *she scolds.* "Durkh shvaygn ken men nit shtaygn.
You can't succeed in this world by being quiet like a mouse." *My father is*
holding his reading glasses like a magnifying lens, studying the daily news-
paper, printed in characters that look like delicate bird tracks on the pages.

She holds my plate in front of my nose, stops, recalling something else
important she must quickly impart. "Beser tsu shtarbn shtey'endik." *She*
pulls the plate back ever so slightly until I listen more carefully. "*It's better*
you should die standing up than live on your knees!"

I don't want to think about how my mother's sand sifted so quickly
through the hourglass. So I get up out of bed.

I go into my study and turn on the television. On the screen, a clock in
the upper right hand corner ticks off the hours, minutes, seconds until the
bombs incinerate their targets. I don't want to watch this happen. I don't
think I can. Throughout my building, every apartment, every house on the
street, everyone is focused on the moment the war will begin, the count-
down ticking as though a glittering ball is dropping on New Year's Eve.

Suddenly, the television screen glows with a blazing image: shock and awe. Baghdad is aflame. I turn away from the television screen toward my window. The sky flashes with lightning. Thunder cracks. It looks and sounds like war. A cry pierces the air, an ancient wail. I pry my window open to listen: a mussein's call. Mohammad leans out his window and shouts: *"Allah akbar! Allah akbar!"* His voice breaks with a sob. Below me, another window opens. Through the grille of the fire escape, I can see Hatem lean out the window and lift his voice to join Mohammad's: *"Allah akbar!"*

"Stop the war!" It isn't until I hear the hoarse cry that I realize it is coming from my own throat. "Stop the war!" I shout again, as shadows of neighbors appear at their windows. A crack of thunder in the sky answers our earthly demand. Lightning flashes, illuminating us all, caught in the resin of this moment.

Rain trickles down my neck, wetting my T-shirt. The street glistens and shimmers with sweeping gusts of rain. I slide down the wall slowly until I'm sitting on the bare wood floor. Elbows propped on my knees, I rest my head in my hands as though in prayer, fingertips burning my forehead like candle flames.

"What do you do when things are like this?" I ask Raisa.

But she does not answer my question for many, many hours, not until I've almost drifted to sleep again.

"Ikh weiss nicht, tayere. *Things have never been like this before,"* she whispers, rocking me. *As she kisses my forehead, I catch a whiff of gardenia.* "I taught you what I learned," *she strokes my hair.* "Now you'll teach me."

I'm being pushed, jostled, in the subway tunnels under Times Square. It's so crowded I can't breathe. I press forward against turbulent currents flowing in every direction. It's Friday evening and day workers are all leaving their jobs. I've got to get out of this underground channel. I struggle to get to the stairwell.

I find the shaft that is bringing people down and I squeeze upward. It's pouring rain, as though the sky is weeping unabashedly while bombs rain down on Baghdad. From every direction, people are pooling like puddles around the subway entrance, jockeying to get downstairs.

Construction trestles along Times Square offer some shelter from the downpour and crowds. I stand under one, between two little waterfalls streaming down from the planks above. As waves of pedestrians surge past me, I am surprised to see how many people have a button pinned to their coat registering their opposition to this war. I can't tell who is here for the demonstration and who just can't remain silent as the battle is joined.

Massive digital commercials flash from the sides of soaring sky-scrapers, colors blazing and bursting in my vision. Text messages crawl from right to left across the buildings. I look north, across the street, expecting the protest to be in the V-shaped wedge in the middle of Times Square. The triangular Army recruiting station there was once the number-one target for our angry demonstrations. But the recruiters are gone—not there, anyway.

Police cars and command trailers are parked everywhere, lights strobing. I thread my way through the dense crowd until I hear voices chanting in unison: "Hey, Bush! What do you say? How many kids have you killed today?"

The chant suddenly connects an old self of who I was once to who I am now, like two globules of mercury reuniting in an instant. Ruby and I chanted in these same streets: "Hey, hey, LBJ!" It was a Democrat in office, then. It was Vietnamese children running from the napalm rain of "liberation."

I can see the protest now. The police have created metal cattle pens along one lane of the street. I try to get closer but a cop orders me away. The other lane is empty—no people, no cars. I try to move quickly to that side of the barricades, but two cops block my way: "Get the fuck off the street!" When I point to the other end of the street as my destination, one of them slaps my chest with her nightstick. "Move it, now, or you're under arrest."

I work my way to the sidewalk, packed with people trying to walk in opposite directions, penned in on one side by metal police barricades and on the other by another construction wall. A woman demonstrator on the other side of the metal grille beckons me and others. "Come over; come inside. Join us!"

Cops move quickly to keep that from happening. "You'll have to go in on the other end."

Someone shouts over my shoulder, "We can't! They told us to come down here!" The police huddle to confer. A cop with gold bars is summoned. They deliver their verdict, pointing to a half empty pen behind the full one. I can see now that pens are set up on every block down the empty expanse of Broadway.

The rally begins with a familiar voice, amplified like a deity's. It's Thor's: "No blood for oil!" The crowd roars. "Stop the bombing, stop the war! Bring the troops home, now!" Cheers of agreement.

A cop steps between me and the metal barricades. "Move!" he barks, sputtering in the rain. "Now!" He wants to arrest me for trying to break into this little prison camp they've set up.

There's nowhere to go except the second pen. It's filling up fast. Instead I retreat across the street to regroup in the entranceway of a corporate office building. My jacket is drenched, my hair plastered to my face, water streaming down my arms and legs. The first pen is brimming with people and bristling with signs. Several teenagers inside move two barricades apart to create an opening and suddenly there's a surge from the sidewalk as more people flow into the pen. The police move in, flailing billy clubs, pushing everyone away until the metal fencing can be resealed.

Those at the front of the rally are chanting, "No justice? No peace! U.S. out of the Middle East!" Those facing off with the police at the rear are rattling the metal grating, shouting, "Whose streets? Our streets!" They rock the barricade, which rolls like a wave until part of it falls over into the street.

A throng of activists pushes past the police and presses south on Broadway. "Whose streets? Our streets!" Police on mounted horseback gallop from around the corner. Foot cops in riot gear rush out from two parked buses nearby. Together they form a new barricade to stop the marchers. Cops on horseback line up in front of them, reining in their jittery steeds. The cops on foot hit their shields with their nightsticks, a drum beat of repression. The marchers, blocked, try to turn east down the side street but are quickly thwarted there, too.

The second pen is almost full now; protesters press up against metal barriers, shouting at the police. The cops try to force the spilled marchers back into the first pen, pushing, knocking people to the ground. Riot cops are hitting an old man splayed facedown on the asphalt. Wrists of others are being cinched in plastic cuffs. People are being dragged away.

"Let them go!" The demand rises like thunder from both pens and everywhere along the sidewalks: "Let them go!"

The police are vastly outnumbered in the tide of protest, contained only by the frail dams of barricades. If we pushed them over, all at once, we could overwhelm them. We need tactical leadership at the back of the pen.

Moments later, the police have regained the upper hand, and a busload of prisoners is on its way to the nearest precinct.

My refuge in the entranceway is getting more crowded. A man in a dripping wet suit and tie next to me lights up a cigarette. He hesitates before putting the pack back in his soggy coat and shakes his head. "They should just let them march."

I nod, shivering from the cold. I hunch over and step back out into the driving rain, working my way to the nearest street corner. The garbage can is filled with sodden handmade signs against the war. A group is marching down the side street toward me. Their banner is so rain slicked it sags, but one of them hands me a palm leaflet: Jews for Palestine.

I hear someone shout my name from down the street. Deacon is calling to me from a small group of people huddled under an awning. They're standing behind a lavender banner that reads Queers Against War & Racism. Everyone squeezes closer together to make room for me as I duck under the awning to get out of the rain. I rub my hands and try to breathe warmth into them.

Deacon takes my raw, bare hands in his gloved palms; I feel his body's heat through the warm leather. Someone next to him says to me, "I'm glad to see you here, Max." She pulls back her poncho hood: it's Jasmine.

Her face contorts. "They just beat a woman on that corner over there, right in front of her child. She was just trying to cross the street. The cops took her away and left her kid screaming on the corner. We couldn't get to the woman or her child in time."

"Yes," Deacon adds, "We were hurrying down the street hollering at them to let her be. But there were too many police in our way. They dragged her off."

I look around. "Where's the kid?"

Jasmine looks at Deacon. "We don't know. The cops were four deep in front of us to hold us back. By the time the cops pulled back, the child was gone. We've been looking for the child while we're marching around."

Silence. Jasmine asks me, guardedly, "Are you going to work tonight?"

I take a deep breath. "I don't know," I answer honestly. "I just don't know yet."

Jasmine sidles over and leans against me. "Think about it, Max. If you can't stand up against a war like this one, what will you stand up against?"

Of course what she's saying is true. I just don't know what to do.

Jasmine starts to speak, but Deacon puts his hand on her shoulder and stills her. "Listen, I know you're worried about Ruby. We're all thinking about Miz Ruby. But life is about always doing the next right thing. And you got to decide what the next right thing is for you to do."

I chew my upper lip. Deacon claps me on my shoulder. "We're all going back to the protest. You coming with us, Mister Max?"

My face is numb, making my smile feel forced. "No. I didn't dress warmly enough for this." I wave good-bye and step out from shelter into the torrential storm.

I'm standing in the alley across from Club Chaos. The rain has stopped, for now.

It's not my head that brought me here, it was my feet, my fear. I didn't think I was coming to work. After all, I wasn't about to open up the place and run it by myself. I just thought maybe if I popped my head inside, Mimi couldn't fire me. And then I'd leave. I argued with myself the whole way here. I knew it was wrong to show up at the job, even if I wasn't there to work. It felt in my gut like selling out.

But I remembered what it is like to be out of work and too queer to hire. I've worked here for such a long time. I can comfortably use the bathroom on the job. And if I got fired now, where is the movement in the streets that will win my job back or find me another one?

And yet, all my arguments felt like copouts.

I told myself I didn't have to decide what to do until I got here. That I'd just scope out the situation. Maybe call in sick from the corner phone.

But when I got here, I saw the sign on the door. A crayoned pink peace symbol with scrawled writing: "Closed tonight. Pray for my kid brother

Frankie. Pray for all our brothers and sisters in uniform." Signed: Mimi, Manager.

The club is closed for the night. And here I am, briny tears of shame sliding down my cheeks. I hunch over in the alley, in the thin space between two brick walls, my hands dug deep in my jeans pockets. I call out to Raisa: "What was I to do?"

She doesn't answer.

"Tell me!" I speak to her too loudly. "Tell me what I'm supposed to do because I don't know. I don't know how to get through this right now."

But Raisa won't come to me now. She thinks I'm a scab. I've crossed an invisible picket line. She's furious with me.

So am I.

I don't pick up the telephone. I don't want to talk to anyone. I lie still, under my covers, and let the machine pick it up.

I hear Thor's voice digitally etch his message: "You won't believe this," he chortles. "The club was closed last night."

Sweat of guilt creates humidity under my quilt.

"So don't worry, buddy. We still got our jobs."

Was it only a dream that I went to work when the others stayed away?

I wear remorse like a shroud. My friends at work are circling me, eyeing me strangely.

"You okay, buddy?" Thor asks.

"Sure," I wave him away, pointing to the line of people waiting to get into the club. "I'm just tired."

"Okay," he says. But he puts his hand on my arm and leaves it there while he examines my eyes like an optometrist.

I turn away and readjust the stanchions. I've evaded everyone's eyes tonight. But it's not working. I feel worse hiding what I did.

"Listen," I say to Thor as he turns to go back inside to work. "I should have told you this before." I press my palms together in an entreaty. "Thor, I came to work last night."

He turns slowly, stiff with new knowledge. His lips press together until they turn white. "What would you have done if the club was open?"

I shrug. "I wasn't thinking that far ahead, Thor. I really wasn't thinking at all. I was just scared. Losing a job is a big deal to me. Especially right now."

"Well," he says finally, "it's a good thing the club was shut down anyway, wasn't it?"

That's all he says. Then he looks at me once more and goes inside. But in that final glance he reassessed me, did another calculation, and arrived at a different sum.

The line of patrons outside the bar shifts and murmurs in frustration, anxious to get inside and begin whatever is to begin.

The door opens. Jasmine stands before me, her arms folded across her body. "I heard," she announces. "Thor told me."

I inhale, but no air comes out of my mouth and nose; the air is lost inside me somewhere. I'm waiting for the blast.

"We haven't proved it to you yet, that's what I think," she begins as though in conversation with herself, not me. "We're not strong enough yet to show you that cooperation is better, is stronger than one person."

"I know that already." I have no excuses.

"No," she bats my statement away. "No, you don't know that yet. We have to show you." These are her final words and then she's gone.

"C'mon, pal," someone in line calls out. "Let us in. It's cold out here." It's time to open up the bar. I beckon to the first in line to come forward.

The door opens again from the inside. Deacon leans out and reaches for my hand—demands my hand. I give it to him willingly. His manner is gentle against the sharp blade of his message. "There are times when you got to be strong enough to stand up for what you believe."

I drop my head and look at the concrete sidewalk.

"Look at me," Deacon demands, with uncharacteristically harsh insistence. "I don't mean the little things in life. I'm talking about the big things. Because if you can't stand up when it matters, you'll lose everything. You'll lose yourself."

I look him in the eye, chew my lower lip, and nod. Then he drops the other shoe. "And you'll be lost to us, too." With those words, Deacon goes inside to start his shift.

The first person in line is visibly anxious to go inside. I wiggle my fingers to come forward. But the front door opens again from the inside. "Oh for Chrissakes," someone in line complains out loud.

It's Thor at the door again, this time holding up his cell phone in the air between us. It's glowing blue, lit and ready for conversation.

"Who is it?" I ask.

He thrusts it toward me wordlessly.

"Hello?" I say the word tentatively.

"Max?" It's Ruby's voice.

"Yeah?"

"Aw, Max," Ruby groans. "Sugar, what the hell were you thinking?"

I don't want to say. "I wasn't thinking," I answer.

She sighs. "You know better."

I barricade myself from her by taking a shot at myself: "Moral cowardice." Bitterness on my lips.

Her voice softens with emphasis. "You are not a coward."

"We both know that's not true." I don't know why I'm taking this path, I don't want to go there.

Ruby's voice rises. "Don't go all History Channel on me now."

"Well," my voice trails off.

"Max, give it a rest. You were fifteen years old."

"I was sixteen," I correct her. "It's just part of who I am, Ruby; you know that. It makes it hard for me to trust myself. In the heat, it feels like I'm doing the right thing when I'm doing the wrong thing."

A moment of silence on the other end of the phone. "Max, tell me something."

"What." My tone turns the word from a question to resignation.

"What was the heat?"

"What?" Now it's a question again.

"You said 'in the heat' you do the wrong thing. What was the heat to make you come to the club last night?"

My mouth is open and I'm looking at the cell phone in my hand. Somebody who knows me really well is on the other end.

11

"Let's go!" Heshie announces. I'm walking around the factory, running my hands over the cold metal contraptions in front of me, their disconnected veins and arteries running in every direction. A tool box lies open, its contents scattered around it.

"Where're we going?" I ask, suspiciously.

"Trust me," he answers brightly. "You'll see."

A most unsatisfying answer. "I'm not a real 'wait and see' kind of person, Hesh." I glance at my watch. It's 7:00 AM. "I've been up at work all night. I've gotta go to bed soon. I'm bushed."

"Okay, then let's go," he reaches for his canes. One is new—a slice of silver, three feet with rubber boots. The other is familiar—black walnut, polished to a warm glow. He struggles to his feet. "C'mon," he says. "If I beat you to the door, what does that say about you?"

He walks to the door with great effort. Every step another hill to climb. I see that the years are taking their toll on his mobility.

I hang back. "Hesh, please. Why the mystery? What's up?"

He's fumbling for the keys to the industrial locks on the door. "C'mon," he cajoles. "I'll tell you when we're in the truck."

"That's really nice of you, Hesh, but I've got a computer already."

Heshie peers out over the hood of his beat-up pickup truck before pulling out of the underground garage into the sunny street. There are few cars and fewer pedestrians on the street at this hour on a Sunday morning.

"This is not going to be just any computer, Rabinowitz," he grins. "What you have is a Dodge Dart. What you're gonna have tonight is a DeLorean!"

"Isn't that the guy that went belly up with his cars?"

He ignores me. "We'll build you a gamer's rig!"

"I just learned the one I got. Besides, where are we going, anyway?"

"To the computer fair out at the Aqueduct racetrack."

"Meadowlands?"

He scoffs. "Queens."

"I've never been to Queens."

As we pause at a red light, Heshie punches buttons on some kind of never-get-lost GPS device stuck to the dashboard of his pickup, wires dangling. Not one to curse, he's mumbling in frustration. "A-q-u-a, right?" he asks.

"A-q-u-E. Sheesh, brilliant techies never can spell. Why is that?"

" 'Cause we're looking at the forest, not the trees."

A mechanical voice, pitched in upper-register tones, dulcet and smooth, advises, "Left turn in point five miles."

I'm not feeling adventurous. I want to go home and to bed. I don't know where I'm headed and that doesn't feel safe. I don't want to fall down the rabbit hole of a computer fair. I don't even really know what a computer fair is. Are there breakneck-speed rides on the information superhighway? Are there Macintosh candied Apples?

Hesh and his talking vehicle have already taken me through the Midtown Tunnel into Queens. It feels familiar; blue-collar Jamaica doesn't look so different than blue-collar Jersey City, except maybe more jerk chicken and goat roti.

Heshie's waxing eloquent about TechExpo at the Javits Center: "There they got so many great vendors, so many tables. And celebrities."

"Hesh, what celebrities come to a computer fair? Like Charlton Heston selling computerized missile systems or something?"

Heshie rolls his eyes. "Computer celebrities."

"So we're not gonna meet Bill Gates today, huh?" I say, to hold up my end of the conversation as we roll through Queens.

Heshie makes a guttural sound in his throat. "Don't get me started on that guy."

"I forgot, Mister Linux." I laugh. "Open source software is where our politics meet." My tone changes. "Hesh, I'll go with you, but I can't afford a computer right now and I don't want you buying anything for me. It doesn't feel right."

Heshie laughs. "It's a *mitsve*."

"Yeah, but, I'm not comfortable with being on the receiving end of somebody else's *mitsve*. I don't want to owe anybody anything."

Heshie speaks, quietly. "You know what I remember about you when we were kids?" My stomach clenches. I don't want him to continue, but he does. "Your humanity."

I burst out laughing, unexpectedly for both of us. He looks hurt. But I can't stop laughing. "I'm sorry, Hesh. It just doesn't sound like me. I was born a cynic."

He frowns. "A cynic? No, that's not right. Even now, you're not optimistic, but you hope for more."

I squirm in my seat, no escape from intimacy.

"I remembered something about when we were kids," he continues, "when you came to stay with us on the Lower East Side that summer. You found me crying, you remember?"

I don't recall and I don't know where this is going.

"I told you some kids were making fun of me, about my body. That they laughed at me for being weak. I can still see your face. You looked so shocked. You said you had been practicing trying to walk like I do. You told me you could only do it for a few minutes; it tired you out. You said to me . . ." Heshie's voice grows thick, "you said to me, 'Your body is strong. You're the strongest one I know.' "

We move slowly through the city without speaking. I'm thinking about my own battles with the same kids. But Heshie isn't finished.

"Something else I remembered on Purim when I was drunk. I remember after your mama died." He adds his hope for her peaceful rest in a whisper under his breath, "*Alav hashalom.*"

My heart clenches. I wasn't prepared for this descent into buried memory.

"Before you went to live with your aunt Raisa, when you were still living with your papa, my mama used to bring over hand-me-down clothes for you."

I fix my stare outside the side window, seeing Heshie looking over at me in the glass reflection.

He pauses. I hope he is finished with this stroll down memory lane. But he goes on. "I thought about how you must have hated our hand-me-downs. And I thought about how you come to me when you need computer parts and I'm still giving you hand-me-downs, thinking—like my mama did—that I am doing a good deed. So I decided, it's time for you to have something new that's all your own. Something I can make for you."

My eyes burn, dry and smoldering. I wait before I say, "It's kind of you, Heshie. But I can't accept it. You and I don't see the world the same way. We've been arguing for almost our whole lives—about Israel, about what it means to be a Jew. I don't want to owe you so big that I have to compromise with you—you know what I'm saying? And there's nothing I can do for you to even it up. It feels unbalanced. I appreciate what you want to do for me. I really do, Hesh. But it doesn't feel right to me."

Heshie shrugs. "So, we keep arguing."

I shake my head slowly. We can't just keep arguing about the Middle East forever. Our beliefs are leading us to a fork up ahead on the road of friendship.

Heshie is undaunted. "Think of it this way, my friend: The good deed is a fortune for the doer. That's what my mother taught me. For this computer, you owe me nothing. This evens up what I owe you. When I was a kid, people treated me differently. Like I was a porcelain doll. They feared my body and despised it. You gave me a gift like nobody gave me before. You looked at me in a different way. More like the way I saw myself. And I never had anything to repay you in kind. I'm going to make you a computer today. A beautiful computer like no other."

The mechanically gendered voice announces "Destination ahead in point five miles."

We drive around and around the vast parking lot, wall-to-wall cars, looking for the closest spot to park. I'm surprised to count only four red-white-and-blue flags flying from car antennas, a far cry from the days immediately after 9/11.

"Aha," Heshie says, stepping on the accelerator. Our truck lurches forward and around a curve, throwing me against the window, and now we are parked right in front of the turnstile gates.

On one side of us is a sprawling outdoor flea market, where shoppers scramble to buy everyday clothing on the cheap. We walk in the opposite direction, toward the sign that reads: Race Fans Only. At the entrance booth Heshie forks over a few bills and hands me a ticket.

The dingy building has seen better days. The escalator isn't working; Hesh has to climb up as though they are stairs. By the time we make our way slowly to the top, he is winded, sweating and panting, and so am I. A young woman at the top of the stairs asks us to show our tickets. I've already misplaced mine, rummaging around in my pockets, embarrassed, until I find it and produce it with a flourish. She stamps our hands—a blue circle on pale flesh—and lets us inside.

I stare at the circle on the back of my hand like it's calling me to solve a mystery.

"What do you see?" Heshie asks.

I smile at him. "I see Pi."

Heshie pats my shoulder and nods approvingly. "C'mon. You can find the answers to the universe later. Let's get to work."

I look around: It's busy, chaotic. But strangely, it doesn't feel tense. It's sneakers and denim, baseball caps worn brim forward and brim backwards. Black, Latino, and Asian; a few multiracial couples holding hands. Heshie and I are among the few whites shopping or working the stalls.

No one is staring at us. They are focused on the gleaming technology around us. And so is Heshie. He is tenderly touching a coiled spiral of copper, a seashell. He holds it up for me to wonder at. "Heat sync," he explains.

"Beautiful." I admire it. I have no idea what it is.

Around me, people are talking to each other and into their cell phones in a language I don't understand—alphanumerics strung together in unfamiliar phrases.

Next to us, a bloody virtual battle to the death between a hypermasculine superhero and a towering muscled ogre is being fought out on an entire wall of video monitors. As I pause to watch, a seller zeros in on me, hungry for a sale. "Don't stop," Heshie tells me. "Keep walking till we've checked out everything."

I widen my view to take in the entire room. There's a booth for every component of a computer: cases, motherboards, processors, RAM, cables, hard drives, DVDs, and CD-ROMs. There're laptops and cell phone accessories—antennas that chirp like birds and flash like disco parties.

One booth has all the television shows from my childhood, transferred onto DVDs: *Burns and Allen*, *Captain Midnight*, *Flash Gordon*. The moment I linger to look, fingers trailing over titles, a seller is glued to me: "Treasure," he enthuses. "Lost gold. Three for twenty dollars."

Heshie tugs at my sleeve. "Look!" He directs me, pulls me in the direction of blaring techno music. Deep inside the throbbing beat, mechanical voices chant technomantras. The corner booth is huge, stacked with computer cases adorned with colorful blinking lights. I touch one—a black case—gently. One side is clear acrylic so you can see the motherboard inside, bathed in an internally mounted blue light. Next to this case is one in lustrous silver. On the front of that case, vertical bars of light shift in hue—red, purple, yellow.

"Look at this," Heshie urges. The sides of the cases he points to have designs—curves like tattoos sliced out of the metal in their sides—with lights inside that flicker and blaze. "Do you like this? I modded my own box like that. The one I game on."

I finger the handle on top of the case. "What's this thing for?"

He laughs. "We bring our computers to LAN parties. The host provides Pepsis, Doritos, and Internet access. We play Quake or RPGs. Or trade 'wares."

I don't even bother asking him to explain his world. I'm just struck by how many realities exist outside my own.

Heshie eagerly pulls me toward a table stacked with pyramids of computer software. He picks up one with a stylized devil on its cover: "Diablo. Number one RPG—role playing game. And this is Quake, the best war game ever. You get a team and you go out fragging—that means a kill. The object of the game is to capture the other team's flag and bring it back to your base. It's a great game; maybe you want to play sometime?"

I shrug off my discomfort noncommittally. "Nah, I don't think so. It's not really my thing. I'm more like the hunted, not the hunter. I'm usually the flag."

Heshie is still exuberant. "But you like to play the games I design!" He hesitates. "You do, don't you?"

"Heshie." I squeeze his arm and give him a little shake. "I love your games. I love them because they're actually vehicles. You physically transport my body to another world, another dimension. You take me someplace where nothing looks the same and all the rules are different. I love that. But I don't want to sit at home in front of my computer screen and shoot and be shot at."

Heshie's joy melts down into that annoyed look he has perfected over the years. "Well, to each his own, my friend. For me, it's my anger management."

He leans forward, picks up another game, and hands the vendor two twenty-dollar bills. His first buy of the day.

"What's that?" I ask.

His frown softens into a little smile. "AvaStar."

"What is it?" I pursue, trying to get past our awkward exchange.

"It's a new game you might like better," is all he says.

Now we've been once around the show and Heshie is ready to buy. Our pace picks up to a whirlwind. He points, negotiates, and hands me packages and bags. He picks through boxes of cables, checks charts listing RAM prices, turns over small devices in his hand like they're supermarket fruit.

Finally, when I'm running out of hands and can't carry another bag, Heshie stops in front of computer cases. "That one," he says to the seller, who begins the elaborate process of packing it up for us.

Heshie scowls in concentration. "You sure you got old cable wires in your apartment?"

I nod. "Pretty sure."

"Then let's go to your house and get started," he says.

His words register like an earthquake on my Richter scale. "My house?"

"Yeah, we'll get you all set up."

I hesitate. I don't bring anyone to my apartment—not even Ruby. My apartment is my solitary refuge from the world, my fortress, my secret hideout.

His smile wavers. "Is there a problem?"

I can't think of an answer. I just stand, fixed like a deer caught in headlights, arms filled with packages.

"Max." He uses my first name for a change, carefully drawing out the single vowel as though it is an answer to this dilemma.

My heart is pounding and my tongue is stuck in the dry well of my mouth. "Okay," I hear myself say. "Let's go."

12

Heshie stands stock-still in my apartment, looking agape at my walls. I am afraid he thinks a wild animal, a *vildekhaye*, lives here. He just stares, astonished. His reaction forces me to see the room through another's eyes. Looking around at the room I fear, too, that I have descended into the madness of alienation and just didn't realize it from the remote depths.

Maybe I'm not just different. Maybe I'm strange.

I lean against the door frame, mired in exhaustion—midday is way past my bedtime. Heshie walks slowly toward the walls. He runs his hand carefully across the script as though he's reading Braille. "This is in Hebrew," he says quietly.

"It's Yiddish."

Heshie whistles through his teeth. "I only remember a little."

Weariness and resentment sharpen the edges of my voice. "This is my world as a Jew, Heshie. Yiddishkeit. You like to think I've abandoned being Jewish. You think I've lost my identity. But we come from different traditions. You don't even see my Jewishness because it doesn't look like yours."

He backs up from the wall and looks at it in awe, still breathless from the climb up five flights of stairs. "Read it to me," he demands. "What does this say?"

"*Ikh heng tsvishn do un dortn,*" I speak awkwardly; I never read these words aloud. "I hang between here and there—*di malke fun stires*, the queen of contradiction."

Heshie is already moving his hand to another poem. "And this one? What does it say?"

"*Zol di eynzamkeyt firn far a hand di neshome*"—the words make my body feel raw as I translate them: "Let loneliness lead a soul by the hand—I still walk faithfully through the wooded gates of Night. Like the rush of wind in your viscera, the life of everything I see rushes through mine, even the images that hover nearby." I hesitate, exposed. Heshie glances at me and back at the wall, and I continue: "I send a prayer to my own body as if to strange, phantastical gods: Make me whole, so I can resolve my simple earthly pleasures on the steps of Night o'er which I clamber."

Heshie points to another expanse of poetry.

"Those are the factory poets." I walk up next to Heshie to stand beside him, recognizing old friends on the plaster wall.

"What will you do when all the walls are full?" he asks.

I shrug. "I usually have to move before that happens."

Heshie backs up from the wall and moves to the hallway. "Is there more like that?" he asks, peeking into the doorway of my bedroom, where the walls and ceiling are painted with cave wall drawings. I wait, braced for his reaction, but he makes no sound at all. Suddenly all the things about my apartment that make it my home, that feel so familiar, seem bizarre and strange, even to me.

"Heshie?" I call to him from the hallway. "There's nothing in the house to eat, really. You want me to order pizza?" No response.

He moves past me on his way to my office. I tag after him, making conversation. "That's where my computer is. You want me to move it?" No answer. I follow him into my office. Virtually every inch of wall space is covered with a mass of maps, bristling with colorful pins, but the first thing Heshie's fingertips rest on is the Palestinian flag.

I step up beside him. My voice is soft. "This is who I am as a Jew, Heshie. This is where my tradition takes me at this moment in history." Heshie studies my face but doesn't speak.

He looks around at all the maps. "What is this?" he asks, very quietly, pointing to the one above my desk.

"*Zelbshuts*—these are all the places where I could find self-defense against pogroms in the nineteenth century."

He moves to the wall across from my desk. "And these?"

"These are all the sites of resistance in Nazi Germany. See these here? These are all the concentration camps where there was resistance. Almost all of them, really."

He pauses beside rows of poetry books in Yiddish. "My mother spoke Yiddish to me." He touches the book bindings tenderly. "But my father said Yiddish is for yentas to gossip. He thought it was a dialect, not a real language."

I try to mask my irritation. "You know what they say, Hesh: a language is a dialect with an army and a navy."

Heshie's laughter sounds a little forced.

I pull out a large volume, three-quarters of a century old, and hand it to Heshie. "Your mama gave this to me, when I graduated from eighth grade."

Heshie takes the book from my hand and touches it gingerly, incredulously, a little bit of his mother unexpectedly returning. He opens the pages to examine the tiny type. "What is it?" he asks.

"*Yidishe Dikhterins:* four centuries of Yiddish poetry by women."

Heshie looks inside the front cover at the inscription his mother penned to me. I wonder if he'll ask me to translate it, but he doesn't. He keeps his head down and closes the cover tenderly.

"You sure you don't want pizza?" I press.

Heshie shakes his head, lost in his work. He is carving a pattern into the side of the computer case with a power drill. My kitchen table is covered with electronic parts, my floor piled up with empty boxes and Styrofoam packing chips.

"Hesh," I point to a tattoo on his forearm, "is that new?" It looks like a big, curvy X.

"Yeah," he stares at his arm. "It's a warchalk: people chalk this on buildings to show where there's free access to open Wi-Fi networks."

"You mean the way hobos chalked the homes that were friendly?"

"Yeah, Rabinowitz." He grins. "Exactly."

Raisa is standing beside my sink, drying the dishes. She nods toward Heshie. "This one is a lonely child," she tells me. I look at my friend and see that she is right.

Heshie looks up from his work. "Did you say something?"

"No, I was just thinking, that's all." I clumsily pick up a computer part.

He snatches it from my hand and gives it back to me, his fingers carefully holding it by the edges, and dives back into his work: "About what?"

"Oh, I don't know. You remember Raisa?"

"Your aunt?" He smiles wryly: "Raisa the Red. I wasn't allowed to play at your house after she came to stay while your mama was," his voice falters.

"When my mother was dying." I finish his thought. "Your parents were afraid my aunt's politics were contagious?" It comes out a little sharper than I'd intended.

"Yeah," he smiles shyly. "Something like that."

"Our whole neighborhood was communist."

"I know," he nods. "But you know, after my mama ran off and married my papa, she and Raisa never got along." He reaches for a screw and places it between his teeth but manages to keep talking. "After your mama—you know, after you went to live with Raisa—I didn't see you for a while. So I never really knew her very well. What made you think of your aunt?"

I don't answer that question. Instead, I tell him, "I remember how when she gave me my first Yiddish book of poems, she dribbled a little drop of honey on the cover. Did your family do that too, with your first book?"

Heshie's smile makes him look young and innocent. "To make learning sweet!"

"Years later I got Raisa her first computer—one of those old ones you had to boot up with two floppy disks, remember?"

Heshie rolls his eyes.

"Raisa was getting a little absentminded about where she left her piles of bills, her grocery lists," I recall out loud. "She kept misplacing little scraps of paper. I was working at a factory in SoHo, stamping out computer parts. I made hundreds of dollars a day in parts for the company, maybe thousands, but I earned so little it took me months to save up for that computer. Anyway, when I gave it to her, I dripped a little honey on the computer screen. I told her: Here's another window to the world."

Heshie stops working. "Did she lick it off?"

"Indeed she did," I laugh.

"Did she learn to use it?"

"Well, yes and no."

Heshie probes gently. "Is she still alive?"

I see Raisa in a floral housedress. "She lives in Coney Island with my uncle."

Heshie frowns. "I thought your uncle died."

I see my uncle Shlomo propped up on a boardwalk bench, wrapped in a wool blanket, staring at the ocean; the sea is boiling. "Yes, he did. A while ago."

"Is your aunt still living there?"

"No, she died too."

Heshie looks at me oddly. "Hand me that screwdriver." He rolls up his sleeves and begins to gather parts and assemble them.

I lean on the table, resting my chin on my arms, drowsing, watching the new machine come together.

"Wake up, my friend!"

I have been sleeping, my head on the kitchen table. It's evening—long, long past my morning bedtime. Heshie has already set up my new computer in the office. I follow him inside, anxious but excited to find a surprise in my own home.

He snaps the switch and the machine whirs and hums to life like a giant insect. I kneel down next to the computer case. The shape of a coiled dragon is carved out of its black metal side. Red light glows from behind its silhouette—fiery breath. I peer into the exposed innards of the computer and suddenly I am Gulliver the giant, looking at a Lilliputian metropolis.

"Heshie," I say. "Wow!"

"Do you like it?" He is proud of his work. Before I can answer, he keeps talking. "It's an excellent motherboard, a really fast processor, RAM up the wazoo, and a good video card—sixteen point seven million colors."

I laugh. "I don't think I'll need the whole palette."

"The human eye can only pick up about 256 colors in the spectrum."

"Then why bother with millions, Hesh?"

Heshie looks exasperated. He holds up his hands in front of him as though he were holding the planet between his palms. "Because the universe has that many colors, even if we don't perceive them all. It's about true life; it's about reality—the real world—whether we see it or not."

He physically droops; he's at the end of his energy spurt. "You're all hooked up with broadband now." He points to the monitor. "And I loaded the game AvaStar for you. Double click on the icon and let it take you someplace new. I've gotta go," he says.

"Heshie, thank you. Nothing like this ever happened to me before," I tell him as we walk to the door.

He waves aside my "thank you" brusquely.

I won't let him. *"A hartsikn dank, Heshele."*

He smiles, letting a little more "thank you" in.

I open the door and lean on the doorjamb. "The lightbulb in the hallway is burned out again," I tell him. "I'll go get a flashlight and go downstairs with you."

"I don't need any help," he snaps.

"Okay," I back off, not wanting to matronize him.

I stand in the doorway listening as he makes his way slowly down the stairwell, one step at a time, a climber carefully descending from the mountain's peak.

13

"I know y'all are not comin' up in here, in my house, and tellin' me what I'm gonna do." Ruby stands in the middle of her living room glaring at Netaji.

Deacon and I are sitting at the kitchen table trying to will ourselves into invisibility.

"Darling," Netaji proffers.

Ruby vogues into a Diana-Ross-stop-in-the-name-of-love stance. "Darling—my sweet, fine ass. I am takin' my damn medicine, I am better and I'm gettin' ready to go back to work. So y'all better wrap your minds around that."

Netaji's hand gesture aims to soothe Ruby. She freezes in her posture to hear him out again. "My love, I am only saying that you have not been well. You had pneumonia. There are so many people who smoke in the club. The air is not good. Please think about your health."

Netaji turns toward the kitchen for support. He does not find it. Deacon is leaning forward on the kitchen table, holding his chin in his hands, staring at the kitchen wall up close, inspecting the paint.

Netaji reaches out his arm toward me. "Max, you tell her."

I know better than to tell Ruby what to do. Ruby swings around toward me. I lift up one hand as though I'm stopping rush hour traffic. Our eyes meet. She surprises me. There's no anger in her gaze. In fact, a smile begins to grow—a sweet smile that twists and turns but can't be suppressed. She's right: in the struggle for her health, Ruby seems to be gaining.

Ruby slowly turns back toward Netaji, arms akimbo. No smile now. She raises one arm toward Netaji, her index finger like a conductor's baton. "Let me tell you this one last time." Her voice is quieter with certainty. "I love you, sugar. You're a mother hen. But I am not a chick. I am goin' back to work and start livin' my life again and not you or no-damn-body is going to tell me I can't. Now, is that clear? Did I make myself understood?"

A moment of silence. Deacon lifts his head from his hands to watch what comes next.

Netaji tenderly takes Ruby's face in his large hands. "Of course, my darling. Yes, my love."

"Business is not good," Mimi tells Ruby.

Jasmine and Thor and I are eavesdropping. Deacon is on a barstool nearby, listening intently.

"So, for tonight, see your friends and relax. Get better, and then we'll talk."

Ruby leans forward. "I am better. We're talkin' now."

Mimi's shoulders rise defensively, aware of her audience. "I was going to discuss this all with you soon, anyway. As you all know, business has slacked off on drag performance nights. We're cutting back."

Ruby moves a step forward; Mimi takes a step back.

"The owners still want to keep the drag shows, don't get me wrong. For now. But they want other formats. They want other theme nights, other music, to bring in new customers. That means different crews."

I can see that Jasmine wants to intervene, but she stills herself.

Ruby nods very slowly. "So what're you sayin', Mimi? Say it so we can all hear you."

"Well," Mimi clears her throat. "I may have to cut all your shifts down to two a week." She hastens to add, "But they're the big-money nights: Friday and Saturday!"

We all draw a collective breath to shout.

As I cross the street and round the corner to go to work I can see something is wrong. Ruby, Jasmine, Thor, and Deacon are outside on the sidewalk in front of Chaos. A handful of other people are just milling around nearby, too, smoking cigarettes and passing a joint, muttering and laughing about their own lives.

"What the hell's going on?" I ask.

Ruby points, with dramatic disgust, at a sign on the door. It reads: Closed for renovations—Management.

There go our jobs.

"Mimi owes us a week's pay," I say quietly, out loud to myself.

Thor thumps on the metal gate protecting the empty club from our wrath.

Ruby sighs bitterly. "Yeah, good luck trying to get it. Mimi won't resurface for a while. And the owners will just tell us to go to hell."

Jasmine sighs in agreement. "There's no paperwork that says we ever even worked here."

I look around at a small group of people nearby loudly debating which restaurant they should eat at. "Hey," I say to one of them, "can I have a cigarette?"

He stares at me like I've asked him for one of his kidneys. "Hey, pal. You know how much a pack of these costs?"

I shrug, "A couple of bucks?"

"What are ya, Fred Flintstone?"

I angrily dig in my pocket and pull out a buck. "Is that enough?"

"Oh, fuck it," he replies, reluctantly pulling out a pack of cigarettes— a brand I used to despise—and extending it to me.

"Thanks," I reply cheerily. "Got a light?"

He's exasperated. "You want me to smoke it for you?"

"Gee," I say, with mock glee, "I never heard that one before. You should write sitcoms." I extend the dollar bill in his direction. He waves it away and herds his friends away from our presence.

I take a drag on the cigarette, strange and familiar in my hand, and cough once. I take another drag deep into my lungs. My body begins to buzz, my vision swirls. It's been a long time since I got high.

I look up and see the faces of my friends, frozen in horror. That makes my next toke on the cigarette more awkward, but not impossible.

"Buddy, what are you doing?" Thor asks, rhetorically.

"You want a drink with that?" Ruby's tone is ominously gentle.

"Hey!" I leave the cigarette dangling between my lips as I hold up both my hands. "I lost my job tonight. I'm sure you all understand, right? So give me a break, okay?" I take one last drag, feeling the rush beginning to ebb. I drop the stub in the gutter and crush it with a twist of my boot. I wonder how much a pack of cigarettes costs now.

Jasmine shakes her head, signaling a new discussion. "We need to figure out what to do next. I'll call the guy who runs Club Pi, Rick, and see if he needs a crew."

Thor pipes up, "Who wants breakfast?"

One by one, we all demur.

I already want another cigarette.

14

"Do you know there's a drink called Sand in Your Butt?" I thump *The Bartender's Bible to Mixed Drinks* on the table of the restaurant booth in frustration.

The waitress looks at me, startled by the thud, as she balances full plates of food on both her arms. "Be with you in a minute, doll. Give me a sec."

"Take your time," I wave my hand.

Thor chortles.

"Don't laugh," I say. "I'll never memorize this in time to be a bartender. Who knew there were so many new ways to get drunk?"

Thor leans back in his chair and smiles. "We'll do fine, buddy. Don't sweat it."

I shake my head, "I'm not so sure. I mean, I've never tended bar before."

"Yeah. So what? You've worked in bars since god was a teenager."

"Yeah," I shrug. "But every job has its secrets and surprises." I slide the bartender's guide toward him on the table. "This is a lot to memorize: Screaming Vikings and Sex on the Beach."

Thor picks up the book and eagerly thumbs through it. "There's Vikings having sex on the beach in your book? Where?" Thor tosses the book back across the table to me. "You wanna know the secret to bartending?" I await his wisdom. "You gotta treat it like it's *Cheers* and you're that Ted Danson guy."

The man and woman at the booth on the other side of the restaurant are gawking at us; he's whispering and laughing in our direction. It's not yet midnight. The yuppies feel emboldened—they think the East Village is theirs. That won't change till after the bars close. I want to go over there and pound the smirk off the guy's arrogant face.

"I most certainly do not want to be Ted Danson." My tone sounds self-righteous.

"Okay." Thor sounds mildly exasperated. "Then be that Woody Harrelson guy."

I see Jasmine coming out of the women's bathroom at the same time that Deacon's coming out of the men's room. "Don't tell Jasmine I'm scared about this, okay?" I make Thor promise. "I don't want her replacing me on the job with somebody else."

Thor pantomimes zipping his lips.

The couple at the table across from us stares at Jasmine, head to toe, and bursts out laughing.

"Hey!" I raise my voice. "You over there." I point to them both. They look surprised that the watched is speaking to the watchers. "Eat your food and mind your own damn business," I shout.

The waitress stops in her tracks, pot of coffee suspended in one hand.

"Go fuck yourself!" the woman at the table answers.

The man laughs as though she's just told a hilarious joke. "Fuckin' freak show," he says, loud enough for us all to hear.

The waitress pulls a pad from her apron pocket, scribbles the tally of their bill, and slaps it down on the table in front of them.

Deacon stands in front of our table like a guard. When they get up to pay, and look our way, Deacon waves his hand at them, "Mind your business, now. Be on your way."

As they leave, Jasmine sits down at our table. She gave us the gist of last night's meeting with our new boss. Deacon will work the hatcheck until he finds another job playing piano. Then Ruby can take over the job from him. It's good tip money when the weather gets cold again. But it's going to be a lousy gig in the summer months. Backpacks, a few hats, meager tips. "We're going to have to split our money as a crew," Jasmine concludes.

We look up at each other and nod in confirmation, again.

The waitress stops at our table. "Anything else I can get cha?"

As we shake our heads, she makes a few computations on our bill and drops it on our table. "Anytime you're ready," she nods toward the cashier.

We crane our necks to check out the bill, digging around for money in pockets, wallets, purses, and drop our share in a little pile in the center of the table.

Deacon wearily lifts his coat from the rack, in no apparent hurry to get home. He puts his hand on Thor's shoulder. "You doing okay?"

Thor pats his hand. "No complaints, my friend."

Deacon turns toward me. "How 'bout you, Mister Max?"

"Well," I smile, "doesn't do any good to complain, does it?"

"No sir," Deacon agrees, "life just flows on."

Thor is feeling the material of Deacon's silk coat with his fingers. "Deacon, tell me you made this yourself."

"Yes, I did." Deacon smoothes the fabric of his coat with a pianist's hand. "When I was a child I wanted more than anything in the world to sew—suits and dresses, all things special. But I learned to play the piano and that just took me this way, instead of the way I thought I'd go." He sighs, "Oh well. I'd best get home now."

Deacon places his fingertips against my cheek, the settling of a bird's wing. "Don't you fret, now, Mister Max. You know you can be a bit of a worrier."

"Who, me?" I smile reluctantly.

Jasmine comes back to the table and divides up all our change. "Here," she tells me, "you put in too much. You only had coffee and a roll. The rest of us had meals."

Jasmine's tone shifts. "I ignore them," she says.

"What?" I'm confused.

She nods toward the table where the man and the woman had been sitting. "It's none of my business what they think of me. I don't care."

I don't think Jasmine understands.

She continues, "Until they step into my circle. And then that's another matter altogether." As she looks up, I realize I am looking into the eyes of a warrior. She does understand. Jasmine heads toward her coat and brings Thor's jacket back with her.

Through the picture window I can see the sky is dark above the trees in the little park across the street; neon constellations surround the black hole of trees and grass. Dawn is hours away; I stretch my arms and yawn. After all these years of working the wrong end of the clock, even after a night shift job ends I can feel exhaustion pulling downward on my body like gravity until the next one begins.

Kisses and hugs good-bye. I'm holding back. I'm not a kisser and a hugger. I saunter toward the door, just ahead of the group.

Thor and I are outside the door into the cool morning. He presses,

"Buddy, all's I'm saying about this bartending gig is you've been doing the sullen bouncer thing for a long time. You've got to lighten up to be a bartender. You've got to relax and listen to people and make small talk."

That's why I'm so worried. It's hard enough for me to do that with my friends at breakfast, let alone with strangers.

"I know," I shrug. "I'm just a little nervous about starting work at a new club, you know? I don't even know which bathroom they'll make me use there."

I'm staring at the screen of my computer. My darkened office eerily glows with phosphorescent light. It's 2:00 AM—tomorrow I start my new job. I'm bored and antsy.

I explore the Internet, looking out the portals of web cams, viewing places and things I've never seen before. A flag stiffened into a permanent wave at a North Pole exploration site. Mist settling its soft blanket over a browning valley. Falcon chicks gobbling whatever is offered from a parental beak.

I'm procrastinating. It's time to click on AvaStar—"the game in which every avatar is a star."

Maybe I'm the only person playing this game who doesn't know what an "avatar" is, so I Google it. The first definition tells me: "From the Sanskrit for the incarnation of Godhead, an avatar is the 'body' you 'wear' in a virtual community—an animated, articulated representation of a human which represents you, the user, in any virtual environment." I click back to the game's gold star icon, flashing in front of me. I'm staring at it as though it is the gateway to hell. Of course, it's just a game and it is online, so I can bail out anytime—no real trail except a few cookie crumbs.

I click on the gold star. My screen fills with bright light, and the airbrushed metallic body of an avatar, like an Oscar award statuette, appears in the middle of my screen, tumbling into yellow cyberspace. A checklist appears with stars to click on: I choose "New Member/Start Game Now."

All light drains from my screen. I think my machine has crashed. Just as I reach to do a warm boot, a cyberscene appears. The background looks like a futuristic Cape Canaveral. Rockets pointing their noses toward chunky asteroids, hovering high beyond reach.

In front of me is a shiny golden door. "Suit up here" the sign above it reads. I'm not sure how to open the door. I click on the door with my mouse. Nothing happens. I double-click—that's the trick. It swings open. Inside, a silver android awaits me. I stare at it. It stares at me. I could go outside in real life for this. I move my cursor over the avatar's metallic muscles. A little dialogue box appears over *hir* head: "FAQ me."

I don't know what questions to ask. I'm tired of this game already, but Heshie urged me to stay with it, so I do.

Unexpectedly, the avatar moves aside and two doors appear.

One door has a "women's" symbol, the other "male." Even in bodiless cyberspace? "You have got to be fucking kidding me," I shout out loud.

I stand outside the doors as I have stood so many times outside bathroom doors with an aching bladder. I don't understand why Heshie would want me to play this game. Surely he recalls having to make this game choice.

I could check them both out. No one knows who I am here. The thought strikes me: No one knows who anyone is here. No bodies with hills and valleys, no resonating timbre of voice. Only cyberpersonas, tried on or shrugged off like a cloak.

I run my cursor over the female symbol. It glows with gold light, but the door remains closed. I double-click on it and it rises to reveal a dressing room. I'm facing a row of lockers. Each one is emblazoned with a label: Faces, bodies, clothes, accessories. I hesitate. A silver android appears with a towel draped on its metal arm. Silver seems to be the color of service worker. "FAQ me" appears as a cartoon balloon over the head of the R2D2 android. I don't want to read the instructions. That's not how I want to play. I click on the locker marked "Faces."

"Choose race" the game demands. It doesn't give me an option to challenge whether "race" really exists. Here, obviously, it does. A glittering futuristic game trapped in the social construction of here and now. "Caucasian, Black, Hispanic, Asian." Those are the choices offered. No room in this game for Mohammad or Hatem. No room for nationality. No room for complexity. I don't understand why there's no space in virtual reality for multiple realities.

It doesn't feel right to go out into this game as an avatar of color and interact with other people. On the other hand, it's creepy to pick being white in a racist world. But I think the only ethical choice for me in this game is to click on "Caucasian."

As I do, a new demand appears: "Child, teenager, adult." Elder doesn't seem to be a choice. I click on "adult."

Now I'm asked to choose my "face." I look at my choices, seeking out some kind of familiarity—something that reminds me of me. There's a long, square face with a kind of a Prince Valiant sort of thing going on with the hair that might work. There's another with a mullet. But I'm not sure I'd wear a mullet, even in cyberspace.

I click on Prince Valiant and move to bodies. The moment I do, I realize this dressing room is not going to work for me. I thought I was going to be a golden avatar, my hills burnished with light, my valleys nestled in darkness.

But the bodies are all slim, hourglass figures, emphasizing hips and breasts. There are no fat bodies here. No bent bodies. No bodies missing limbs.

I click on "Clothes" to see if I could layer the figure to create another embodiment. But the clothing fits on the body like the tabbed, form-fitted outfits on the paper dolls of my childhood.

Now I want to check out the male dressing room, but I can't figure out how to exit backwards. The only way to get out of this dressing room, it seems, is to exit the game and log in again.

My phone rings in the living room. When I hear Ruby's voice on the machine, I run in and pick up the receiver.

"Max. Are you awake, sugar?"

"Yeah, I'm here."

"You sleeping?"

"No. I'm just playing a game."

Silence. "With anybody I know?"

"No," I laugh. "I'm playing in cyberspace."

"Uh-huh. Then I guess I don't have to tell you to play safe."

"I'm playin' this game Heshie gave me. It's one of those role-playing things. AvaStar. Guess what the first thing they make me pick is?"

"Boy or girl!"

"Bingo," I laugh. "Then they make you pick your race."

She doesn't laugh. She doesn't say a word.

"I got hung up trying to figure out what to do about that."

She pauses. "So what'd you decide?"

"I picked what I am. But it felt extremely distasteful to choose white."

"Uh-huh. They got 'Queer' in la-la land?"

"They've got gay and lesbian. Heshie says they even have clubs with go-go boys. You pick whether you want to be female or male. But I can't find any room for gender queer. You can't mix and match anything. I'm still trying to figure out who I'm going in as."

"You payin' for that game? You're already playin' it."

How did I get this far in the game without being asked about payment information? Did Heshie remember I don't have credit cards? Has he prepaid?

"Anyway," I sigh, "I wonder if they got police in this game."

"Sugar, if they got go-go, they got po-po."

A fire engine siren screams down the street outside. The sound enters my open living room window and fills my apartment.

"Max," Ruby hesitates. "Do me a favor? Call Estelle and kinda nudge her about Vickie's memorial."

That's not something I'm anxious to do. "She told me she wasn't ready."

Ruby sighs. "I know. But this has gone on too long now. For real."

"But if she's not ready, how can I push her?"

"Listen, sugar, talk to her. Tell her we'll all help her." Ruby is talking to herself now. "It feels like Vickie just up and disappeared. Some of us need some damn closure."

"Yeah," I resign myself. "I'll call Estelle soon. I'll feel it out with her."

"That's it. That's right. Thank you, sugar."

"Don't hang up, yet, okay?" I ask her, not wanting to sit in lonely silence after hearing Ruby's voice.

"What's goin' on with you, Max?" She doesn't wait for me to answer. "You still smokin'?"

"Not in the house."

"Not yet. You had a drink?"

"No." I say the word as though the question is absurd.

"You're on a slippery slope, sugar. You've been here before."

"We both have," I say, barricading myself.

"You want me to say you need a meetin'?" I groan in exasperation. She pursues. "I'm just sayin'."

Now my tone is flat and cold. "Don't twelve-step me."

"I'm just sayin'."

I can hear her television. "What are you listening to?"

She sighs, audibly annoyed that I am changing the subject. "I'm sittin' here watchin' another goddamn war. It's a crime what they're doin' to those people who didn't do a damn thing to us." Her voice grates, "I'm so angry. They got all this money for bombs to grab that oil, and my friends got to take up a collection for my medicine. Now that's a damn crime, too."

I can hear explosions in the background behind her voice. "When we met it was Vietnam," I remember. "The marches were still small."

Ruby laughs unexpectedly. "Oh, lord, remember that time we were comin' back from D.C. in the snowstorm and the bus got stuck and they closed the turnpike?"

I remember us huddled together for warmth on that cold, cold bus. "Yeah," I recall, "and the toilet broke. Yuck."

Ruby emits a mock scream, "I forgot that. Half the women on the bus were on their moons. By the time the tow truck got there all the snow around the bus looked like *Chainsaw Massacre*."

We laugh together, looking at the same memory from different vantage points.

Ruby's tone shifts gear. "You goin' to the antiwar march in D.C. next weekend?"

"I can't. I'm starting this new job." As the words come out of my mouth, I think they may make Ruby feel left out.

"You startin' that new job tomorrow, huh?" She asks casually, "You think they're gonna need me? I could try to find work someplace else."

"I think they will. Deacon's lookin' for a music gig. And when the cigarette ban starts the club won't be so smoky. You may as well take this time to get some rest. It's been a long time since you got any rest."

We sit without speaking.

"I have value," she says softly; an affirmation. "I have worth."

"Yes," I whisper in agreement. "Like no other."

A train is passing on the tracks down the hill. I can hear the unearthly keening of the rails.

Ruby's voice lifts. "We need to have a party soon. Remember the parties we had, back in the day? We had some mad fun. Remember how we'd be up on the roof dancing all night long until someone called the cops on us? Remember how we used to string up Christmas lights and those little paper lanterns—till the super figured out whose electricity we were tapping into?

"Mmm," Ruby tastes the past. "And Angel would get so mad if anybody said his music was salsa. 'Salsa is something you put on your food! These young ones comin' up got to know this is Afro-Cuban music!' I can't believe that Angel's dead. Those times don't feel so long gone."

"We're the sunset of another ordinary day." Essex Hemphill's words on my lips.

Ruby's voice, stony and cold, says what's true: "Essex is dead. Audre's gone, Assotto, Marlon. And almost every single friend I ever had. They're all dead now."

"Yeah," my voice is soft with loss. "And Angel."

"Call Estelle," Ruby commands me. "We got to do that memorial for Vickie soon."

15

"Move, move, move," I'm muttering under my breath at the tourists who are mall-walking two and three abreast. I'm out of breath, heading east on my way to the new job. It's nine o'clock and the night is so unseasonably temperate that the streets and sidewalks are packed. I'm due at work now. Jasmine will be furious with me.

I race past Cooper Union, toward St. Marks Place, and all the memories of the stories Raisa told me about the uprising here of 20,000 women garment workers come back to me in a rush. I wish there was an uprising right this moment. Something so big that it would shut everything down and I wouldn't have to start a new job tonight. Something so big that it would change everything, and I'd be a part of it.

As I head east on Eighth Street, I see how these streets have changed since I was a kid. I'm surrounded by an oddly mixed crowd—counterculture grunge and affluent casual—milling around the shopping stalls piled high with multicolored socks and scarves, T-shirts emblazoned with clever insults and simple expletives. As I work my way around foot traffic, I notice how many people are still wearing "No war on Iraq" buttons pinned to worn denim, scuffed leather, soft cashmere.

Headed east across Second Avenue—the Jewish theater district of my childhood—I cross against the light, jogging across the street, warding off honking taxis and cars with an outstretched arm like a Heisman Trophy winner. I cut over a block, leaving behind the Off-Off Broadway theaters, egg creams, and crème brulée.

Halfway down the block, I thrust two crumpled dollar bills through a tiny takeout window and get a Chinese bun and a nickel change. I pull off steaming pieces with my fingers and wolf it down as I hustle to make up for the stop, noshing on the soft, fresh dough smeared with sweet red bean paste—taste delicious as touch.

I slow down again at a newsstand to toss quarters on the counter and grab a daily newspaper. I read as I walk: stock market down, dogs of war straining at the leash. Reports that the CIA has an Arab guy in custody they say is al-Qaeda. The newspaper is taking a poll: how many think we should torture him?

By First Avenue, the coldwater tenements are now being rented out as fancy townhouses. Bodegas flashing with neon primary colors are being eclipsed by wine bars bathed in muted teal or burgundy light.

As I near the alphabet avenues—A, B, C—strings of little white holiday lights still twinkle this late into springtime, ensnared in the limbs of budding boughs. I hang a right at Tompkins Square Park and head deeper into Loisada. New high-rise apartment buildings ascend from the lots on which community gardens once grew. Most of the bright Puerto Rican murals are painted over now. Saabs, Acuras, and SUVs line the curbs.

But at Avenue D, the blue, red, and white bandera of Puerto Rico still blazes from walls here and there. Lampposts are plastered with posters demanding ¡No Guerra!

I am panting as I pick up my pace. Groups begin to gather in the huge world of the projects, and outside restaurants, stores, and clubs. All across Gotham the night trade is readying to commence. The exchange of commodities never sleeps.

I head south, across Houston, deeper into the Lower East Side of my grandparents. I am on my way to a new job, and I am late.

"Handsome, buddy! You look real nice." Thor fingers my sharkskin lapel and skinny black tie as I fasten the last button on my white shirt collar.

I look down at my clothes. "Secondhand treasures." I smile, still trying to catch my breath.

"Max!" My name is being shouted as a curse. Jasmine is headed for me like a storm. Thor pats my arm for comfort and courage. I put my hands up in front of me to ward her off.

"How could you show up late your first night and risk spoiling things for all of us?"

I don't answer. I feel defensive, on edge, and there's not much to say. "I called Estelle before I left. The call took longer than I thought."

Jasmine crosses her arms across her chest. Her anger drops a notch. "Why couldn't you have waited until morning to call her, Max?"

I don't answer. What's done is done.

"How was she?" Jasmine asks.

I shrug. "She was sobbing when she picked up the phone. I didn't know how to hang up while she was crying so hard. I knew I was running late, but I couldn't hang up."

Jasmine drops her gaze to the floor. Now she gears herself up again. "Don't let it happen again, Max, you hear me? If you don't want to be part of this team, tell me now. Do you hear me, Max?"

I don't answer. I'm not a child.

An unfamiliar, burly man looms behind Jasmine. "What's the problem?" he asks.

Jasmine spins around at the sound of his voice. "No problem, Rick."

He scrutinizes me and Thor. "Who are these two?"

Jasmine points to her clipboard. "These two will take the little bar downstairs."

He looks us up and down so long I'm ready to go for his throat. Thor must be reading my mind because he raises his hand ever so slightly toward me to cool me out.

Rick talks to Jasmine about us like we're not there. "These are drag kings?"

Jasmine smiles politely without speaking.

"Old school and new school," Thor answers, enigmatically.

Rick is already bored by the conversation. He half turns to walk away and then swings back to face us. "You want to work for me, you get a couple a things straight, you got me? There's no comp drinks for your pals, you got that? At the end of your shift, when the money gets tallied, if there's a drink not paid for it comes out of your pocket. And no buy-backs. You understand?"

Rick holds up his arm and taps his watch face with a fingernail.

"C'mon," Jasmine rounds us up. "Let's go."

The club is spacious and dark, lit here and there with neon torches. Spots of color chase each other in circles around the floor. Jasmine beckons us down a narrow stairway into the lower level. It's small and even darker. One whole wall is a screen on which an old David Bowie concert is flickering, but the sound system is blaring the Pointer Sisters singing "I'm So Excited."

Jasmine explains, "When you start your setup, go get the things that are farthest from your bar and work your way closer. You get the ash trays, napkins, paper towels over there," she nods toward a stockroom door with a flimsy padlock. She instructs us on the setup of swizzle sticks, lemons and limes, olives and cherries, spigots for beer and soda pop, garbage bags, cartons for empty bottles. She holds up a stack of plastic cups: "No chilled glasses for martinis in a club this size."

"A club this sleazy," I mutter to Thor.

Jasmine bangs an ashtray on the bar. "Max, this is not a game."

I know that, but I feel childish right now. And I can't snap myself out of it.

Thor moves between us. "How long does the setup take?"

"That depends," she tells him, "on how it was left the night before." She ticks off on the fingers of one hand: "Top shelf liquor seven dollars, well drinks four. Bottled beer is six and draft is four. Got that? Max, you'll need to start cutting up some limes now, before the doors open. First, let me show you both the register."

I feel overwhelmed by fatigue. I want to go home.

"Max, are you listening?"

Jasmine is on my last nerve. She picks up a clipboard. "I need you to sign these tax forms; put your Social Security numbers here and sign them here."

I panic. "This isn't off the books?"

Thor holds back Jasmine's response. "No, buddy. This is on the up-and-up."

My head swirls. "I don't file taxes. I don't exist as far as the world's concerned. I wouldn't have a telephone if it wasn't in your name, Thor." He nods in understanding and holds up his hands for me to stop, but I'm on a roll. "Are we getting paid by check? I can't even cash a check without ID!"

Jasmine tries to reassure me. "Well, you're only getting fifteen dollars on the books for the night."

"Total?" My voice rises. "I make ten an hour bouncing!"

Jasmine is visibly annoyed, but her response is still in her quiet range. "Yes. But the money is in the tips. You're supposed to report them, by law. You can save up the nightly pay and get it in one check. I could cash that out for you at the bar. But you'll have to report your tips at the end of the year and file taxes. Are you willing to do that?"

Thor pats me on the back. "C'mon buddy, we'll figure it out as we go along, yes?"

I exhale—long, slow, audible. "Okay."

"Well, don't do us favors, Max." Jasmine picks up her clipboard and walks past us to go. She stops in front of me and pokes my breastbone with her index finger. "There's too much at stake for all of us."

I don't answer. She looks me in the eye, wordlessly repeating what she's just said, and walks away.

"Hey, buddy," Thor splashes me from the sink to get my attention. "You're gonna have to get serious about this job."

I shrug off his words, annoyed that he's siding with Jasmine. "I don't know why I'm being so cranky with Jasmine. I just got hooked when I came in late and I couldn't snap myself out of it."

There's warning in Thor's smile. "Well, snap out of it."

Jasmine's voice travels down the stairwell: "House doors opening!"

"And what the hell is a buy-back?" I ask him, holding my dripping hands like a scrubbed-up surgeon.

"Who cares," he laughs, tossing me a roll of paper towels, "because we don't have it here!"

"What's a 'well' drink?" I ask, as I slice limes into little wedges.

Thor runs his fingertips along the bottom row of upright bottles of booze: "House liquor; generic. Not the good stuff."

I'm not ready to deal with people, but clearly there's no choice. We don't hear anything upstairs. No crush of people piling in on a Thursday night. Soon, though, people make their way down the stairs. I stand straight as a ramrod with my arms folded across my chest. Thor wipes the bar and throws the dishrag over his shoulder.

"Beer," someone orders.

"What kind?" I sound annoyed.

Thor sidles next to me: "We got draft, bottled beer. Imported, domestic."

Another voice: "I'll take a Dos Equis."

I feel lost. Thor points to the array of beer brands.

More people are streaming downstairs: young gender queers of all nationalities, gay men—Black and white—playfully relating to each other, a handful of white women whose sexuality I would not presume to guess, and a whole lot of white East Village metrosexuals who can afford to go any place that piques their fancy.

Thor and I bump into each other as we speed up behind the bar. "We'll get this down, buddy, don't worry." He tries to put me at ease.

"Hey," a familiar voice shouts over the music.

This is the last person from Club Chaos I would have wished to see again. "Weasel. What are you doing here?"

"My name is Wolf! You know that. Now gimme an old-fashioned."

I can't for the life of me remember what the mix is. "What's in it?" I ask.

Weasel smiles slyly. "You're supposed to know that, aren't you, Max? You are a bartender right? You got a certificate and everything?"

I prepare to lunge across the bar, but Thor steps in. "Hey, Weasel, what's up?"

"Max doesn't know how to make an old-fashioned."

Thor snaps his damp dish towel toward the little rodent, making Weasel step back, and polishes the dark surface of the wood bar counter. "Max and I are busy right now, Weaz. It's rush hour. So make it simple and easy, and make it fast."

Weasel shrugs. "I'll take a draft."

"You see, Weaz," Thor leans forward toward Weasel, sounding like Mister Rogers, "that wasn't so hard, was it?"

"My name is Wolf!" Weazel pouts.

An angry voice interrupts. "Who do I have to fuck to get a beer around here?" I look up at a face more bored than angry. But I'm pissed at being shouted at. Thor moves in smoothly with a plastic cup of draft beer and nudges me away from the interaction. More people are bellying up to the bar. A DJ starts mixing music, turned up loud, loud, loud. The mirrored moon on the ceiling turns, pulling constellations of light in its orbit. Bright lights begin to strobe, like paparazzi popping flashbulbs at every turn. Hands wave for my attention, reach across the bar for drinks, extend money in my direction. One anxious hand misses the bar, slapping money on my forearm instead. I spill the shot of rum I'm pouring on my other hand, the liquor running down my wrist, seeping into my shirt cuff. I'm too rushed to roll up my sleeves.

I turn toward the cash register quickly and collide with Thor. Foamy waves of beer pour down the front of our shirts. I feel the liquid seeping down into my trousers, my briefs. Wearing vintage suit-trousers that need dry cleaning wasn't such a good idea. Maybe tomorrow night I can get away with wearing black jeans.

I try to find my rhythm at this job—I, who prided myself as a teenager on being able to make quota at any factory sweatshop, from Manhattan to Newark. But people keep interrupting my work. They are unpredictable, demanding, and increasingly drunk. They are my work.

Jasmine is bent over the bar, a pencil behind each ear, punching a calculator with the same index finger she poked me with. Thor and I are leaning on the corner of the bar, waiting.

"I gotta get off my feet," I whisper.

"I'm hungry as all hell," Thor responds.

Jasmine opens the cash register with a ka-ching, and counts bills carefully into piles.

"How long does this part take," I moan quietly.

Jasmine answers, "As long as it takes." She counts out stacks of money, and slides one to Thor and the other to me. I lick the tips of my fingers and leaf though the bills. I am incredulous. "I did all that work for this?"

Jasmine slams down a roll of pennies. "Max!" She turns and putters around the register, her back half turned toward me. Her body language is angry, a flash in the sky before a summer storm.

I'm eager to argue.

Thor says out loud, "Uh-oh."

I look back toward Jasmine at the register and catch sight of my own reflection in the mirror over the bar. My body looks like hers: barricaded and defended, angry and wounded. Familiar.

I hold my fire. My anger drains, leaving the silt of emotional exhaustion and regret. I don't want to argue with Jasmine. She's mad at me because I've been screwing up. And she feels disrespected.

Thor says, "I'll meet you both upstairs. Hurry up, I'm starving."

Once Thor leaves, and Jasmine and I are alone, we look anywhere but at each other. When I speak my voice sounds hollow, resigned. "I messed up tonight. I'm sorry."

Jasmine turns her body to face mine, fixing me with her gaze, searching out something in my eyes.

I say quietly, "I'm not trying to disrespect you, Jasmine. I'm sorry I got off rocky with you tonight, you know? Vickie, then Ruby. All this change and having to interact with people. It's just not easy for me, you know?"

Jasmine's voice is hard but her body softens. "It's not easy for any of us."

I nod. "I know. I don't want to fight with you."

Jasmine takes a deep breath. "The whole crew is trying to work hard and split the take with enough for Ruby. That's what it's all about, isn't it? We're all trying to help each other."

I sit down heavily on a bar stool. "I guess I'm used to Ruby being the quarterback and I'm her wide receiver. Now she's sidelined, and I don't know quite what to do."

Jasmine doesn't blink. "Well, the question for you is, are you ready to play with a relief quarterback?"

I look up at her with a smile, but her eyes aren't smiling. They're still smoldering coals.

I think about her question and answer seriously. "I can be a team player."

Jasmine nods. "Good," she says. "Me, too." She pokes me lightly with her fingertip. "You could make a lot more money doing this if you'd lighten up a little."

I smile, tentatively. "You could too—lighten up, I mean."

We can't hold each other's gaze; we look away. I ask her, "You got any advice for a new bartender?"

She looks around the bar. "Yes, Max. It's not about memorizing how to make the drinks. It's about knowing where everything is." That's actually very helpful. "And it's about people," she adds. "It's people skills."

"Well, I might figure out the part about knowing where everything is first."

Jasmine shakes her head in mock frustration. "I've got to go."

We move slowly toward the stairs and climb up out of the small grotto. I realize how hungry I am. "You want to get something to eat?"

"No, thanks," she says. "I'm tired."

"Which way you headed?"

"Chinatown. I'm going to see my sister."

I nod my head slowly, not sure what else to say. "I'll see you tonight, okay?"

She pokes my chest, very lightly, with her index finger. "Don't be late."

* * *

Opponents line up opposite me. There's been no time for a huddle—I don't know what to do. As I see the snap of the ball, I weave around the human obstacles in front of me, run, and then turn. The football is spiraling toward me. Foes are closing in on me, their faces covered by darkened visors. I feel the ball dance on my outstretched fingertips. If I drop the ball, something terrible will happen. I reach higher, higher, until the rawhide slaps my palms. I pull the ball down into the crook of my arm.

I pivot and turn, the precious responsibility tucked tightly against my body. I'm running now. Running for my life, the cheers thundering in my chest. I'm running faster and faster; I can hear the tacklers panting behind me. I can see the goal line, closer, closer. With a burst of speed I cross the chalked boundary. The crowd is on its feet, roaring. I spike the ball, and dance in triumph.

My friends rush toward me, jump on me, hug me, squeeze me.

I awaken reluctantly from the familiar dream. My old fantasy lived in the vision of sleep. The dream never changes much. Except this time, anonymous teammates were transformed into recognizable faces.

I get up to get a glass of water, pretending that it's the middle of the night, and not noontime. I need to get back to sleep, soon. It's going to be a busy night—the first drag king performance at the club.

But as I walk to the kitchen to get something to drink, the euphoria of the dream loosens up my body; there's still a little cakewalk in my hips.

16

As I open the door to the barber shop, a bell rings. All the banter inside the bright, warm room halts, as though someone has pressed a pause button. Two barbers, each with their scissors in midair.

There are only three chairs for those waiting for a haircut. I make a place for myself, wedged between two men—one reading the daily tabloid, the other reading *Sports Illustrated*. They look at me; they look at each other. It's only a judgment being rendered with a glance, over my head, but verdicts can lead to sentencing. Should I leave?

No one is talking. Even the television is on mute. Snipping and buzzing—those are the only sounds. I smell alcohol and talcum powder, shaving cream and bay rum.

The young man in the barber chair, now shorn, examines himself in the mirror and nods once to signal satisfaction. The barber pulls the cloth off him with a flourish, snapping out any leftover curls and locks, whirling the fabric like a matador.

"Next!" he orders.

I look around at the others who were here long before me. They look at me. No one moves. I get up and go sit down, filling the empty chair. The barber looks around at the other men, as though this is haircut by consensus. Some kind of agreement has been reached. This haircut will be conducted amid smirks and sneers.

"I don't usually cut lady hair," he announces. "You have to tell me what you want."

"Here's what I want." My tone is get-down-to-business. "I want a zero fade on the sides—not skin, zero. Make the top flat, down to a 'one' in the middle. And pull up the front nice and short."

It's still quiet, but the silence has changed. In the mirror in front of me, I can see the men behind me roll their eyes at each other and go back to reading.

I face the barber in the reflection, eye to eye: "You got that?"

"Nice haircut, dude." John D. Arc compliments me. "New barber?"

"Still breaking in a new barber," I snort. "You want another beer?"

"Naw, thanks, dude. I gotta perform soon." John is wearing paste-on sideburns, the kind I wore decades ago when Ruby and I did an act together on a bar stage.

Thor stops slicing limes and wipes his hands on a bar towel before shaking John D.'s hand. "I caught your one-person show last week," Thor enthuses. "Your stuff on sexism was brilliant. Cutting-edge stuff, buddy. And your work is really personally brave, too. I've got a lot of respect for you!"

John D. grabs a handful of Thor's hair and pulls him forward, kissing him on the lips. Thor blushes and grins.

John D. slaps a couple of dollar bills on the bar. I slide them back at him. "Break a leg, brother!"

Thor and I are working the big room upstairs at Club Pi tonight for the premiere of the drag king show. The room is packed with people, their backs to us as they whistle, hoot, stomp, and applaud in approval. I can just about catch a glimpse of the action on stage, over their heads, if I stand on tiptoe.

A roar goes up. "Who's that?"

Thor has dragged a stool behind the bar. "It's Grand Mister Flesh and Elle Elle Kewl Gay. They've both got their fedoras pulled low over their eyes and they're rapping at each other—dueling rhyme. I can't hear it over the noise. People are eatin' it up. This is great!"

The MC announces the next performer, John D. Arc. The room quiets down long enough for me to make out the first words before cheers rise:

> *Ma'am, sir, ma'am, sir, isn't that what you said?*
> *Now it's not just me, it's you, that's turnin' all red.*
> *Ma'am, sir, ma'am, sir—that's what they taught you to say.*
> *But all you had to say was "Have a nice day!"*

The crowd in front of me, densely packed together, parts as one of the other performers, Def, makes *hir* way gently between them. Amidst the din, Def looks relaxed. *Ze* gives me a little salute, points toward the stage, and flashes a thumbs-up.

I give *hir* a big, wordless smile, hold up an empty cup, and point to the draft beer spigot.

Ze nods *hir* head emphatically, up and down.

Def sips the beer, unable to see the stage from here. I see *hir* studying the crowd, very carefully. Def should be up onstage right about now. I'm surprised *ze*'s calmly drinking at the bar. How will *ze* ever get through this crowd in time?

Def takes another swallow of beer, places the plastic cup carefully on the bar, and takes out *hir* wallet. I shake my head—it's on the house.

Def looks me in the eyes, flashes me a sweet smile, and smoothly slips out of sight between people.

"Hey, pal!" Someone else is standing in Def's place at the bar. "Gimme a rum and coke." This guy is close to not needing another drink. He's well-dressed, manicured, and trimmed. He's the kind that loves an argument like a dog loves a bone. He gestures toward the stage, "Are those guys?" he shouts.

I pour his drink as fast as I can. "Some of 'em are."

His focus shifts to me and Thor. "What about you two? What are you?" I pretend not to hear him. But he is not deterred. He leans across the bar and yells near my ear, "Are you a guy, or what?"

Thor makes eye contact: *Everything under control?*

I shrug: *I'll let you know.*

"Mister," I say, plucking the ten-dollar bill from his fist. "You see that poster?" The big advertisement for this event has been hanging over the bar and on lampposts in the East Village for weeks.

"Yeah, I see it."

"You see what it says?" I yell over John D.'s gender rap and the wildly enthusiastic audience response.

"Yeah, so?"

"My eyes aren't so good anymore. Read me the description."

He just stares at me—he's not about to do anything I ask him to.

"Let me see if I can read it," I say, as though I'm adjusting a pair of invisible glasses.

Thor is miming doubled-over laughter. He knows what I'm doing.

"Let's see, it says: drag kings, tranny bois, transmen, butches, he-she's, morphers, gender-benders, bi-genders, shape shifters, cross-dressers, Two Spirits. . . ."

I'm not half-way finished before he interrupts me. "Yeah, what's your point?"

"My point is, pal," I say the last word as hard as I'm slamming his change down on the bar, "why come to an event like this and ask anybody if they're 'a guy or what?' Why don't you just stay home and watch reruns of *Baywatch*?"

The guy readies himself to shout something back at me, when suddenly the room falls silent.

I hear applause and then quiet again. The crowd is motionless. Scattered shouts of appreciation and then silence. Thor is balancing on the rung of the bar stool. "You got to see this, buddy. Def is amazing!"

I can see silent images projected behind Def onto the curtain of elephants making music, drumsticks and tambourines in their trunks. Now I hear an eerie sound, whale song vibrating through my bones. The chirp of dolphins. "What's Def saying? I mean signing?" I ask Thor.

"You can read it if you get up here," Thor says. "The words are being projected on the screen. But you got to see Def to get it."

I climb up the other side of the stool, holding on to the bar with one hand for support. "What's it about?"

"This is fucking amazing. Def is signing to the animals, like an emissary, telling them: Hearing world doesn't understand you, the way I do. Hearing people teach you sign language. They're just making words with their hands. But you and I can talk about the world around us, our dreams, and things they don't yet understand."

I can't take my eyes off Def, bigger than life onstage, holding us all in thrall. *Ze*'s in perpetual motion—striding across the stage, reaching toward the slide images on the screen, and patting *hir* chest, windmilling arms, fluttering fingers, face a kaleidoscope of emotion. As a performer, Def is way beyond the slides and the signing, making me feel connection, longing.

I don't understand how *ze* can express all this without words. I don't know where Def draws that power from. I wish I could reach down deep inside myself and find it too. Someone tugs my pant leg.

"What?" I demand, annoyed at the interruption.

"Are you people on vacation? I want a drink!"

Loud shouts outside my bedroom window drag me, unwilling, from a sweet dream. My body feels sensuous, riding a wave of physical pleasure I don't want to abandon. A warm breeze billows the curtains. The earth is tilting toward another season. I get up in my underwear and peek out the window. The sun is high up in the sky above me.

I see a young Latino boy—maybe ten, eleven years old—on his knees. A white cop is standing over him, shouting, "That's right, kiss my dick, you little pussy. Kiss my dick, you little cocksucker."

A row of teenage boys and one girl, all youths of color, are lined up against the side of the brick building across the street, their hands against the wall, their legs spread wide apart. They turn their heads, worriedly, in the direction of this youngest one as other cops pat them down and dig in their pockets.

Mohammad is arguing with the police from the stoop of his store, "What did they do? Tell me! They are just children!"

Hatem comes out of our apartment building waving his arms. "Wait, stop!" he says with such authority that the officers look in his direction.

I open the window further and lean out, straining to hear.

Hatem points to the teenagers lined up against the wall. "I do not believe this is a legal search. You are going through their pockets." He addresses those with their hands against the wall: "Did you give the police your consent to go through your pockets?"

All heads shake back and forth vehemently: *No!*

"And this!" Hatem points to the cop who is leaning over the young boy. He stretches his hand out to the youth and helps him to his feet.

Mohammad looks up and sees me. We look at each other with mouths slightly agape, waiting for the storm. It builds slowly.

"Who the fuck," the cop who stood over the boy begins to challenge, "are you?"

The other police had looked stunned, frozen for an instant. But not for long. The cops jump Hatem and wrestle him toward the wall. He is thrown against the bricks with such force that I can hear it from my window. "Stop!" I shout, but no one looks in my direction.

Mohammad runs toward Hatem. "What are you doing to him?"

I shout out the window, "Leave him alone!" but my words have no impact. As the cops drag Hatem toward the squad car, I get dressed, flying through the house, pulling on pants and a shirt, sneakers without socks. I run down the stairs, two at a time, swerving at high speed around the landings. I open the front door of the apartment building and look around. There's no one there. No Hatem, no Mohammad, no police, no teenagers, no squad cars. Just a balmy day, people going about their business as usual.

Did I dream this?

Once I get inside Mohammad's store, I know what I saw was real. Mohammad is shouting in Arabic on his cell phone.

Alma is nodding as though she understands every word. "Did you see that?" I ask her. She's our building super. She sees everything.

Alma sighs with disgust. "They do it all the time to these kids."

"What happened?" I ask.

She makes a face. "The cop says someone stole his wife's car radio. They live over there." She points her finger in the direction of loaves of bread stacked on the nearby shelf.

"Where is everybody?"

"They drew their guns and told the kids to get lost. Those kids were gone like that." She snaps her fingers.

"What about Hatem?"

Alma looks at Mohammad, who is listening to someone at this point, his lips pressed tight. Mohammad shakes his head slowly, from side to side.

"I gotta go," Alma says. "The electric company guy is coming to check the meters. Tell Mohammad I'll be back, *más tarde*. I'll check on Hatem's sister. I'll stay with her until her family gets here."

Mohammad covers his face with one hand; his other hand keeps the cell phone pressed to his ear. Tears slide down his cheeks below his hand.

The television is on, always on. A Pentagon general, standing ramrod stiff in front of a map of someone else's country, says the bad guys are on the run.

Mohammad looks at the cell phone, clicks it off, and turns away from me to make coffee. He blots his eyes with a napkin. "You want some coffee, my friend?" he asks without looking at me.

"Sure, yes. Thank you."

He turns to me with two cardboard cups of coffee, both light and sweet. We sip our coffee in silence, as questions circle us in the room.

I speak gently, carefully. "Mohammad, is Hatem okay? If he's under arrest, I have a little money. I could put in for the bail."

Mohammad lifts his hand to stop me. He fumbles for his crumpled pack of cigarettes and offers me one.

"Yes, please," I reach gratefully for a cigarette.

In unison, we each tamp one end of our cigarette on the countertop and then place it between our lips. He flips open his Zippo and lights mine first, then his. I can see his hands tremble. We each take a deep drag and exhale gray smoke.

"He's not under arrest," Mohammad says quietly.

I smile, elated. "That's good news!"

Mohammad draws more smoke from his cigarette and exhales.

"Is he okay?" I ask. My skin begins to crawl. "Is he hurt?"

Mohammad crushes out his cigarette and looks at the television screen as though it were a crystal ball. "I don't know," he tells me. "He is not arrested. He is not at the police station. I called. They don't know anything about him. They say nothing happened here on this corner this afternoon. They say the police were never here."

His words stun me. "What? What does that mean?"

"It means," Mohammad says, "Hatem has disappeared, like many others."

He whispers, in a quieter voice, "Like my brother-in-law."

"Did they call his consulate?" Thor presses me.

"Well, Hatem's Palestinian," I tell him. "I don't know if they have a consulate in this country."

"I thought he was Egyptian." Thor is trying to get the picture as we hurry down the street to Ruby's apartment for dinner.

"No." I shake my head as we dodge traffic to cross the street. "Mohammad, the guy who runs the grocery store, is Egyptian. His brother-in-law is Pakistani. The guy went to pick up his daughter from school one day and never got there. He hasn't been heard from since. Mohammad thinks he got disappeared by the feds."

Thor chews his lip. "A lot of Muslims are getting rounded up."

"I read about one guy in the Jersey newspaper," I recall with rage. "Until he died in custody, nobody knew he had been in jail. The feds said the guy asked them not to notify his family or his consulate."

Thor snorts. "Easy for them to say. He's dead."

"Yeah! Who gets arrested and asks the cops not to tell anyone? The article said he wasn't charged with any crime. Somebody in his family who finally got to see his body said he had been tortured."

Thor clenches his fists in anger. "They're all 'suspects.' There's no charges. No lawyers. They don't have any rights."

"How many people have been rounded up?"

Thor shakes his head. "We don't know. It's a secret. We've been demonstrating outside the detention centers in Brooklyn and in New Jersey where we think they're being held. We're demanding to know the names of who's in there and what the charges are."

I nod, slowly. "This is someone I know."

Thor nods. "There's a demonstration coming up soon."

I'm thinking about Hatem, my neighbor. "I've got to do something."

My printer is so slow it's making me pace around my office. I tug the last couple of pages out the moment the white edges emerge. The pages are still warm from the machine's hot belly.

I take a last look at my work. The leaflet is simple text. Big headline: Where is Hatem Ashrawi? Last seen in police custody.

Smaller line in the middle: Remember Japanese-Americans interned in concentration camps during WWII? This is how it begins.

Bold type on the bottom: Stop the roundup of Arab, Muslim, and South Asian people!

I jog the leaflets, wrap them up in newspaper, and stuff them in my backpack with rolls of tape. I'll take it all with me to work and tape the leaflets up in the neighborhood just before dawn, when I'm heading home.

I think maybe I should make some leaflets about Mohammad's brother-in-law. But I should talk to Mohammad first. Two days ago someone lettered an ugly slur across the metal gate of his store in paint as red as drawn blood. I saw Mohammad cleaning it with a rag and turpentine when I came home from work. I offered to help, but he shook his head, grim-faced as he thanked me. I think he might have been uncomfortable having me stand around while he rubbed at the epithet. That night when I left the house to go to work, I saw he'd hung a U.S. flag over the door of the store.

I think I'd better check with him before I do anything in the neighborhood that might draw the dragon's breath in his direction.

I'm ready to go home and lie down to sleep as the sun is rising to find me. But anxiety is slapping like waves in my belly as I'm taping up the posters in the early dawn light, fearing I'll be caught.

The need for a cigarette is gnawing at me and won't let me be. The liquor store/deli at the PATH station is open twenty-four hours. It's a long walk back. The light is coming up. I should go back home to sleep. But instead, I stuff my posters and tape into my backpack and walk back to the store at the PATH station.

I'd forgotten how awful it feels to be squeezed in the tight-fisted grip of addiction. Ruby is right: It's a slippery slope. And I've been on it before. At first, the liquor warmed me, like Raisa's embrace. At first. By the end I was holed up alone in my apartment, in cold isolation. It was Ruby who came and took me with her to my first meeting in a crowded hall on Eighth Street. "I'm your friend, so I'm doin' this, one time and one time only," she told me. "Here's the first step. I took it. We all took it. Now all you got to do to stay on this path is just do the next right thing."

Now I'm taking a step in the opposite direction, telling myself that it's just a cigarette. But I'm flirting with it all. I'm pulling the wool over my own eyes, telling myself, "Just one more. I'll deal with it. Just not right now."

17

I arrive at Club Pi huffing and puffing because I'm running a few minutes late. At the nightclub door I take a lungful of air to slow my breathing and walk in to find boss-man Rick glaring at me, his fists on his hips. Thor and Jasmine are hovering uneasily nearby.

It's not my fault. I left my house early but the damn PATH service was suspended because of signal trouble. I had to take a dollar-ride jitney, which got bogged down in unexpected evening street traffic between Journal Square and Manhattan.

Rick and I both check our watches for dramatic purposes.

"Five minutes late!" His gesture attacks.

"Five minutes late!" My gesture defends.

He speaks, "The next time you're late, you're history. Got that?"

Thor and Jasmine swing their gaze toward me as though this was a tennis match.

A curt nod is all I'll give him.

"Okay, everybody's here," Rick announces unnecessarily. "I've got something to say to you all. Everybody over here in front of me where you can hear me."

We move closer to him, trying not to line up like schoolchildren.

"Listen up," he begins, "Like this war or not, now our boys are over there and we have to support them in doing their job."

Where the hell is this going?

Thor takes a step forward, "Support them how? Being cannon fodder? Killing or being killed? We're supporting them by demanding: Bring them home, right now!"

Jasmine lightly touches the back of her hand to the inside of Thor's elbow; gentle restraint. "What is it you're trying to tell us?" she asks Rick in a tone that would make a diplomat green with envy.

Rick's index finger jabs toward our bodies. "I want those buttons off."

We all look down at ourselves. My Queers United antiwar button is pinned to my denim jacket over my heart. Jasmine and Thor are wearing the fluorescent green People's Fightback Network buttons, and Thor is also wearing a brass peace-symbol belt buckle.

"I don't want to see one of those in my club again," he says with finality, "or you're all out of here."

"We have a right!" Thor sizzles with anger.

The back of Jasmine's fingertips continue their caress of Thor's arm. At this moment she has become our spokesperson.

"Well, Rick," she begins slowly, "you are the boss. So if you say we can't wear our buttons at work, then we will not."

Thor and I both look at her, aghast. Maybe she's not our spokesperson.

"But," she says, instantly restoring our confidence, "just as you have your views, and they are very strong, we have very strong views, too. You will not see our views on our clothes during our shift. But"—she points to my coat without looking at it—"you will see our views when we come to work and when we leave. And we will not be silent about our views at work."

Rick starts to stammer in disapproval but he's silenced by Jasmine's raised hand. "Talking to customers is part of our job. That's what we do. If asked our opinions, we will not be quiet about them. And," she takes another breath, "there is no reason that Thor should not be able to continue to wear a peace sign as his belt buckle. It is a universal symbol for peace that is as recognizable and common as an antismoking symbol, which you will have on these walls soon. Is that agreed?"

The three of us stand tall together in front of Rick.

He waves his hand in disgust. "It's a free country," he says. But rather than leave that lie at rest, he adds, "I think you're being unpatriotic. If 9/11 didn't teach you anything, then you don't deserve to live in this country."

I catch a glimpse of Jasmine just as her jaw sets squarely. She doesn't need to hold us back. We are all a wall of silence until Rick turns on his heel, shaking his head in contempt, and walks away.

"Hey, buddy," Thor pokes the person slumping on our bar. "Last call."

I'm anxious to get out of here and go see if my leaflets have stayed up on the lampposts.

Thor's words rouse the last barfly, who lifts *hir* head and points an index finger toward the ceiling to make a point. "Do you think," *ze* asks us, "that Superman turned his X-ray vision on and off, or did it stay on all the time?"

Jasmine has her back to us, getting an early start tallying the night's receipts.

I roll my eyes. Thor digs into the subject. "It stayed on, for sure. That's not the kind of thing you can switch on and off like a light."

"But," *ze* counters, "he'd melt his ice palace."

Thor shakes his head. "That's his heat ray, not his X ray."

I'm wondering: If Superman's X-ray vision stayed on all the time, why didn't his heat ray? However, the person who started the conversation begins to crumple forward until *hir* forehead is resting on the bar. Jasmine turns on her heel and heads upstairs to get a bouncer.

"I don't know," I continue the conversation with Thor, as though I care. "Superman was always trying to be an ethical person. I don't think he would look through women's clothing—I mean, I was led to assume he was straight. That whole Lois Lane thing, you know."

Thor considers this and responds earnestly. "Well, maybe if you're looking through everything in the world with X-ray vision then it's not salacious. It's different than selective abuse of a power."

I shake my head. "I don't think he had it on all the time. I mean, his whole pain, his burden, was that he was living in somebody's else's world. He was never going to fit, you know? That's why he did that Clark Kent thing part time. Otherwise he could've just lived in that spectacular ice palace in the frozen tundra. But he was lonely."

Thor frowns, "So? I don't get you."

"So if he was going to live in this world with humans, then he would have to look at people as they are. You can't always be examining people with X-ray vision. He'd have to turn it off to see the world as it really is."

Thor shakes his head. "Naw, I don't agree. It's a superpower, buddy. You can't tell it when to come or go."

Two burly white men in black Club Pi logo T-shirts grab the drunken customer by *hir* elbows and drag *hir* off the stool.

"Hey, hey, hey! Easy does it!" Thor and I shout at the two bouncers. They appear not to hear us.

Jasmine looks over her shoulder to see what the ruckus is. She walks over to us and hands us each our earnings. "The real question is," she says, fatigue clouding her voice, "did Superman ever sleep?"

* * *

The sun is already partially visible on the horizon as I emerge from the PATH station, on my way home to bed. I fire up a cigarette; its tip glows like the dawn's red sun.

I stop at each metal lamppost to see if my posters have been torn down. I already see one on the sidewalk, ripped up. But nearby, tacked with staples to a wooden pole, a goldenrod leaflet catches my eye. There's a photo of a man, a woman, and two children, squeezing together, all smiles. They are dressed up and sitting very tall and proud.

Beneath the photo are the words: "Have you seen Shahzeb? Loving husband and father. Last seen January 3."

Across the street, parked alongside the old courthouse, two white men are sitting in a black sedan. They don't seem to pay any attention to me as I walk past, but a moment later I hear their car engine start up. I glance back to see if they've pulled away. But they've done a U-turn and now they are driving slowly behind me.

My heartbeat is pounding in my skull. I don't have anything on me that could be used against me: no leaflets or tape; I left my backpack at home last night. I'm not carrying a knife. But I am always a crime walking. I slow down my pace every so slightly. Hurrying will not help me. It will only signal desperation and panic.

I turn the corner where I live and climb the stairs of my tenement. I don't see them pass by. I pause for a moment at the front door of my building.

They are nowhere to be seen.

18

I'm keeping one eye on the clock as I log on to AvaStar. I have time before I have to leave for work, but not much.

This time I double-click on the golden door with the male symbol hammered into it. As it lifts, the scene is the same. Same silver servant. Same options.

I double-click on white faces to see if there's one in which I can find some resemblance to my own. The cartoonish faces that look back at me are blank and expressionless. Few choices: different color hair; different lengths. No balding here. Some faces have facial hair; some are smooth-cheeked.

The bodies: flat chests, slight bulges in the codpiece. Wide shoulders, slim hips. They are as decidedly male as an avatar can be. There is no ambiguity. They are not me. And neither were any of the female cyber bodies. How can I possibly interact with others when the avatar has already introduced me as someone else? I don't know how to play this game.

"*If I would be like someone else,*" I hear *my mother sigh,* "ver vet zayn vi ich? *Who will be like me?*"

I glance at the clock. It's time to go and I'm still in my underwear.

I log off the game with a click and race around my apartment. I chug down a viscous, premixed protein drink as I rummage through my closet for black jeans, black shirt, skinny silver tie, thick black sweat socks to make standing all night easier, black boots with padded insoles.

I grab my keys. I run back to my bedroom to find my wallet. I'm ten minutes late, but I'm ready to go.

I'm out the door and I turn to lock the top lock. My stomach flips. Taped up on my apartment door is one of my own leaflets: "Where is Hatem Ashrawi? Last seen in police custody."

"You can't just up and go all Che Guevara on us all by yourself!" Ruby leans forward across the restaurant booth with such velocity that Thor and Jasmine and Deacon lean back with equal speed. "What were you thinking? You can't make a damn revolution all by yourself! You hanging up one leaflet is not gonna change the world. It's just gonna bring down heat on you and nobody's gonna know what happened to you. Put your energy into the struggle, sugar. Make it count!"

Ruby sits back, exasperated. She gears up to say something else. But Jasmine leans toward me to intervene. "It's a limitation of individual action," she says more gently.

That stings. I know that. I was just trying to do—something.

Deacon pats my hand that's resting on the tabletop. "Some good white people tried to do some good things in their own way during segregation."

Ruby crosses her arms across her chest. "But it took a whole lot of people coming together to hammer a stake into old Jim Crow's heart, and he's not dead yet."

Thor waxes philosophical. "Yeah, but sometimes people just feel like they've gotta do something."

I thump the tabletop with my palm. "Right!"

Ruby taps the tabletop with a long, strong nail. "It's one thing when there's nobody protesting. But now there's people out in the streets against this war and about what they're doin' to these immigrants, too. This is no damn time to be a hot dog."

I sit back, crushed.

Thor urges, "Come leaflet with us, as a team. We go out postering in squads, with a lookout. Help build the weekly demonstrations and rallies outside the detention centers. You can speak out there about Hatem and Netaji. We've got to build this movement, buddy. We need to show our strength together. That's what's gonna make a difference."

"Netaji?" I say, surprised.

The others look at each other, from face to face. They know something I don't.

Ruby speaks first. "Before you got here and laid this bomb on us about what you've been up to, Thor called Netaji's sister because he heard her family was gettin' harassed in Queens. And she said she hasn't seen Netaji since Friday. He didn't come home after his shift."

Deacon whispers, "Oh Lord, Lord."

I don't understand what's happening. "Netaji's not Muslim."

Thor shakes his head. "It's a big dragnet. Lots of people are getting caught in it."

Thor is at home in the office of the People's Fightback Network. As I watch people greet him and confer with him, I realize that we—his Queer family—are just one small part of his life. I'm flushed with jealousy. Is that because I wish these people respected me and cared about me the way they do Thor? Or because they clearly mean so much to him?

"Hey, buddy." Thor welcomes me. "I'm glad you made it." He helps me off with my jacket and drapes it over the back of a chair.

The walls are covered with posters and flags: Palestine, Puerto Rico, First Nation. People of different ages and nationalities and genders are answering phones, working on computers, running off leaflets. This isn't what antiwar coalition offices looked like in the '60s when I used to go buy bus tickets.

I look at my watch. "I got a couple of hours."

"Great," he says. "There's a lot to do. You're gonna be there next week, yes?"

He beams at me, until he hears my answer. "I'm not sure."

"What do you mean?"

"Deacon's meeting with a lawyer Saturday. He's due in Housing Court that Monday. The landlord's trying to evict him because he's illegally subletting. He asked me to come with him both days. So Jasmine and Ruby are coming to the rally, and if Deacon and I are done with the lawyer in time we'll take a cab."

Thor doesn't look happy about it, but he doesn't argue. "Let me know how it goes in court. If it doesn't go well, there's people around here who can help."

"He'll be glad to hear that. Hey, have you found out anything about Netaji?"

I'm facing posters demanding freedom for political prisoners—Leonard Peltier, Mumia Abu-Jamal, the Cuban Five. Where is Netaji right now? Is he behind bars?

Thor folds him arms. "His lawyer, Miriam, thinks he may have been forcibly deported. She says you'd be shocked at how many thousands of people are being deported. It's mostly Pakistanis, Muslims. But a lot of people are vulnerable."

I know this is an emergency for a lot of people, but right now I'm just trying to picture where my friend is, and what he's going through.

Thor points to placards demanding justice for Netaji. "We're getting placards ready for the demo Saturday. Do you know Hatem's last name? We can make some signs demanding his release."

"Yeah, Ashrawi."

Thor points to someone who is bent over, inking placards. "Rae-Rae can letter the placards." He sounds rushed, excited. "Can you help staple the signs on cardboard poles? The poles are over there in the corner."

"Sure. But where's a bathroom?"

Thor frowns. "They're both out in the hall. Other businesses on the floor use them, too. The keys are hanging up over there."

"Which should I use?"

He shrugs. "Either one. The men's is multiple occupancy; the stalls have doors. If you use the women's room, just be ready for an argument from the Democratic Club down the hall. There's no reason it should matter to them—it's single occupancy with a door that locks. It's just gender-phobia." He adds, bitterly, "They don't seem to care so much when it's the super or one of the men from the other companies who uses the single occupancy. They only get up in arms if it's the gender queers."

"Oh, Thor," I sigh as I pick up a stapler. "We have got a lot of work to do."

"Yeah," he smiles wryly, "if it was just all of us against the powers that be, it'd be over by dinnertime. But there's all these obstacles in between."

My laughter is tinged with bitterness. "That's why they call it 'the struggle'!"

19

A night off work—I have a little time to play AvaStar. But I can only think of one way for me to get into the game. I click on the men's symbol on the dressing room door, and enter.

The male avatar faces are blank masks, revolving like little planets on my screen. I double-click on the most nonthreatening-looking male face I can find. The constellation of other faces disappears. Now if only I could find a heavenly body. Instead, I pick one that is the most nondescript.

The face and body are joined, rotating for my approval. With a double click, an airbrushed body and blank face stand in front of me but do not reflect me.

I need clothing. The selection is ample, but not that varied. Not unless I want to go for a bell-bottom, hippie fringe look, and I passed that one up decades ago. I select a pair of light-color denim jeans and a sky-blue T-shirt. I find a motorcycle jacket and a pair of chunky black boots. But

I look a little too much like a Ken doll doing a revival of Brando in *On the Waterfront*. So I take off the motorcycle jacket and leave the boots on.

This avatar doesn't look all that different from me. I can squint and kind of see myself. But nobody else is going to see me when they look at him.

It's time for the naming. I need to "queer" this avatar. As I type in the name, I feel a little chill of anxiety. I can always log off. I can always change avatars.

I take a breath and click "enter." There I am, standing on new ground, in jeans and a T-shirt, next to a posted map and a group of rocket ships. Gold stars are throbbing in a cybersky.

The announcement on the screen reads: "Welcome, Pollygender. Our newest Star."

I awaken with a start in the twilight. Instead of getting up, I roll over, burying my face in the warmth of my pillow. Everything is caressing me—the futon holds my body like gentle hands; the sheets a lighter touch. My body is yearning. My skin aches and I feel a throb between my legs. I must have been dreaming about sex. I roll over on my back, settle into the futon, and let myself drift back. I can almost touch the dream it's so close.

Suspended in air, turning, turning. My shoulders are burnished copper wings, patina of silk, and strong. Currents of wind around my body, lifting me higher. Yearning rising from my groin up into my throat like a song coming from me. My body vibrating with the music. The heat of the sun, drawing me in. Sweat running like rivulets down my curves, into my valleys. On fire, thrilled to be consumed by flame.

I feel the intimate breath of another body on mine. My mouth making wet, warm love with another mouth. The feel of our bodies twisting with need. Fingertips, beads of sweat, trailing down the small of my back like rain drops. No fear, no shame, only want. My hands in another's hair, I pull my lover's head back to see hir *face.*

My eyes open with an electric jolt; I sit bolt upright in bed, breathing hard. Jasmine.

"Look out for the birdcage," Thor warns me as I walk into his living room. It's too late, I've already sent it into a wild swing by banging it with my forehead.

"You okay, buddy?" he reaches out for my head.

I cover the point of impact. "Yeah, I'm okay. How's the bird?"

"No bird," he says, departing into another room.

I wait for him to return. I'm tempted to talk to Thor about the dream I had. I don't know why I want to tell him about it, I just do. Maybe when he comes back into the room I'll say something.

It seems ironic that soon we'll be on our way to Ruby's apartment to give her a hand with her seasonal heavy housecleaning when her home is so neat and organized and Thor's is just the opposite.

There's very little living room in Thor's living room. Very little space to move around. So I stand near the exercise bike with jackets and sweaters hanging from its handles, and survey my surroundings.

No plaster wall or spackled ceiling is visible. The room is walled with books—shelved from floor to ceiling, double rows on every bolted metal shelf. My fingers trail across the Renaissance. I stand stock-still in front of another shelf while my eyes unsuccessfully try to convert Gaelic titles into meaning. Shelves lined with Marx and Lenin, Nkrumah and Mao, Fidel and Ho Chi Minh.

The floor is wall-to-wall rug from another land; Persian maybe. Maroons and gold and a little blue. The rug is matted with hair. Either Thor has a dog or he's shedding.

Fabric covers the ceiling. This material hails from farther East. India,

I'd guess. It's got more cerulean. The fabric is tacked up in a few places, sagging like a pitched tent after a heavy rain.

Thor calls in from the kitchen, "You thirsty, buddy? Can I make you anything to eat?"

"No, I'm set, thanks," I call back.

I hear him open and close the refrigerator. "C'mon in here," he shouts. "Keep me company."

The kitchen is a yellow world: walls, ceiling—everything is painted yellow. The cupboards and table and chairs are all yellow, with a little sponged red, like sea anemones.

Every horizontal surface has piles on it. Dirty dishes crest in the sink, a zenith of clean ones on a dish towel next to them.

"Whatcha doin'?" I ask.

Thor is gently picking dry seeds off a towel and putting them into a handmade white paper packet. "Storing precious diversity," he says, absentmindedly, wiping his hands on his jeans.

The table is heaped with newspapers, periodicals, and 'zines, unopened mail, stacks of antiwar leaflets, and rolled-up posters. Thor sweeps them to one side with his forearm, raising the heap to a new height.

A bright yellow rubber duck sits atop the reams of leaflets. I lift it up and look at its face—painted innocence. Thor moves quickly to take the duck from my hand and place it back on its makeshift throne. He turns away from me, back to the sink and the seeds. "Do you know who Thor was?" he asks me out of the blue.

All I can conjure up in memory is a red-bearded sky deity wielding an iron hammer. "Tell me," I say.

Thor turns around and leans against the sink. He looks down at his hands and wipes them on his jeans again. "He lived in the land of strength. He wore iron gloves and a belt of power. And he wielded a hammer of power called Mjollnir."

He fingers the mallet amulet hanging on a chain around his neck as he continues to speak, as though describing a vision he can see. "His chariot wheels created thunder in the heavens. He was the only god forbidden to cross the bridge between the human world and the realm of the gods because the inferno of his lightning would set it aflame."

Thor paces around the little kitchen as though he's looking for something. "He was the most popular god of the people." He speaks quickly. "They would call on him to bring them fertility. They wore these amulets, even after Christianity gripped Scandinavia. I have this book." He looks around and then falls into silence for a moment.

"Hey, Thor." I fill the void. "What's going on with you, my friend?"

Thor picks up the rubber duck. "Thursday," he says, using the little latex bird to stab at the air near my face with its beak.

"Thursday is named for Thor." I'm proud to recall something from all those years of sitting in a classroom, staring at the ticking clock.

"This Thursday is the day the courts gave my ex full custody of my child."

I want to rush to Thor and hold him. But the anger in his body is like a force field, holding me back. "When the judge said he was granting custody to the father, I almost shouted with joy. And then I realized he didn't mean me.

"There I was with my piercings and my tattoos, and all my fatness." Thor grabs the flesh of his belly with both hands. "I was dressed in clothes I'd spent weeks picking out so that I could be myself that day, I could truly be proud, and there was my child who is of my flesh," Thor sucks in breath, "and they ripped us apart like we were a piece of paper—I could feel my skin tearing." Thor exhales and swings his gaze up toward the ceiling. "Where was my hammer then?"

Thor drops his eyes back down to mine. I have to fight the urge to turn away from the pain in his eyes. His upper lip curls in an unfamiliarly bitter smile. "The giants feared Thor. He was their enemy."

I look Thor in the eye—a long look—and I recognize the fury I see as my own. I don't have any words in the anguish of this moment. And I can't tell if he wants to be touched yet or not.

Thor breaks the gaze first by swinging around toward the refrigerator. I almost didn't recognize the appliance—it looks like a bulletin board, layered with clippings and leaflets and xeroxed pages from books and magazines. Thor takes a bottle of beer out of the fridge. He turns to me and extends the bottle. "You want one, buddy?"

Thor knows I don't drink. The bottle does look tempting at this moment: cold enough to perspire in the room's heat. But my smoking is regression enough. I don't need another problem right now.

"Oh, sorry, buddy," he says, recoiling the bottle back toward his body. "I forgot." Thor leans back against the sink, uses a dish towel to unscrew the cap, and drains half the bottle in his first swig. Two more short swigs and the beer is history.

We just stand there, in silence, together. I don't know what to do. Should I just stand here or sit down? I'm itchy for a cigarette. "Thor, you got a fire escape I can smoke on?"

Thor looks around as though he's not sure where he left the fire escape. "Yeah, sure," he says. "C'mon, I'll sit with you while you smoke."

That's a surprise. Thor hates cigarette smoke. He grabs a fresh bottle of beer from the fridge and waves, "C'mon," over his shoulder.

Thor's bedroom is another surprise. It's an orderly sexual playground. As he opens bolt locks on the window to the fire escape I look around at the racks of neatly arranged sex-toy equipment on the walls surrounding his four-poster bed.

Thor opens the window and gestures. "C'mon out on my balcony."

I climb out behind him, the sounds of this Brooklyn neighborhood so much quieter than Jersey City. Not far off in the distance I can see a spiderweb bridge that spans to Manhattan.

"I love that bridge," Thor and I both say at once and then laugh.

Thor sips his beer, surveying the landscape. His body appears to be relaxing, like a heap of fiery tension reduced to ash.

I dig in my shirt pocket for a crumpled pack of cigarettes and pull out the book of matches I've wedged into the cellophane skin that surrounds it. Already this ritual has become habitual and repugnant.

Thor watches me light up. He holds the neck of his beer bottle between two fingers and studies my face. "What's up with you, buddy?"

It's a real question. He's shifted his focus outward, to me. I shrug, just enough to buy time, not to dismiss the question entirely. "I don't know." I stall. I'm still tempted to talk to Thor about my dream, the one about sex. But maybe this isn't a good time, not with everything he's going through right now.

Thor drinks the last of his beer and leans forward, hugging his knees. "I told you what was going on with me. What's up with you?"

I fix my gaze far off, over tenement rooftops. "I had this dream," I begin.

Thor rests his chin on his knees; just listens.

"It was sexual, sort of."

Thor lifts his face up, his eyebrows rise, "Ahh," he says, like he's channeling Freud. "Is that a problem?" he continues in his psychoanalytic mode.

"If it's just a dream, no. If it means my body is waking up, yes."

Thor nods and lets his chin settle back on his knees.

"I mean," I struggle for words. I can feel my heart pounding wildly. "For me, it's a lot easier for me when I don't feel anything. When I don't have to deal with sex." My vocal cords sound strained.

Thor leans back against the wrought iron. "How long's it been?"

I hate to say it out loud. I wish I hadn't said anything about this. It was better left unsaid. "I don't know. Ten years. More." It's been longer than that.

Thor is running his thumb around the mouth of his beer bottle, which looks obscenely sexual to me at this moment. "Anyway," I shift gears, "That's not how I want to relate to Jasmine."

The moment her name escapes my lips, I regret it.

"Jasmine!" Thor leans forward. "You dreamed about Jasmine? I'll be damned! But you two—oh, well, I guess it makes sense. I've seen the sparks fly."

I emit a short little laugh, more like a strangled gasp. "I'm not sure she even likes me."

Thor smiles sweetly. "I could pass her a note in study hall and find out."

"This is serious, Thor. I'm not about to sexualize or exoticize her."

Thor leans back and places the beer bottle on its side, between two rods of iron. "Do you think you're exoticizing her?"

I swear he's really in a shrink mode. I've never heard Thor talk like this before. Maybe he's just trying to be careful with me, but it's really irritating.

"I just think she's an amazing, complicated human being. I don't have any indication that she's attracted to me. I've been in an emotional abyss. I have a hard enough time with intimacy. I'm not ready for sex. And I figure it's best if I don't even think about acting on this in any way. It's best if I just forget about it."

"So it's not just a dream?"

"Well, having a dream can change things. It can change the way you relate to people."

Thor smiles and nods as he picks gently at the label on the beer bottle with his thumbnail. "Do you want things to stay the way they've been?"

"Yes," I answer emphatically. "Yes and no," I amend more quietly.

Thor doesn't speak, waiting for me to elaborate.

"It's just." This sentence withers on its vine. I begin a new sentence. One that I know is true. "The world is full of danger for me, Thor. And when it strikes, it always aims between my legs. I'm barricaded for safety. It's not a choice. It's just the way it is."

"But does your body have to be the barricade?"

"My whole being is the barricade."

Thor whistles in appreciation. "I know that war."

I think: It's different for him. That's why he can stay sexual.

"It's different for me," he says out loud, as though he's answering me. "I think I couldn't survive without my connection with other human beings. That's what I love about sex. It makes me feel whole again. It makes me feel my humanness. For me the shutdown is around intimacy, not sex. For you, it seems like it's just the opposite."

I laugh, thinking he's being sarcastic, but he's not. "Intimacy? Me?"

"Oh, yes," Thor says seriously. "You're real with people. That's one of the things I like about you. You're conscious and connected every moment, in every interaction. I guess that's part of how you've had to stay alert to survive. You're in the moment with people in everyday life the way I am with sex. I admire that about you, buddy, I really do. I wish I could be more like that."

I don't know if any of this is true or if he's just therapizing me. I don't feel as though I am intimate with people or that he is not. I just sit and look out toward the bridge, wishing I could find an overpass to other people as easy to cross.

Thor shifts on the metal grating. "My butt is starting to hurt. Let's go inside," he says. "I know what would make us both feel better."

I can't imagine what. "We're supposed to be at Ruby's soon."

Thor is already climbing back inside his apartment. I follow him into his living room. He's pecking away at a computer that's nearly hidden under a ridge of papers sprouting yellow Post-Its. He nods with satisfaction, walks toward me, and cocks one ear until the first notes of music come through his computer speakers.

In a sulky growl, the Righteous Brothers accuse me of having lost that loving feeling. Thor opens his arms to me. "C'mon buddy, dance with me."

My body chills, like I've been dunked in icy water. "No, thanks, Thor."

He wiggles the fingers of both hands. "C'mon, I won't bite you."

I take a half step backward and hold up both my hands, as though I'm warding off an aggressive physical move, not a gentle invitation.

Thor lets his hands drop to his sides. "C'mon buddy, it's just a dance."

I approach him tentatively, as though he is sizzling with electricity. But as I let my body meet his, and fall against him, his belly is comforting, his body soft and sweet. His back is roped with muscle. His hands, warm and strong, rest gently on my back.

I don't know what to do. There are no rules for this dance. I pull my head back to look at his face, so close to mine. "What do we do now?" I ask. "How do we do this?"

Thor smiles as he sways to the music, as though he finds my question odd. "Let's just dance."

I don't know what to do and I feel awkward with my arms wrapped around my friend with the music playing in a living room that is not mine. Ever so gently, Thor pulls me closer and we nestle against each other. He smells sweet: stewed tomatoes and Drakkar Noir aftershave.

What we are doing now, I would not call dancing—not exactly. We are moving to the music in a pattern we have claimed as our own.

I can't recall how long it's been since I danced with anyone. And it's been much, much longer than that since anyone held me in their arms, let me press my body against theirs.

For just a moment, I feel almost human.

Then I start thinking and quickly I realize that I can't think and dance at the same time. I start moving in the direction I think Thor's gonna go, and he goes another way. He pulls back but doesn't let me go. "You okay, buddy?" he asks quietly.

The song ends and we stop moving, still holding each other loosely. Then another song begins: Marvin Gaye's voice, soaring high, sweeter than honey, telling me that when he gets that feeling he wants sexual healing.

Thor smiles—mock-wicked. I laugh. He opens his arms wider to reinvite me in. I accept. I get braver. "You lead," I order.

He grins and I feel our body momentum shift in a slightly new and unexpected direction. I vow not to think, just to feel his motion. His hands, his arms, take me with him, wherever he goes.

We sway and we move in half circles, pulled by combined centrifugal force. As we turn, I feel a hard cock against my thigh, and involuntarily, I pull away from him.

Thor takes my left hand in his right hand and dances in a more formal stance. Without me consciously realizing, we have shifted to a new dance; he is letting me lead.

"It's not a weapon," he says, looking me in the eyes.

I try to rest my face against the side of his, but he pulls back his head to hold my gaze. "It's not a clenched fist," he says.

I try to smile. "I know."

He waits.

I shrug. "Involuntary reflex."

He never takes his eyes off me. "I understand, buddy. I understand like nobody else in this world does."

His compassion fills my eyes with tears; his intimacy congests my chest with fear. I want to stop dancing, but I don't want a breach between us. I wonder how many songs are programmed to play in this loop of computerized music.

He presses against me gently. "It's a part of me, buddy. And you know me. You know all of me. I would never hurt you. Not if I could help it."

My smile is lopsided. "I know that. I know you, Thor. You know I love you; I love who you are."

Thor blushes and drops his eyes for a moment. When he looks up at me again, the shy smile has become more playfully coy. He squeezes my shoulder. "I'm not used to being with a top, you know."

I miss the next beat, but Thor shakes me and laughs. "You see," he says, "I went right from being intimate to being sexual. That's my thing. Sorry, buddy. I didn't mean to shake you up."

I get my back up a little. "I'm not shaken up," I say haughtily. That's not really honest. Flirtation, even lighthearted sexual teasing, is more than I can handle right now. "I just didn't realize I was leading till you said that." Actually that's not true, either. I was aware of the comfort and familiarity of leading.

Thor's serious now. "I like it. I'm not used to it, but I like falling into it. There's nobody else I can think of that I'd trust as a top. I'm really the only top I trust." He cocks one ear toward the song. "Was Marvin family?"

"Who knows," I sigh. "You hear things. There's so many famous people out there that, when they die, people are gonna be shocked to find out who is trans this or trans that."

Thor smiles wistfully. "I wonder if anyone will remember me after I'm gone."

I'm so surprised. I've never heard Thor say something like that. I don't want to mention his child. Not right now.

"Don't worry," I whisper, as our bodies whirl. "You're a warrior. You'll live on, in the thunder."

20

"Max!" Estelle sounds buoyed to hear from me. I'm afraid she is going to deflate when she hears why I am calling.

"How're you doing, Estelle?"

"Oh, Max." She pauses. "I've been weeding all day." Her laughter sounds artificial. "I heard that one of my neighbors was trying to organize the others to make me cut back all the wildness. I just couldn't have that conflict going on in my life right now." Her voice drops, "Not with everything else."

"That's none of their business," I say rhetorically.

"Well, I understand," her tone is singsong again. "Property values. She's trying to sell her house." And then, with quiet incredulity, Estelle whispers, "She's a widow."

"You need any help in the backyard?"

Her words are tender now. "Oh Max. My dear, dear Max. No, I'm fine. Really, I am. It's just," her words trail off wistfully. "No more wildness."

"You know—" Estelle sounds as if she's in a reverie—"Vickie always used to tell me, 'You take a stand when it's for other people's lives, but you give in when it's your own.' I used to tell her, 'Dear, that's because I don't want to fight, I just want to live.' And you know what Vickie would say to that?"

I respond from my own philosophy: "Sometimes you have to fight for the right to just live."

"Yes, that's exactly what she'd tell me! And here I am now. Nobody's letting me just live. I am under attack. I've lost my partner to it. It menaces me, too. Now I've even lost my untamed refuge in my own backyard. I used to stand up to things for other people. I was a fighter for just causes. Why aren't I fighting back now?"

I'm lost for an appropriate answer.

"Why aren't I doing—something?" She's talking to herself now, not me.

I pause, and very gently say, "Well, Estelle. Maybe it's time to organize a memorial for Vickie, to bring us all together."

"Max," Estelle says with finality. "You're right. You're absolutely right."

Now that I know the memorial will be a reality, I can't sleep. Instead, I sit in front of my computer, the face that stares but does not turn away from me, nervously tapping my bare feet on the cold wooden floor.

The world outside that took Vickie away from me is a dangerous place. But cyberspace doesn't feel so safe, either. Knives and guns can't kill my avatar. But it's the same people, with the same attitudes, sitting in front of their computers playing this game in real time. And I can't even read those android expressions for telltale signs, the way I scan faces in the line waiting to get into the bar.

Yet hunger for more human interaction is gnawing at me as the clock nears midnight. At least in this computer world, I can try to connect with strangers, and log off if it doesn't go well.

I click my way into AvaStar, hesitating for a moment as I type in my *nom de 'Net*.

Now here "I" am, Pollygender, an awkward avatar in jeans and a T-shirt, standing next to a row of rockets and a roster of celestial destinations tacked up on a cyberbulletin board. Around me are male and female avatars, all of them clothed in the same limited mix-and-match choices in the locker rooms. If I pass my cursor over their cyberbodies, their chosen monikers pop up above their heads: out2lunch, bikerbob, grrl2watch4, sneakypete. These are my crewmates.

I huddle in with the group crowded around the rota of possible journeys to the different planets to check out the choices. One by one, the other avatars take steps away and stare at me. A corner of my control panel on the bottom of my screen flashes—once, twice, three times. Other cursors are passing over my body, registering my cybercontradiction.

I study the roster: singles, adult only, lesbian, gay. I guess "adult" must mean heterosexual. And I guess bisexuals have to shuttle back and forth between planets.

I turn around and see small groups of avatars talking, some looking at me. No reason to be paranoid in cyberspace, I remind myself. What's the worst they can do to me here?

One avatar is alone, checking me out from a distance. The name pops up on my screen: sylphboy.

The ringing of my telephone, in real time in the next room, jangles me. I tilt my head to listen to the message.

"Hey, buddy," Thor's voice booms in my apartment, "I was just thinking. About the other day." He sounds dreamy. I get up and walk toward the phone, wondering if I should pick up. "I was thinking about what you said. And I was thinking about things you didn't say, and thinking about things I wish I had said." He must be stoned. I can hear music in the background—the thump of bass, an occasional tinkle of notes. "I don't know what goes on in your head when you have sex."

I decide not to pick up.

"But for me it's all about the music. I don't think, I just feel the music. I mean I actually feel it in my body, making a different kind of music as it runs through me. And then I try to listen to the music in the other person's body and harmonize with it. And there's just nothing bad that can get inside when that melody takes over. And when there's more than one person, well, that's a symphony. But that's another subject, buddy, for another night. I gotta go to bed now."

The machine registers the end of the call with a loud click. I stand in stillness, unready to talk about this right now with Thor, yet strangely pleased about at least beginning a conversation about sex with someone who doesn't seem to feel too much shame or humiliation to talk about it.

I walk back to my office and sit down in front of my computer. A new group is lining up for the rockets ready to blast off to other planets. The gender-queer avatar is nowhere to be seen. Up in the golden sky, three-dimensional planets turn slowly on programmed cyberaxes.

21

It seems silly to me that I've showered and brushed my teeth and put on freshly laundered underwear to sit down in the dark in front of the phosphorescent glow of my computer monitor. I am about to venture out again into the daylight of a virtual world. I want to visit the lesbian star. It's been such a long time since I've set foot on that home planet.

I'm at the rocket ships, looking up at the planets in a shimmering sky. They're just chat rooms, really. My breath is quickening: why should cyberrejection hurt any less?

I take a deep breath and check out the rocket ship scheduled to go to Planet Lesbos. Three or four avatars are chatting—nonsensical text in dialogue bubbles over their heads. According to the game rules, until an avatar gives permission for contact, the conversations of others appear in an unintelligible hieroglyph.

I walk slowly toward the line and wait patiently for the ship to board.

One avatar leans way, way back to look at me. The group conversation has paused as the other avatars check me out. After a long moment, they give the equivalent of a shrug.

Blinking lights on the shiny ship alert me that it's time to board. I wait till the others are up the gangway. The steps glitter like golden steel. I'm worried that the game regulations won't let a "male" avatar visit a lesbian planet. But at the top of the stairs, a silver service android wearing a chauffeur's cap taps *hir* brim as I step onto the main deck.

Although the availability roster had shown Planet Lesbos was crowded this time of night, only half a dozen seats on board are filled. Attentive cybereyes watch me pass. I take an aisle seat, in the back. When the flashing sign announces it's time to buckle up I do so, despite wondering what harm could possibly come to me if I do not.

I watch the glyph dialogue of others nearby, trying to decode it. I see that even this seemingly unreadable language could probably be understood with study—its patterns and repetitions. I settle back in the soft seat as the ship shimmies and shakes. Outside the round portal, programmed plumes of rocket exhaust trail behind us.

Relief floods me as our ship passes from the eggshell blue of earth to the blackness of space. Golden stars shoot past us, leaving blazing trails. I would be happy just to voyage on this ride tonight, a quiet journey to another domain. But in moments, we have arrived.

I wait in the back of the ship to disembark. As I leave, the silver android nods at me, touching the brim of *hir* cap again. I step gingerly down the gangway, clicking on a step at a time, blinking in the golden light. Over the horizon of the orb on which I stand, I see the earth, turning slowly in space. A nearby rocket ship, steaming in the luminosity of this bright atmosphere, waits to take me to other planets.

A short distance from where I stand, female avatars are crowded around a redwood tree. With a click of my cursor, I can read what's posted on the tree without pressing forward to look. It's a list of discussion groups at Lesbos Academy: feminism in the twenty-first century, sex and the single lesbian, same-sex marriage, domestic violence, safer sex tips, how to lobby your local politician, femme identity, butch–femme roles.

I hear a familiar sound—the crack of a wooden bat against a rawhide ball. All our pixeled heads turn at once toward the sound. We all head up the nearby lavender hill. I lumber, learning to walk as a newcomer in the atmosphere of this particular planet.

Over the hill I hear cheers and watch the runner round third base, heading for home. The little avatars sitting on bleacher seats under the twin golden suns rise and raise their arms, excited conversation blurbs popping like balloons. Those sitting on the grass at the base of the hill, or lingering at the edge of verdant woods, slowly swivel their heads to follow the runner's trajectory.

I walk halfway down the hill and crouch in the purple dirt to study the players and the crowd. At least three players and two fans have found a way to place a cap brim-backwards on their heads. Lots of jeans and T-shirts and sneakers. A few tight sweaters and skirts. All of the bodies were selected from the girls' locker room. In the Dick-and-Jane AvaStar universe, these are all Janes. At least at first glance. Animating each of these avatars is someone sitting in a darkened room, the way I am. And who knows who they are? Complex people playing this simple game together.

I wave my cursor over the players and their nearby fans like a divining rod. One of the players is named "Mikey233Avatar." One of the fans is "Tony1792."

A roar overhead pulls all our gazes up toward the sky. Two small-engine craft—like airborne jet skis—race each other overhead, leaving trails of rainbow exhaust in their wake. The game stops as we shield our eyes from the double glare of the sun, and watch as silver androids, gold badges large as battle shields across their smooth chests, appear above to block the sky race.

Suddenly my screen freezes and a text message appears, trimmed in gold: Action delay. Players expelled.

The scene of the baseball game resumes, although players and onlookers are not moving—momentarily stunned. Murmuring bubbles simmer in the crowd.

As I turn to go back up the hill I discover another avatar standing right behind me. This face is not like any of the other androids. This is a complexly human face, digitally rendered, on a female avatar. We pass the wand of our cursors over each other. A name appears: Two-EaglesSoaring.

My screen goes dark for a moment and a message appears: "No more racist mascots!" Now I'm back on the hill and the face before me softens into something like a cyber smile.

"How did you do that?" I ask.

The figure points toward my control panel. The blurb above hir head is garbled. I don't know how to allow access for communication. I fumble around my control panel, clicking on things that may turn it on.

A box appears between us: Another AvaStar would like to communicate with you. Accept? Decline?

I click "accept."

A new box appears: Out of this world? Real time?

I don't know what that means. I click on "out of this world." My screen changes into nothing more than a typed line of text:

TwoEaglesSoaring: new here?

Pollygender: Yes and no.

TwoEaglesSoaring: u get the hang of it . . . it's easy.

Pollygender: How did you create a real face on your avatar? And how do you smile? How do you show emotion?

TwoEaglesSoaring: u learn . . . ask the silver people . . . they'll tell u . . . hard thing is the clothes . . . crappy choices . . . like a utah ywca . . . best I could find is this fringe. I look like an old hippie.

I pause, not knowing what to type.

TwoEaglesSoaring: i have a ? 4 you.

Pollygender: Ok.

TwoEaglesSoaring: this a.m. i saw this silver and turquoise belt . . . powerful old stones . . . in a pawnshop window . . . really, really cheap . . . I'm not sure . . . think i should buy it?

This seems like a very odd question to ask a stranger. I'm not sure if I should be honest or not.

Pollygender: I couldn't buy it.

TwoEaglesSoaring: y not?

Pollygender: Pawnshop. I couldn't buy someone else's tears.

No answer. Maybe that was too honest.

TwoEaglesSoaring: 2 much sorrow.

Pollygender: Yes.

TwoEaglesSoaring: i could tell u might be worth talkin 2.

Oh, it was a test.

TwoEaglesSoaring: where's yr home?

Pollygender: I live in Jersey City.

TwoEaglesSoaring: that's where u live . . . where's yr home?

The question hurls me into a tailspin.

Pollygender: Hard question.

TwoEaglesSoaring: u lost?

Pollygender: Maybe. Are you lost if nobody's found you?

TwoEaglesSoaring: no . . . u lost if u don't know where u r.

Pollygender: I'm near the sea. Where are you?

TwoEaglesSoaring: u want to feel the power of the ocean, u should come here. . . .

For a moment, a photo of the desert canyon walls, carved by long-receded waters, fills my computer screen.

Pollygender: How did you do that?

TwoEaglesSoaring: like i told u . . . when u c the metal people, ask 'em.

Pollygender: I guess people use photos so you know who you're talking to.

TwoEaglesSoaring: u never really know.

Another photo appears, sepia with age. Someone has handwritten the words—*boarding school, 1956*—across the bottom. Indian youth are posed in three rows in front of a dormitory building, their eyes smoldering with rage. Two priests flank them, holding their crosses in front of their bodies like conquistador armor. The image dissolves.

TwoEaglesSoaring: . . . i met this dude from germany today . . . a tourist . . . he asked me 2 take a pic of him and his boyfriend . . . so i took the pic . . . then he goes and tries to hand me a dollar . . . i told him i didn't want that president when he was alive . . . so he takes this button off his backpack . . . it was in german i couldn't read it . . . he tells me the buttons says everybody is a foreigner most places . . . hey u ever go 2 day of mourning?

Pollygender: What's that?

TwoEaglesSoaring: turkey day . . . folks who are feeling no thanksgiving go to plymouth rock . . . make a circle of truth around it . . . we get to tell our truth.

Pollygender: How do you find out how to get there and what time?

TwoEaglesSoaring: do what every1 does who isn't on the moccasin telegraph.

Pollygender: What's that?

TwoEaglesSoaring: google . . . i might go next year . . . may b i see u

Pollygender: I'd recognize you. But how would you recognize me?

TwoEaglesSoaring: i recognized you here.

My telephone rings in the other room. I ignore it until I hear Jasmine's voice on my message machine: "Max? Are you there? Pick up, pick up. Max." She repeats my name, in a way that makes me stiffen. "It's Thor. He's been arrested."

I type: emergency, be right back.

I run into the bedroom and pick up the receiver. "What?" My voice rises in panic. "What happened?"

"He left the protest at the detention center alone to go to the bathroom. The cops followed him and busted him in the john."

I've been arrested in public toilets. I know the cops are going to do everything they can to humiliate Thor. Jasmine says, "We're calling everybody we can think of to use their phone trees to get as many people outside the jail as fast as we can."

"Does he have a lawyer?"

"Yes, she's there already."

"Where should I meet you?"

"Get off at the Christopher Street station. We've got a car. We'll drive out to the precinct together. That's safest."

"Okay, I'll hurry up and get dressed. I can be there in about forty-five minutes."

I hang up, ready to put on clothes and go out the door. TwoEaglesSoaring—I'm still online! I run back to my office and bend over my keyboard.

Pollygender: I'm really sorry there's an emergency here. My friend just got busted. I'm scared for him. I've got to go.

My cursor blinks back at me: no reply.

Pollygender: Are you still there?

TwoEaglesSoaring: yeah.

Pollygender: Can I meet you online again?

TwoEaglesSoaring: maybe . . . see u around. . . .

A text message pops up: TwoEaglesSoaring has left this planet.

22

As the dark sky behind the police fortress fades into the promise of dawn, I realize we've been waiting for Thor's release for more than twenty-four hours. His lawyer, Miriam, said the cops are still considering serious charges against him. That's when I knew, even before Miriam told us, that they'd hurt Thor.

The cops had pushed us across the street from the precinct more than an hour ago, when our numbers dwindled as some drifted off to catch a few winks in their nearby parked cars, or ran to get a bite of breakfast and hurry back. But now, as people are returning, this sidewalk won't hold us all.

A few young tranny bois and Radical Cheerleaders of all sexes are schmoozing in the street near the curb, slowly repositioning closer to the bastion.

Guarding the entrance to the jail, like mythical sentry creatures, is a double row of cops in riot gear. Their faces are screened by darkened helmet visors, except for one. Visor up, she holds her club in both hands horizontally across her waist, surveying us with revulsion and hatred, her eyes wild like a police horse in a noisy crowd.

But we are quiet. Conserving our strength. A silent, uneasy standoff.

Ruby and Jasmine are conferring near the curb, their foreheads almost touching. Deacon and I are standing next to each other, wordlessly staring at the granite and steel edifice.

I take a last drag on my cigarette, crush it out against my heel, and toss it toward the curb. "It's a scary place," I whisper. I nod toward the jail.

Deacon rolls his head to one side to look at me. "Yes it is. But we can't let our fear of that place keep us from doing what needs to be done."

Def and John D. Arc arrive with other drag king performers, direct from their appearance at a downtown club. They're still bristling with spirit-gummed sideburns and mustaches, handsome in suits and ties. They've brought cardboard trays of coffee, handing out steaming cups of caffeine and balking at any coins or dollar bills extended to them. I gingerly hug John, so that none of the coffee spills. He pushes back the brim of his fedora and leans toward me. "Any word?" he asks, worry weighing on his tone.

I shake my head. "Not yet. His lawyer's in there arguing with the cops."

"Bastards," John mutters as he offers me a cup of coffee.

I peel back the plastic lid and smell the chemical aroma of energy. "Thanks." I toast him with the cup.

Def looks me in the eye for information. I shrug and shake my head, helplessly. Def presses *hir* lips together and nods. Then *ze* looks me up and down, like a tailor about to fit me for a suit. Def places both palms of *hir* hands near *hir* thighs, and as *ze* runs *hir* hands upward, *hir* whole body lifts.

It's not until Def does this that I realize how slouched over I am. I raise myself up dramatically. Def nods in approval and thumps *hir* chest.

Then I slump, theatrically. Def laughs and nods again, this time in understanding. *Ze* takes my right hand in *hirs* and folds it into a fist. *Ze* picks
up my arm and shakes my raised fist at the police station. I laugh. Def
pats my back and walks away.

Ginger Vitus arrives, still spangled from performance. She makes a
beeline for me. "Got a ciggie?" I take out my pack and offer her one. It's
an excuse for me to smoke another. The whites of Ginger's eyes are red
with intoxication; a thin film of sweat makes her face gleam under her
streaking makeup. She looks so frayed, so world-weary. And yet, under it
all, I see such dignity.

She fumbles for a light. I give her my matches.

"Anybody know anything yet?" she asks, her voice quavering.

I shake my head slowly from side to side.

She turns from me abruptly and heads over to Ruby and Jasmine,
huddling with them in the flow of tactics.

More people have arrived in the morning light, and they're standing
on the sidewalk in front of the precinct. These are people I've never seen
before; they're a mix of ages, nationalities. Maybe some are from the immigrant rights movement; maybe some from Thor's antiwar organizing.

Others arrive with People's Fightback Network placards, similar to
the ones I helped make. These hastily inked posters demand: Stop the
War & Free Thor!

For those of us who have been standing here so long that the balls of
our feet ache and our knee joints are frozen, the sight of fresh forces
renews our vigor. Those who have just arrived position themselves on the
sidewalk in front of the precinct. The police cordon, shifting anxiously
from foot to foot, has not yet received orders to push them back across
the street with the rest of us.

Ruby lifts her head and looks around, wordlessly drawing our attention. She nods toward the police station. As if in slow motion, we begin

to glide, a step or two at a time, to coalesce on the sidewalk in front of the precinct.

But no movement is small enough, nonthreatening enough, to keep the cops from reacting. They change position, holding their clubs across their bodies as though in preparation for an onslaught. Do they really think that we are plotting to storm the citadel, wrest the cell keys from them, and spirit Thor away with us? Certainly not with the numbers we have here this morning.

Radical Cheerleaders, most in pink tutus, form a line in front of the steps to the precinct, their backs to the blue forces. They've got guts. They pass a whisper along the line, readying to raise our spirits.

Ruby sidles up to me. "Keep an eye on the pigs. They ain't bacon yet."

I lean closer. "You're making me hungry."

Ruby shakes her head. "For real."

The chant is not particularly threatening in any way. But many of the cops appear visibly agitated—is it the cheer that alarms them or the cheerleaders?

> *Gender, gender, fuck it we say.*
> *Life's more fun with gender play.*
> *Gender, gender, it's not what's down there,*
> *Assigning strict roles, that ain't fair.*

Jasmine joins us, nodding toward the cops. "They're getting riled. I'm a little concerned because we've got, what, how many people do you think? Close to a hundred?"

I look around. She's right.

"It's amazing." I'm thinking out loud. "This many people. Thor must work with so many groups."

"But," Jasmine amends, "it's people who haven't worked together

before. We don't know each other. There's no communication. It's easier
for the cops to bust us up. We need a plan if we're all going to stay here
in front of the station."

The cheerleaders are chanting:

> *If I wanna wear whitey-tighties with my dress,*
> *Who are you, messing with my happiness?*
> *If I wanna wear high heels and I got a dick,*
> *Leave me alone, don't be a gender prick.*
> *So I've got short hair and a big strap-on,*
> *You have no right saying it's wrong.*

Ruby leans closer to us, in order to be heard over the chant. "Look
around, everyone likes this. Well," she smiles in the direction of the cops,
"all the people like it." Jasmine looks around, quietly evaluating. The
chant dies down. A cop with gold bars on his uniform stands behind the
row of riot cops, silently assessing.

Ruby whispers to Jasmine. With a short nod, they begin to chant, each
word strong and decisive: "We want Thor! Let our brother go!"

We all raise our voices, loud: "We want Thor! Let our brother go!"

As though we conjured them, people begin streaming in from unseen
directions to swell our ranks. Our voices grow as our numbers build in
size and strength.

"What the hell?" I ask Ruby. "Where are all these people coming from?"

She looks over my head as she answers. "Jasmine and I phoned the
Fightback Network office. They said someone had put out an e-mail last
night to meet at the courthouse. So they've got someone over at the
courthouse building telling everyone who shows up there to come here
to the precinct."

"We want Thor! Let our brother go!"

At the sound of the new chant drawing closer, we all turn. A large group shouting "Stop the war! Free Thor!" is marching down the street toward us.

Ruby beams at Jasmine. "You were right to call the Fightback office."

Jasmine laughs. "I believe that was your idea."

They wrap their arms around each other's waists and join in the new chant, bouncing like the Radical Cheerleaders: "Stop the war! Free Thor!" The two groups cheer each other as we merge.

Deacon points to the top of the stairs. I swing around, fully expecting to ward off a billy club. But it's Thor's attorney emerging from the station. She walks halfway down the steps and stops.

I tug on Deacon's coat, "Is she a good lawyer?"

He nods. "Supposed to be. She used to work with Miz Vickie."

Miriam raises her hands to speak and we quiet down. "As some of you already know, the police were considering bringing felony charges against Thor."

Someone shouts out, "For peeing?"

The lawyer answers indirectly. "Thor's face is badly bruised. And his shoulder appears to be dislocated. He has refused to go to the hospital until he is released from police custody."

My whole body aches thinking about Thor in there, wounded.

Ruby audibly exhales. "They hurt Thor. That's why they want to charge him with assault." Ruby rubs her face hard with her hands, and when she looks up again to listen, I see her face glistening with smeared tears.

"But," Miriam holds up her hands to quiet the audible anger, "all of you being here has been important to the process. The police chief has informed me that they may be about to release Thor on his own recognizance. I've spoken with Thor and told him you're all out here. That really helped raise his spirits." She drops her professional demeanor for just a heartbeat: "And mine, too. Thank you."

Miriam turns and goes back up the stairs. The police close ranks

and bar her way, looking behind them for a higher-up to tell them
what to do.

She turns back toward the crowd. "I am going inside the precinct now
to escort my client outside."

Ruby starts the chant, "No justice? No peace!"

The demand appears to part the row of police, creating enough space
to let the lawyer through. But just as she leans forward and opens the
heavy glass door, Thor appears in the doorway.

"There he is!" someone shouts.

Jasmine begins a chant, over our cheers, "The people, united, will
never be defeated! *Los pueblos, unidos, jamás serán vencidos!*"

But I can't raise my voice; it's stuck in my throat as I look at Thor. Half of
his face is a mottled bruise, purple and red; like the Phantom of the Opera—
a mask of pain. He has a cut over his eyebrow that's bled down to stain his T-
shirt. His left shoulder looks crumpled like a broken wing. His eyes look
away from all of us, then down at his feet, and back up toward us with a
strong smile. But in that moment, I know that not all his wounds are visible.

He lifts one arm, wincing, and tries to shout out, "Thank you!" But
he can't. He physically begins to fold. Miriam tries to support him down
the steps.

Jasmine and Ruby and I run to help. I get one arm around his waist.
Jasmine's arms steady him. Ruby hesitates—she's on the side of his body
that's wounded.

Ruby coos to Thor, "You'll be okay, sugar. We got you now."

Thor's head has dropped forward. He nods a little.

Jasmine ducks forward to look at his face. "We need to get you to the
hospital."

I whisper, "We'll stay with you, don't worry. Whatever you need, we'll
all be there."

Thor squeezes my body, just a little. "Thanks, buddy."

* * *

The hospital security guard is glowering at us. He smirks at me and draws his index finger across his throat.

I laugh out loud. He's a rent-a-cop with a Ken doll hairpiece pasted on top of his head. What's he going to do, beat me to death with his bad toupee?

We've been sitting for hours in this crowded emergency room waiting area. I try not to look at the television suspended above us, volume turned down. It's the Jerry Springer show. It's too painful to watch. People set up to fistfight or pull their pants down, and the crowd whipped up to call for blood and more degradation.

I can't stand waiting much longer. I want to crawl out of my skin. "I need a cigarette," I announce.

No one moves or speaks.

Ruby looks up from fretting. "Sugar, you got to put that poison down."

"Yeah," I admit, to ward off the suggestion, "but not right now."

Ruby shakes her head in disgust. She knows this routine.

Miriam appears in the doorway. "They're bringing him out now."

A nurse in pink scrubs rolls a wheelchair with Thor slumped in it into the waiting area. The nurse rests his hand on Thor's forearm and bends over to flip up the footrests and help Thor slowly rise to his feet.

Thor's arm is in a sling, tightly bound to his body. There are several tiny pale blue sutures, like ghostly railroad tracks, across his bruised cheek, and the wound is glistening with ointment.

We cluster close to him.

"You hungry?" I ask gently. "Or you want to be home and we could make you something to eat?"

Thor appears to be an avatar that has just landed on this planet, confused and afraid. He sounds weary: "I just want to go home and be by myself."

23

"I don't want to go in yet." I verbally dig in my heels. "I'm not ready." I reach into my suitcoat pocket for my pack of cigarettes and matches. It's so warm and bright out here. Near my cheek, a few tiny white blossoms remain on the branches of a pear tree.

Ruby is not in a mood to be messed with. "Max, don't you start with me, now. Don't even bother lighting that up. You hear me? Don't go all Marlboro Man on me now. I am not gonna be late to Vickie's funeral and I am not gonna go in that church alone. Now pull yourself together, sugar. We are goin' inside."

I salute her with the two fingers that could be holding a cigarette right now.

As we get closer to the little West Village church, it seems to rise above me like a towering Gothic tree growing upward in time-lapse speed. My legs wobble and I slow down a little.

"I don't do well at sharing grief," I remind Ruby.

"News flash," she snaps back. Ruby admonishes me without ever breaking her stride. "Do not trifle with me, sugar! I am in no mood."

"Why is this being held in a church?" I complain. "They're secular Jews!"

She shrugs. "Don't ask me. Maybe 'cause everybody's so used to comin' here when one of us dies."

Ruby and I walk through the open oak doors. We clutch each other like we're marching toward our own funerals. Hundreds of people are already inside, sitting in pews, and milling about. Lots of older white Jews from Vickie's and my generation. That I expected. But there are also many Latinos of all ages. And a few people who appear to be Arab and South Asian. I recognize dozens of people I know from the bars, including a lot of the Black drag queens and transwomen, and few white "old gay" butches I've known for decades. As I look around the room at the white men who appear to be "straight" I can see, by the momentary cut of a glance or the grace of a gesture, that there are a lot of cross-dressers here.

The pulpit, surrounded by flowers, is covered with a lavender cloth with a graphic of a clenched fist stenciled on it, covering any religious symbol that may be underneath.

The organ pipes open their throats. I am surprised to see Deacon playing the organ. Someone who looks familiar begins to sing an aria.

I ask, "The person singing. What *hir* name?"

"That's Lady Night," Ruby answers. "She used to sing at the old Phoenix. Never lip-synched. Brought the house down every time. She could've been a famous opera singer if she wasn't one of us, if she wasn't family."

The sung refrain asserts itself: "Remember me, remember me!"

The song raises goose bumps on my forearms.

When I am laid in earth:
May my wrongs create
No trouble in thy breast;
Remember me, but ah!
Forget my fate.

Thor stands in front of us, dressed in a hand-stitched black suit, rose silk shirt, and maroon tie. I wonder if Deacon made that fine suit for him. No more stitches on his cheek, just a red scar, a remembrance of what is still healing.

Thor kisses Ruby; she whispers something in his ear. He nods without smiling.

Thor grabs my hand and squeezes it tight. "How're you holdin' up, buddy?" he asks.

I shrug. "I'm okay. How're you doing, Thor?"

He looks over my shoulder, "Okay. I'm doin' okay." He hands us each a program. He's doing his organizer thing.

I flip through the program to see what it is I'm listening to. I nod toward Lady Night, "This is beautiful."

Thor lowers his head to listen to the refrain. "*Dido and Aeneas,*" he sighs. "Yes, it's beautiful. But it scares me a little that Estelle picked it out. Dido killed herself when her lover sailed away."

My skin crawls. I hope Estelle can survive this pain.

Ruby tugs my arm. "Let's go find a place to sit."

"Back here?" I point to open pews.

"Up there." Ruby pulls me toward the front pew where I can already see Estelle talking with other mourners, her body frozen, her manner gracious. My gait slows as we move closer to Estelle. Ruby begins to drag me and then releases me. She stands back and signals the direction forward with her hands like I'm an airplane that she's guiding toward the runway: "Go on. Go on, now."

This is too hard. It was painful enough that Vickie was killed, that I've lost her. But now we have to look the horror and grief in the face, in each other's faces. And worst of all, we have to talk about it.

I peer around for an escape, but Estelle recognizes me from behind her facade of geniality. Her smile is generous and real, and my body relaxes a little. "Max." She kisses my cheek as we hug, leaving a light dusting of makeup on my face. She clenches my arm too tightly. "Thank you for coming. I'm so glad you're here."

My face feels stiff with unexpressed emotion. "Of course I'm here, Estelle," I reply.

She smiles, takes my hand in both of hers and pumps it up and down, and then she turns away. Ruby waits a long moment before touching Estelle's sleeve. Estelle makes a little cry of recognition. They hold each other, rocking back and forth slightly, body to body. Ruby whispers, bringing a little gurgle like laughter from Estelle's throat. Ruby murmurs something else and Estelle nods and they leave each other's embrace, slowly, reluctantly.

Ruby comes back to me. "C'mon," she says. "Let's go look at the photos."

She directs me toward a table displaying Vickie's pictures in the back of the church. Ruby and I burrow our way between people to look at more than a quarter century of Vickie's photojournalism.

I remember Vickie told me that when her draft notice first came, she was terrified. She held hope that the experience might turn her into a "real" man, but she was afraid she'd be bayoneted in her sleep if her femininity betrayed her. The Army taught her to take pictures and then sent her out to the battlefield to document their war. But Vickie saw the battle through her own lens.

I see two photos from Vietnam on this table. The first is of a GI, his head back in a full scream of grief, as he rocks another soldier, lifeless in his arms. The second is a photo of an old Vietnamese woman looking directly at the camera—a challenge to the viewer to search for their own humanity, to stop being the enemy.

Vickie did. She shot herself in the thigh. Almost bled to death. She said she hadn't really thought it out, she just had to do something to get the hell out of there. She was still in a brace and on crutches when I met her marching in the streets against the war with a North Vietnamese flag pinned to the back of her denim jacket.

Here on the table, I see us all—the way we looked to Vickie, the moments we raised up to our highest selves to protest—captured in black and white. I'd forgotten how the changes going on in the world around me then had awakened me from slumber. How the seeds of my own consciousness traveled on those winds. I study our faces: were we all so strong and so beautiful then, or was Vickie just a great photographer? I pull Ruby over to see the one of her and me marching in front of a bright orange Youth Against War & Fascism banner: Stop the War against Black America!

"Lord," she studies the picture, hands on hips. "Look at us now. We're old as dirt!"

Thor comes up beside me and points to one of the prints. I wouldn't have recognized him in the photograph. He's linking arms with others in front of the entrance to a building, wearing a button with one word on it: Divest!

"That's where I met Vickie," Thor says. "We started talking. I can't believe she stayed friends with me after what I said to her that day." He shakes his head as though he can dislodge the memory.

"What?"

"It's so arrogant I hate to even repeat it. She was a stranger to me and I was pontificating. I told her Black people in South Africa should take the moral high road by rejecting armed struggle and choose nonviolent civil disobedience, like we were doing.

"And she was furious. She said, 'You mean they should arrange to get arrested, like you are? Do you know what the South African police did to Stephen Biko? Why would anyone who is oppressed want to put themselves into police custody?'

"I told her, 'History will condemn any struggle that resorts to violence.' And I added, a little haughtily, 'I go by the name Thoreau.'

"And she said to me, 'History is always written by the victor. And my name is Victor.' " My laughter seems to make Thor more embarrassed.

"That night Vickie gave me Henry David Thoreau's public defense of John Brown. Then we argued for about a year after that. And later I changed my name from Thoreau to Thor."

"I never knew that story!" Thor was Thor by the time I'd met him.

Thor looks at the photo, connecting with a moment long past. "That's what memorials are for, I guess. Well, I gotta go help hand out these programs."

Someone next to me says proudly, "That's me." I do a quick scan of his face and then look at the photo: Farm workers, their faces creased by the sun, battling hand-to-hand against men with short clubs. "Sí, se puede!" reads the farm workers' signs in the fray. "It can be done."

I point to a snapshot of Ruby, Angel, and me, collapsed in exhaustion on the lawn of the Ellipse behind the White House. Angel is lying on the grass with his placard resting on his belly: "Big firms get rich, GIs die!"

The stranger nods, our introduction complete.

Although Vickie must have taken a lot of photos of Estelle, there's only one snapshot at the end of the display where the guest book waits for our signatures. Estelle is sitting on a blanket at the beach, the wind tossing her hair, her smile bold, looking directly into Vickie's lens, her eyes making a silent pact.

The music stops. Deacon remains seated at the organ, as though it is a home away from home. The crowd noise quiets. Ruby tugs me again. "Let's go sit." She points to the first pew where Estelle is sitting with her body bowed forward.

The seating is more like a wedding than a funeral. Those who knew their friend as Vic mostly sit on the side where Estelle sits; those who knew her as Vickie on the other. Ruby and I are the crossovers.

Thor steps to the pulpit. His voice is low and quiet. "All of us here loved an extraordinary human being. An immigrant rights lawyer, a tireless political activist, a photographer who chronicled more than one struggle for justice, a friend, a life partner," Thor looks up at the many hundreds gathered, "and a cross-dresser."

I respect Thor for waiting a moment before he speaks again. He lets the words reverberate in this cavernous room. "Some of us are here to remember our friend Vic. Some of us are here to honor our friend Vickie. But because we've come together here, all of us, we are bringing together two parts of one life that cannot be understood in disconnection. Today, we will all come closer to understanding the person we loved in *hir* entirety.

"And we are here to stand with Estelle."

I cringe a little, wondering how that sounds to the guy in a wheelchair next to our pew.

"Estelle," Thor speaks directly to her, "we love you and we are with you."

The soft sob of pigeons in the windowsill nearby is the only sound echoing in the yawning space. The audience sits, still and quiet.

Thor continues. "We would like to thank the Immigrant Workers' Alliance for arranging this space for us all, a space in which we hoped many communities would feel comfortable because each has been welcomed here so many times in the past."

I lean against Ruby and whisper, "Is there an order to who speaks today?"

Ruby shushes me. "Just get ready, sugar. You'll be up soon. Do you know what you're gonna say?"

I swallow down my fear. "Yes, I've gone over it in my head a hundred times. I just wish I didn't have to get up there in front of all these people and say it."

Thor keeps talking and I'm trying to pay attention, but I'm tuning in and out, wondering am I up next?

The audience draws a collective, audible gasp.

"What did he say?" I jiggle Ruby's arm.

She leans her head toward mine. "Thor said sometimes he asks himself if Vickie's death had anything to do with the 'war on terror,' 'cause some of the cases she was lawyering for were big political cases. I don't think he should've said that. We got no proof."

But the idea has been said out loud and it shakes me. Is it possible that Vickie wasn't murdered by strangers who had no idea who she was?

Someone else is at the podium now. An older white woman. But I can't really hear her. I'm asking myself questions that I may never have answers for—and I really want answers.

The church resounds with applause.

I tug Ruby's sleeve. "What did she say that made people clap?"

"She said Vickie would've been tellin' us to bring the troops home right now. Excuse me, are you listening—at all?"

I ignore her sarcasm. "I didn't know you were allowed to applaud in church."

"Shush," she swipes lightly at my hand.

"Hey," I protest. "I'm whispering over the applause. Why are you telling me to be quiet?"

She pats my withdrawn hand. "I'm trying to think about what I'm gonna say."

The stranger who pointed to himself in the photo of California farm workers walks slowly to the pulpit and begins to speak haltingly. "I didn't know about Victor's, um."

"Uh-oh." Ruby sighs.

The man inhales deeply and continues. "I didn't know about Victor's ways. About his way in the world, you know? Not until after he died, until Estelle told me. We worked together for many years. He was my friend. I can't believe he never told me. Maybe he thought I wouldn't understand.

"After Estelle told me, I was sorry I knew, because it changed how I thought about him, you know? I wanted him to stay the way I remembered him. And he wasn't around to talk to about it. But Estelle told me if I wanted to come to the memorial with all of you I should understand this.

"I was scared to come." He takes off his glasses and wipes his eyes. "I didn't want to come here. I didn't know how to think about all this. But I always respected him very much. Victor was there for me when *La Migra* killed my brother for crossing the border. I don't know how I got through those days after my brother was killed. Victor came by the house every day. Every day for a long time.

"After Victor was killed, so viciously, Estelle said she wasn't trying to say that the killing of my brother and Victor were the same thing. But, she told me, 'They killed your brother for crossing a border that shouldn't be there. And they killed Victor for crossing a border that shouldn't be there.'

"It made me think. About how no human being is illegal. No human being is an 'alien.'

"And when I heard that my friend had another name that I didn't know, I thought about how the people who know me as George don't know Jorge.

"My mother used to tell me when I was little: *Cada cabeza es un mundo.*" He taps his forehead with an index finger: "Each head is a world. I know this: We lost a beautiful world. A bigger world than I understood."

Jorge gulps a breath of air and raises his fist and concludes, "Victor Siegel, presente!" He pauses, gripping the pulpit with two hands, draws another breath, and says more softly: "Vickie Siegel, presente!"

"That guy is a *mentsh*," I murmur to Ruby. "He's a beautiful human being."

Thor motions for me to come to the dais to speak. I panic. I'm not ready.

"Just keep it real," Ruby nudges me to get up. "It's not gonna get any easier to wait."

I make my way up the carpeted stairs, woozy with fright. I had no idea how many people were in the room until I stand here facing them. But I know this is the only way to make what happened with me and Vickie right, at least with myself.

I tap the microphone and whisper, "Good morning."

A few voices respond, "Good morning."

"I was the last friend to," I hesitate, "to be with Vickie. Just before she got on the train to leave me, she asked me a simple question. She asked me where I live in relation to where we were standing. I told her it wasn't far, just a few blocks away.

"But I've gone over and over that question in my mind since her death—thinking about where I live in relation to her life. And now I wish I could go back to that moment and answer her differently."

Everyone in the church is watching me. It's so quiet in the room.

"I live in Jersey City on a corner where two streets meet: Maple and Birch. I'm on Maple when I'm in my living room, and Birch when I eat my breakfast. Across from my window I can look out and see the skyline of Manhattan. Most days I spend more hours on that side of the Hudson River than I do in Jersey.

"But as I kept hearing Vickie's question in my head, I began to dig deeper. And the more I searched, the more I discovered that I live where flesh has been torn and scars still bleed. And scars are memories.

"I discovered that I live on top of a seam of pulverized rock that may be the wound where Africa and North America tore apart 220 million years ago. It's a giant geological scar where red-hot magma bled, and when it cooled, it rose to form the precipice on which I live.

"I live on land where, just a few hundreds years ago, the Lenni-Lenape still hunted in the forests. Their blood, spilled by settlers, still drenches the soil. And a short walk from my apartment is a small, overgrown park where the end of slavery was first announced in my town. All around that little park today live people who still yearn for freedom.

"That one simple question Vickie asked me just before her death led me to feel connected to this past. To see how it shapes my present. I'm lost until I figure out where I live in relation to others.

"But my relationship to Vickie, that was hard for me to figure out. Vickie was the kind of person other people just couldn't help but respect. She was so principled. So clear in her political vision. I loved that about her. And I loved her as a friend. But deep down, I never felt a connection with her as a cross-dresser.

"Which you might think would be the most obvious." I look down at my own suit and tie, "because so am I.

"But Vickie and I weren't the same kind of cross-dressers. She was fluent in two gendered languages. That's how she conveyed who she was. But this is the only way I articulate who I am."

Estelle nods, head still down.

I take a deep breath. "I regret my last interaction with Vickie. I saw her going home to a good job, to someone who adored her."

Estelle looks up at me, yearning for more information, her hands tightly clasped in her on her lap.

"And in that instant, jealousy flared up in me because I thought that she could just take off her wig and her dress and move through the world another way—a way I thought of as closeted. But it takes two pronouns to even approximate Vickie's life. And she wasn't just half and half of anything. She was trying to be understood for the whole of who she was.

"Now I wish that Vickie could ask me again, once more, where I live. I would tell her: I live at the intersection of oppression. And you and I were neighbors. The same sky above us. The same earth. The same red blood, metallic tasting on our tongues. You lived under the sun. I live under the moon. I was sometimes envious that you could walk in the daylight, welcomed by smiling strangers. And I wasn't a very good neighbor sometimes. For that, I am truly sorry, Vickie.

"My aunt Raisa taught me an old Sephardic Jewish proverb: *Dime con quién conoscas, te diré quién sois*—Tell me who you know; I'll tell you who you are."

My voice cracks. "I knew Vickie."

I don't have anything else to say. There's no sound as I walk down the carpeted steps. A middle-aged white woman holding the hand of a young white teenager passes me on her way up to speak.

As I pass Estelle, I lean forward to kiss her tear-streaked cheek. She reaches up for me. "And I know you, Max," she whispers.

Ruby leans against me as I sit down and puts her arm through mine. "At first I thought you were goin' all MapQuest on us."

"I am Victor's youngest sister," the woman begins. "And I didn't expect," the woman chokes up. "I didn't realize," she covers her face with one hand. "I'm so glad he had such a big family to love him." She breaks down and cries, hard. She holds on to the podium. Estelle is up at her side, quickly, as the woman's body begins to sink into a kneeling position.

Thor looks to Deacon, who strikes up chords of a familiar spiritual— slow and strong and emotional—to give her time to speak again, or to step down. As the music swells, Ruby sings, softly, next to me. Lady Night stands up near the front of the church, her voice rises, low and sweet like Ruby's, translating for the whole church the longing of the music into spoken desire: Swing low, sweet chariot, comin' for to carry me home! This is what we sang at Marsha "Pay It No Mind" Johnson's memorial after she was found floating in the Hudson River. I remember how I cried that day. I don't want to break down now.

If you get to heaven before I do
tell all my friends I'll be comin' after you.

Sweat beads on my forehead and a little wave of nausea rises in my belly. I scoot out of the pew as unobtrusively as I can, creeping hurriedly and quietly toward the back of the church and out the front door.

I bend over the iron railing and throw up the cup of coffee I drank before coming here, the brown acid seeping into the roots of the forsythia bushes blooming bright as ballpark mustard along the foundation of the church.

I spit once and wipe my mouth with the back of my hand. I slip off my suit jacket. The warmth of sunlight is comforting. I pull out a cigarette and light up, taking a couple of long, deep drags before tossing it in the gutter.

I feel better now. Like I threw up something old and rotten in my gut. I run across the street to the store to buy a pack of gum and chew a stick hurriedly before going back inside.

A man is concluding at the podium. "I came here to remember an old friend." He shakes his head as though he's confused. "And I met this new one."

As I sit down at the front pew, Ruby hisses, "Where've you been?" She doesn't wait for an answer. "Oh, out smokin'. I should've known."

She stands up to speak. I tug on her sleeve. "I threw up."

"Oh," her tone softens. "Well then that's okay."

Ruby strides with a steady gait, heels clicking; she circumvents the strips of carpet on the little steps. She grips the pulpit between her hands and lifts her head to speak. I recall the times I've seen her do that before, at rallies, just before she begins. A summoning of spirit.

"I'm angry." As Ruby says it, I feel my own fury, churning in my empty stomach.

"They snuffed out this precious life. They took Vickie away from me.

"Vickie and I understood each other. We knew why we were angry people. I'm angry 'cause I get treated like less than human all the time. Vickie was angry 'cause she got treated less than human part of the time. You might think that she'd be glad she sometimes got a little break from it all. But when she was bein' Vic, and people treated her well—the same people who would spit if she passed by in her finery—that just made her madder. After all, she was the same person, worthy of the best, like us all."

Ruby nods toward the photo display. "That's why she took those pictures of us. She wanted to show us we were fierce," Ruby smiles, "and foxy and fine.

"And she was puttin' us back in the history we helped make, showing the world we were there.

"Vickie always defended people like me—she was the one you could call when the cops busted you, even if it was three in the morning. And she defended immigrants, too. She was always there for all the people who don't have papers, don't have passbooks. People who can't pull out their ID when the cops demand to see it. They can arrest us anytime they want, and they do. And they do whatever they please to us when they got us, too."

Estelle slides over closer to me. "Did Ruby tell you what she's going to propose?"

"No," I reply, startled.

"Listen," Estelle says.

Ruby's voice builds. "We got lots of immigrants in our Queer family, too. Like our friend Netaji. He just got snatched up. They just disappeared him, and a lot of other people, too. When Netaji didn't show up for work, Vickie would've been who we called. But she was already gone.

"Before she got killed, Vickie warned us about this so-called war on terror. She never stopped reminding everybody that the real terrorists were sittin' up there in the White House and Congress, in the Pentagon and the In-Justice Department. She warned everybody that while they were makin' war over there they were gonna step up the war on all of us here. All that Code Orange and Code Red—she was nobody's fool—she knew that's just a code for racism. And she warned us when they start demanding more ID and searching people's bodies, and pokin' around in our lives and takin' away what few rights we won, folks like us are all gonna feel it first."

Estelle pokes me lightly. "This is it!"

Why didn't Ruby talk to me about whatever she was going to say?

"She didn't have to tell me that we got to fight the war right here, too. I knew that already. I've known that all my life. I hear a lot of folks talk about 'peace.' Well, I want some damn peace. But even in between these wars I've lived through, I never got any peace. The police have been treatin' me like the enemy since I was born. I can hardly make a living. I get hounded from pillar to post.

"I am glad that nine judges in tacky black robes finally decided that we're not criminals just because we have sex with each other. Hallelujah. We won it because we won't stay put and we won't be quiet. We keep comin' out of the closets sayin' we got a right to live, and live proud. Maybe that Pride march last week was the biggest ever, I don't know.

"But I know this: It ain't over. Not by a long shot. I can still get arrested at the drop of a hat just for bein' who I am. I get treated like I'm illegal just for walkin' down the street. All the cops have to do is say they saw me tryin' to turn some trick. My friend Thor here got beat up and thrown in jail, and for what? For goin' to the bathroom!

"And racism keeps rearin' up its ugly head. I have to deal with it every day. And that's what these people who are gettin' rounded up are dealin' with.

"So what are we gonna do about all of this? We gotta defend our lives, yes, we do. But we gotta defend each other's lives, too. We got to show that we know when they start coming for immigrants, saying their papers aren't all in order and what not, then we all got to get together and say, 'Hell no!'"

Estelle leans forward, nodding, hands tightly clenched.

"I'm inspired by those people fightin' back in Iraq. They're takin' on the empire. They got to. It's not just their country they're fighting for. It's their lives. And we got to fight for our lives, too. It's all one big fight.

"So I say what if we were to call a protest march in Sheridan Square? Right there where we made the Stonewall Uprising. And we bring signs with pictures of Vickie and Netaji. And we bring signs for young Takeesha Johnson, a fifteen-year-old AG who got shot to death while she was just walking with her femme and their friends near the Christopher Street piers.

"And we bring signs that say: Stop rounding up our Muslim sisters and brothers! And we bring signs that say, like the sister up here said before: Stop the war! Bring those troops back now!'

"And when people say, 'What's the connection?' we tell them what my mama taught me when I was knee high: a house divided cannot stand.

"We can't let them divide us. Vickie brought us here together. And you know Vickie. She never brought people together without a purpose. If she called you up and asked you to come to a birthday party, you better bring your purse with you, 'cause she was going to hit you up for some good cause.

"And if she knew we were here, all of us people who've never been together in a room before, and she thought we were gonna leave here without doin' what needs to be done, well, I think she would," Ruby snaps her fingers in an arc over her head, "read us the riot act.

"So I say: Vickie, we're gonna march. All of us together. And we're gonna keep marching. We're not gonna rest until freedom's won, for everybody. And on that day you'll be with us all, just like you're with us here today."

The audience stirs as Ruby steps down. Estelle stands and slowly claps her hands together. Others stand, one after another, until most everyone in the room is on their feet. The applause is measured and determined, sustained and building in strength.

I clap my hands as Ruby approaches. "That was great!"

She demurs. "For real?"

"For real."

Estelle walks slowly toward the podium. She is holding a thin volume tightly in her hand. She stands, unsteadily, as Thor adjusts the microphone to her height. Like me, she taps it once, with her fingernail, to make sure it is on. She draws herself upright, as if to open up a resounding speech: "Thank you, Ruby." She smiles in Ruby's direction. "Thank you for your leadership. I will be there.

"Well," she deflates almost immediately, "I just don't know what to say. I've gone over this in my mind almost endlessly since Vic's . . . since Vic was killed. Since Vickie was killed." She enunciates the last four words with precision.

"I listened to what Ruby said, and I thought to myself, 'The best of what I loved in my Vickie is still here in these people around me. I want to be a part of organizing, not just for the life of my partner, but for Takeesha Johnson and all the lives that are so dear and are being cut so short. And why are we losing these precious people?" she asks. Then asks again, "Why?"

Estelle drops her head, her mouth too close to the microphone. "If only Vickie could see me now." She leans her head back, too far from the mike. "I think she'd really see a lot of change."

Estelle frowns, lost in her train of thought. "Of course, the greatest change is that I am without him, after all these years."

She looks far away at her own past. "Victor told me about himself on our fourth date. Told me he liked to wear women's clothes, I mean. And I thought to myself, 'I knew this handsome young man was too good to be true. I knew there was a blemish there somewhere.'

"A blemish," she shakes her head. "I can't believe that's how I thought about it when I first heard, but it's true. I thought it was a fault. A failing. An impulse that could, and should, be controlled.

"I said to him, 'I knew you were gay when you didn't try to get fresh with me after three dates.'

"But he smiled and shook his head: 'I didn't try to get fresh with you because I thought you were the one. And I wanted to tell you before this got more serious.' "

Estelle wraps her arms tightly around her own body. "And I was so thrilled that this man who was so smart and funny and sweet and gentle thought I might be the one.

"I tried to get him to assure me that he wasn't gay. But he wouldn't. He said he couldn't do that to his gay friends—that it would be like pushing them away to say 'I'm not like that.' I was shocked. Not that he had gay friends. I knew people who were gay. But they didn't say they were.

"Victor just told me, over and over, 'I'll just say this: You're the one who knocks my socks off!' "

Estelle covers her face with one hand and sobs—once, twice. "When I married Victor I knew that people believed I'd found the perfect mate. But I thought: if I could just keep this terrible secret. I was such a martyr, then. What a fool I was. I would run around the house, picking up any telltale sign before my family came to visit: an oversized shoe. A tube of lipstick that wasn't my color.

"And then one day, Vic sat me down at the dining room table and asked me such a simple question: 'Are you ashamed of me?' "

Estelle opens her mouth, but no words come out. She turns her head from side to side as though she could shake the words out. "I, I said," she stammers. "I said 'No!' I remember, so clearly, he dropped his head on his arms because I had so disappointed him with my lie. And then I said, 'Yes.' And Vic got up and walked away from me.

"Suddenly I realized that I was going to lose him, this person I loved most on the face of the earth, if I didn't take a good long look at myself. I'd lose him if I didn't love him for who he was, and not in spite of who he was.

"I found him in our bedroom, curled up on our bed. He looked so small lying there. I thought to myself, 'Oh, I've really hurt him. I haven't loved him the way he has loved me—generously and unconditionally. And he so deserves to be loved.

"And so I sat down on the bed and used the name he'd asked me to use once or twice before. I said, 'Vickie?'

"And she came out to me in a timorous way and said, 'Yes?'

"I said, 'I'd like to get to know you better. Perhaps it's time we dated. Is there a night, soon, that you might be free?' "

A soft ripple of audible emotion appears to awaken Estelle, startled, from the trance of her past.

"Shortly after that, I told my family about Vickie. My mother, of course, was very angry. Well, you'd have to know my mother. She thought that he'd tricked me. She thought I was being cheated, somehow. She could not understand why I would want to stay with my husband after knowing what I knew."

Estelle's voice rises, defiantly. "I told her, 'I am the luckiest person in

the world because I am loved for all of who I am, and I love this magnificent person with all my heart. And I wouldn't trade this amazing life for
any other.'

"I asked her that night how she would feel if her husband—my
father—could come back to life and be with her again. What if they
could be together again, but sometimes, when they sat listening to the
radio, he might be wearing a dress or makeup. Wouldn't she want him
back at her side?' "

"My mother didn't say a word when I asked her that. She stormed out
of my house that night and did not speak to me again, ever, for the rest
of her days.

"For a long time I asked myself: Am I such a bad daughter? Such a bad
person that she will not speak to me? And then I realized, I understood,
that she would rather never speak to me again than have to answer that
question.

"Now I have lost Vic, and Vickie. And I'm afraid I'll lose you all now,
too." She smiles down on us. "When you are not around me, I lose a part
of myself. And you lose my love. You don't get the chance to see, reflected
in my being, just how beautiful you each are."

Estelle reaches for the book on the pulpit, "Every year on Vic's—" her
smile trembles, "—and Vickie's birthday, she would read these wonderful
words from Walt Whitman aloud. It was her little ritual of affirmation.

"This year," Estelle stops; her face twists and contorts. Her voice
sounds strained. "This year I will read these words to you."

She opens the book. "This is what you shall do: Love the earth and
sun and the animals, despise riches, give alms to everyone that asks, stand
up for the stupid and crazy, devote your income and labor to others. . . ."

As Estelle reads, Ruby stands and slowly waves one arm over her head,
her hand floating like a leaf.

"hate tyrants, argue not concerning God, have patience and indulgence toward the people, take off your hat to nothing known or unknown or to any man or number of men, go freely with powerful uneducated persons and with the young and with the mothers of families. . . ."

I rise and stand next to Ruby, our bodies swaying together.

"read these leaves in the open air every season of every year of your life, re-examine all you have been told at school or church or in any book, dismiss whatever insults your own soul. . . ."

I look around and see that each person is standing, as though Vickie is among us now, being welcomed by our silent ovation.

"and your very flesh shall be a great poem and have the richest fluency not only in its words but in the silent lines of its lips and face and between the lashes of your eyes and in every motion and joint of your body."

Estelle wavers, teetering back and forth. Ruby and I rush forward to take her hands as she lurches down the steps.

Thor calls on Vickie's uncle, Moishe, to close the memorial with a song.

The old man climbs up the steps slowly, with great effort and determination. He turns to face us, almost angrily. "Why?" he demands. "Why won't anyone say Victor was a communist?"

Estelle looks up, stricken.

"You say he stood up against injustice? That he fought back? Yes, he did that. But he knew the whole *megile* is rotten. He knew in his heart we have to fight for a whole new way to live. Victor wanted something so simple: a society where people can sit down to plan what's needed. Where people can have what they want. This is a crime? To want a society like that? Then this is what made him a criminal!

"I carried him," Moishe's voice breaks up. "When he was a little boy, too little to walk, I carried him on my shoulders to marches and picket lines. I sang him this song, from the Spanish Civil War. And this," he wipes away his tears, "is the last time I can ever sing it to him again."

Emotion traps Moishe's voice. Thor moves close to him and rests his hand on Moishe's forearm. To my surprise, Moishe puts his hand on top of Thor's and presses it to keep it there. Everyone stands up again, in silence, and faces him.

Estelle moves next to me and squeezes my hand so tightly it hurts. "Oh, Max! How could I have forgotten to talk about what made Vic who he was? What he believed in? How could I forget that?"

"It's okay." I try to gently pry her grasp open. "That's what a memorial is. Everybody puts their piece in and makes something whole."

Estelle is still gripping my hand, shaking her head, angry with herself.

Moishe lifts his head and begins to sing, a capella, his voice off-key and cracking:

To you beloved comrade, we make this solemn vow.

I know this song! Raisa sang it to me when I was young.

The fight will go on—the fight will still go on.

I look up at Moishe and see Raisa standing next to him, comforting him. She is looking at Estelle, Ruby and Thor, Jasmine and Deacon. She is singing to them:

Sleep well, beloved comrade, our work will just begin.
The fight will go on—till we win—until we win.

Raisa is singing to her comrades. I have not been her comrade—not for many years now. I was once, when I was that person in the photo display, out in the streets in the '60s. Awake. Full of conviction and determination. When did I change? When did I fall back asleep?

The song ends. Raisa vanishes without a farewell.

Deacon strikes the first chord of "Solidarity Forever." People whose bodies are numb from hours of sitting on bare wood stand up and stretch and begin to talk to each other in low murmurs.

Ruby walks back toward me, exhausted.

"Ruby," I ask her, "what happened to me?"

"What?"

"It seems like such a long time ago that you and I were up all night on buses going to D.C. for marches, or sleeping on church floors the night before. I was tired, but it was different then. I didn't feel so worn out. I had so much energy, so much optimism."

Ruby shrugs. "The revolution didn't come fast enough for you."

"No," I shake my head. "The movement filled up with people who didn't want you and me in it."

Ruby brushes off my excuse. "You don't leave the movement because some people don't want you in it. If you're still waitin' for the Welcome Wagon ladies, you may as well give it up. The movement got up and moved along."

"I want to work on the march you called for in Sheridan Square. I want to help."

Her face lights up as though an old friend walked in the door. "Are you comin' back, Max? Are you comin' home?"

I shake my head slowly, "I don't know what home is. But I'm sick and tired of being sick and tired."

24

Ruby and Jasmine lean their heads back against the red plastic of the restaurant booth. Deacon is dozing, slumped in the corner. Thor's awake, I think, but he's folded his arms around the stack of leaflets on the tabletop, resting his head on the flyers as a pillow.

I press back against the padded plastic hide of the booth and yawn, louder than I mean to, without covering my mouth. I startle the waitress. I can see weariness weigh her body down as her shift draws to a close.

The overhead fluorescents are switched off. Through the picture window I can see the cars and buses whiz past us, people of all ages hurrying to school or to work.

I sip the last cold dregs of milky coffee. The waitress is next to me with an outstretched steaming pot. I lift my cup toward her offer. Everyone at our table awakens, roused by the aroma of roasted caffeine. All our cups are outstretched toward her like a plea for alms.

We have become an instant meeting—just add coffee.

Thor rubs his face with the heels of his hands. "Should we try to get a permit to march?"

Deacon reaches out, wordlessly, for the bowl of half-and-half containers.

Ruby passes it to him as she considers the question out loud. "Well, if we get a couple a dozen people, we can just rally. If we get a couple a hundred, maybe we could march someplace."

Deacon pours half-and-half into his coffee and stirs, creating galaxies in the little dark universe. "I don't expect they'll be givin' us a permit anytime soon."

Jasmine shakes her head, "They're not giving anybody a permit."

Ruby laughs bitterly. "Yeah, they got this catch-twenty-two kinda thang goin' on. You can't march without a permit and you can't get a permit to march."

I sip at my coffee, too drowsy to consider this problem any further. I have to pee and right now I wish I had a permit to use a public toilet without fear of arrest. If I use the women's stall I could get busted. If I use the men's, I may have to fight my way out of there.

I look around the restaurant. Two old white women who know each other well enough not to have to talk are sipping their tea in the booth behind ours. Both of them are gray-headed, but one's hair has yellowed and the other's is rinsed with blue, which looks kind of post-punk nowadays.

The booth in the corner is packed with transit workers, Black and white, still smudged with tunnel labor. A metal wrench half my height is leaning against their table. Their tool belts sag from coat hooks on the wall nearby. One of the white guys notices us and nudges the Black man next to him. They look at each other's faces wordlessly and shrug.

Something hits me in the back of the head. I paw my neck until I feel something unfamiliar in my hand. It's a balled up, soggy straw wrapper—a spitball. I turn around and glare at the three white girls in the booth behind us. They are giggling like young teenagers, but they're older than that. The disarray of their hair and clothing tells me they've been out all night.

Ruby casts an index finger in their direction like a fly rod. "You girls better straighten up."

"We will when you will," one of them baits, as they all guffaw.

The waitress arrives at their table in an instant, slapping their check down on the table in front of them. "We're not done yet," one of them says, her voice syrup sweet, behind me. "We'd like an order of French fries."

The waitress slouches off, filling their order with great physical reluctance. I like her. I wish I knew her name. I hate lifting my hand in the air to get her attention. But I wouldn't like it if someone at the bar asked my name. I'd be suspicious about why they were trying to get close.

"I could paste up some of these leaflets near the Community Center if someone would come with me," Thor offers.

Deacon silently raises one hand to volunteer, while lifting his coffee cup to his lips with his other hand.

"I could put up some around the piers and up and down Christopher Street," I offer. "If some one else wants to do it with me," I drag out the last word, "as a team."

Ruby smiles, her sweetest diplomacy, "Now there you go, sugar. I'll do it with you."

A little piece of hamburger bun lands on the table in front of us. I look at Jasmine; she has the girls behind us trapped in her stare.

Thor is lost in planning. "We need to make a list of all the places to drop off or tape up leaflets and then list all the places we've already done."

The cold liquid splashing on my neck is such a jolt that I shout out loud. Shock and rage pull me to my feet. The girls are laughing, uproariously. Cola is sliding down my neck and arm.

The waitress is in front of their table. She picks up the check on their table and slaps it back down again.

"We're not done yet," one of the girls says, between snorts and hoots of laughter.

"Oh, honey, you're done." The waitress slaps the tabletop. "You're out of here, now." I'm behind the waitress. Jasmine is already at my side, her hand resting on my shoulder, part support, part restraint.

I look up and catch the stare of the two transit workers. I'm afraid they're going to avenge the honor of these young women. For a moment, we all look at the wrench leaning against the table. The white worker glances at the Black worker. They both look at the wrench and then back at me. They shake their heads slowly.

I'm so mad and so tired and my neck is so sticky that I'm afraid I'll lash out in anger and do something that someone else will make me regret. Even a fuss in public that brings the cops will land me in jail before my coffee gets cold.

The two old women at the table shake their heads and cluck and tsk-tsk. I wonder who they're disgusted with. Blue Rinse leans forward. "Those girls are trouble," she confides to me. "I knew it the moment they walked in."

Jasmine, Ruby, and Thor form a wall in front of me as the girls walk past us, pelting us with jeers. "Faggots!" "Fudge packers!" "Perverts!"

When they leave, the restaurant is deathly still. For a moment I feel like all the epithets they hurled at me. But everyone goes back to their meals, and their discussions and debates, and my friends and I are left standing. We signal the waitress for our check, but she won't hear of it. "It's on the house," she calls out, loud enough for everyone to hear.

Thor tugs my sleeve. "Hey, buddy," he says to me. "Can I talk to you for a minute?"

"Sure," I say. "What's up?"

"Would you hook up with me tomorrow? Like late afternoon?"

"Sure. Where?"

"Meet me at Forty-second and Twelfth."

I try to picture where he's talking about. "Up where the *Intrepid* is docked? You want to meet me at an aircraft carrier?" For all I know he's going to tell me that the antiwar movement is planning to sink the damn thing.

"It's the Circle Line boats. It's gonna be a beautiful day tomorrow. Let's take a boat ride around the island."

I don't want to get on a boat. "I don't know, Thor. Can't we meet someplace else? What's up, anyway?"

Thor looks grim. "Do this for me, buddy, okay? Just meet me tomorrow, around three."

Thor has already bought the tickets for the boat ride, so it's too late for me to try to convince him to just walk alongside the river. We wait in a winding ticket holders line.

"Look," he indicates with a nod of his head, "there's family." A butch–femme lesbian couple is in line up ahead of us and there's a small group of women and men, all wearing rainbow buttons, chatting excitedly with each other.

The sun is beating down, hot on my neck, bright in my eyes. I'm a little cranky: I don't want to be in a long line of tourists. And boats are not my mode of transportation. The line begins to move. If I'm going to turn back, now's the time.

"What's the matter, Max?"

"Let's go someplace else," I propose.

"C'mon, buddy," he waves the tickets. "It'll give us a chance to talk."

Thor seems lost in thought until the boat, unmoored, begins to drift from the pier. We sit in our own little row of wooden chairs near a scratched Plexiglas window. He looks out over the Hudson.

Thor turns to me. "I have to quit my job at Club Pi," he says, as though we were midstream in a conversation. "I'm leaving the night shift. I just can't do it anymore."

How could Thor just up and leave me stranded at work, stranded as a friend? "Why?" I sound like I'm winding up for a tantrum.

His touch on my arm is so light that I shake it off with my shoulder as an irritant.

"Buddy," he says softly, "listen to me. I'm trying to tell you something important. Something you need to know about me."

I rein in my anger, just a bit.

"Max, I love working with you all. The nighttime has been my whole world for a long time, too."

My face feels flat and cold. But I don't interrupt him. He's being honest about something. So honest I'm not sure I'm up to spending two hours with this level of intimacy on wooden chairs in a slow boat full of tourists.

"Max, buddy, I've been gettin' high. A lot. I can't even remember when it started. But stopping it—that's the number-one priority in my life right now. I'm trying not to make a whole lot of changes right now. But I have to make this big one—I have to get off night shift."

The hard buds of my knuckles relax and my palm opens to touch his face; I open my arms—Thor is in them. He buries his face in my shoulder. I stroke his hair. "Good for you, Thor. I'm proud of you. Will dayside be easier?"

His shoulders rise and fall. "Yes. No." He pulls away from my shoulder a little and I see his eyes are swollen with emotion. His face flushes, making the pink scar on his cheek almost seem to disappear. "All I know is I can't work in a bar right now and it's easier to find meetings in the daytime. And that's what I've got to do now, Max. I've gotta make meetings."

He hasn't talked to me about what the cops did to him in jail. I want to ask him, but I don't want to violate his privacy, or invoke the nightmare all over again. So I ask gingerly, "Thor, I'm just wondering. Does this have anything to do with your political work?"

"Yes," he says enthusiastically. "It does. I finally found my place. It feels so good. I love the work I'm doing. That's the part of my life that feels right—that I want to hold on to."

I look out over the horizon. "No, I mean, does this have anything to do with getting arrested?"

Thor leans forward, elbows on his knees. "Well, it didn't help. But you know, I've been busted before. We all have. I'll get busted if I don't do political work and I'll get busted if I do. The difference is now that I'm an activist, I'm not alone. That's what coming outside the jail and seeing you all out there waiting for me really brought home. I don't want to be isolated any more. I don't want to isolate."

I pull him closer and kiss his hair. His face reddens again and we embrace, holding each other tightly. He's sweating and panting, like he fell overboard and was coming back up over the side, pulling himself up, hand over hand.

The tour guide's disembodied voice, coming from somewhere on the boat, directs us to headquarters of companies whose owners scrape their names into the sky. I can see the shipyards, the factories along the river banks, rotting away or revamped as luxury housing.

I see that the tourists nearest us have recoiled, their chairs pulled away from us, so that the area around Thor and me looks like a big crop circle. Several tourists are already on their feet, agog, pitching and rolling as the deck undulates. I address them all with a glare: Get over yourselves. We're gonna be doing this for a while. They are missing an amazing view of the lattices of the Brooklyn Bridge. But the tour guide can't hold a candle to our spectacle.

"C'mon," I urge Thor, "let's go out on the deck."

It's cooler out here. The bow is empty since the Statue of Liberty digital photograph frenzy has subsided and the group is wearying of the Garrison Keillor–like patter. The boat chugs its way north up the east side of the island, stalls out in the water in front of the United Nations building, then slowly turns. We won't be sailing up the east side of Manhattan to the Gold Coast. Instead, the motor growls as the boat turns around in busy East River traffic and heads back toward the financial district.

"Max," he pulls back his face to look at me. "You don't drink anymore, do you?"

"No, not for a long, long time."

"Can I ask you somethin', buddy? How do you do it now? At the bar, I mean. How do you handle that stuff all night and not have it soak into your whole life?"

I think before I speak, trying to be honest with myself. "When I first got sober, years ago, everything felt new and fresh, like a good rain that washes all the grime away. Ruby used to warn me that I couldn't stay up there on a pink cloud forever. She kept waiting for me to come down. I think I've come down. Since she got sick, I feel like I'm fraying."

The boat pitches and rolls. We're motoring against the incoming tide. "It's been getting hard lately," I continue. "It was a lot easier outside the bar as a bouncer than it is as a bartender. It makes me feel sick inside. I reek from alcohol. But what else am I gonna do for a living?"

Waves eddy around us; gulls hang low in the sky. I talk to myself out loud. "Where else will I find a job with a bathroom that I can use, you know?"

"Testosterone?" he asks, tentatively.

"Naw, not now," I answer. "Hormones won't take me home, the way they do for the guys. They leave me in exile."

I wish I was off this boat now but we are just rounding the southern tip of the island. I want to go sink into Ruby's overstuffed couch and tell her how much emptier my life will feel without Thor around.

"Well," he says, "at least there's one good thing'll come out of this. Ruby can take my job as bartender. You'll be back working together: the queen and the king." He bends in a little mock bow to me.

I smile in spite of myself: It will feel good to work with Ruby every night again. But it just won't be the same to go to work and know that Thor won't be there. Once people go over to dayside, it's like they step into another dimension. No matter how much we all promise to keep in touch, after a while we lose our connection.

I look out over the railing as New Jersey sails past us. Past the Colgate clock—"the largest in the country"—the Circle Line narrator tells us for the second time. It's 5:30 PM and no sign of dusk. The hot klieg lights of summer are ablaze. We watch in silence as we drift past the Jersey City financial towers that block the view of my tenement home. The tide is behind us, pushing us past Christopher Street, back to our midtown berth. Geese fly low over the water, their wedge reflected in its sparkling surface. They lift up in formation almost within arms' reach above our heads on quiet wings: a rustle of silk. The tour guide's voice wearily points to the headquarters of companies, again—he named them all earlier. I realize it's his route of travel that triggers his story. "Did I ever tell you about the Aboriginal song lines in Australia?" I ask Thor.

He just looks at me, waiting.

"As best I can understand, it's a giant song map of every rock, and water hole, and gum-tree. Each person goes on Walkabouts, singing their part of a song. As people walk, they sing what they see. If they're in a car, they sing faster. They can actually measure the distance from here and there with their piece of song. The song connects every one to each other, to the land."

The wind is picking up behind us. Thor leans closer to me on the rail. He nudges me with his body. "Why are you telling me this right now, buddy?"

"Because," I say, hearing desperation in my voice, "you're leaving. And without your song, I'm afraid I'll be lost."

25

A chat invitation appears on my computer monitor from Femmeangel. I've seen *hir* at the cybersoftball games. Last weekend I watched *hir* from the farthest edges of the AvaStar Saturday night lesbian party. Many cursors probed my identity; no one asked me to dance.

I had checked out Femmeangel's "Star Bio." The self-description read: "Old-fashioned femme: lipstick, dresses, tough as nails."

Filled with longing, a kind of homesickness, I had wished Femmeangel would ask me for a dance, but *ze* didn't seem to notice me. Later that night, I added some key words to my own online bio: "Suit-and-tie butch; bad-ass bulldagger, old-gay drag king."

None of those phrases would win me a dance with those whose bios instructed: "No druggies, no butches," but I wouldn't care to dance with them, either.

Now *hir* invitation to talk offers me two choices: Real time or Tree House chat? I click on Tree House.

I'm transported to an old-growth forest: tall, tall trees whose leafy tops are hidden in mist pierced here and there by the rays of the suns. I look deep into the woods. A golden star is flashing on a tree up ahead.

I click my cursor on the star, but nothing happens. I walk around the base of the tree, looking for a button to push.

Femmeangel leans over the edge of a tree house. "Hi!" I can actually hear the spoken word coming through my computer speakers. The voice sounds decidedly female.

I lean back and look up. "Hi!" I shout up.

Femmeangel is sitting in the tree house—a platform balanced on two sturdy boughs.

She points to her ear. "I can't hear you!" Her voice enters the silent space of my office. "Can you hear me?"

My avatar nods for me.

"Go to your control panel," she instructs. "Your outgoing sound is turned off."

I poke around the control panel with my cursor, as though it were an index finger, until I find: Audio. The moment I click on background volume control, the sounds of the forest come alive in my darkened room: I hear a bird trill, high up in the trees. A small creature skitters in the leaves nearby.

"Hey there!" I hear her voice. "Did you turn on your sound?" As she speaks, the sound meters on my control panel register like swarms of locusts. But the monitor for outgoing sound doesn't register, no matter how loud I raise my voice.

"My sound isn't working," I shout as I type. "How do I get up there?"

Femmeangel leans over the rail. "I've seen you watching me lately. Have you been following me?"

"I'm not a stalker, if that's what you mean."

"Do stalkers ever SAY they're stalkers?" She laughs, a little uneasily.

"You invited ME, right?"

She continues to lean over the railing, without saying a word. But I hear a mechanical growl: an elevator, planked with wood, descends to ground level.

I step onto the elevator and it rises, slowly. At first, I see the forest spread out before me, and the snowcapped mountains beyond. Now I am covered in mist, colors bending and refracting into rainbows in the vapor. Now a platform porch appears, with two wicker rocking chairs.

Femmeangel's avatar is rocking back and forth, one bare foot up under her on the seat. Before I can step off the elevator she holds up one hand to stop me. "It just makes me a little nervous that you say your outgoing sound isn't working. How do I know whether you're some guy trying to get his rocks off with a lesbian if I can't hear your voice?"

"You don't know, really," I type. "You'll only know by how we interact."

"Okay, I guess that's true." She pauses for a moment. "Then let me ask you a question: do you know what a femme is?" Her voice is still distrustful.

"Hmm," I answer. "Well, there's a whole lot of different types of femmes. And no two femmes I've ever known have been alike. But I gotta tell you, if I've learned anything in life from femmes, it's to let them define themselves."

Femmeangel smiles. "That was good—I think. I can't tell if you're ducking the question, though. If so, you're smooth and that's scary."

"Then ask me something else. Ask me something hard."

"Okay. Tell me what you think is the toughest thing that a femme has to deal with?"

"That's easy," I type. "Other people's assumptions."

Femmeangel sits up, putting her feet on the wooden floor. "Come in, pull up a chair!" She ushers me in with one hand.

But I don't move. "Now I want to ask you a question."

The pixels of her smile waver. "Okay," she says.

I wonder if her wariness is fear of rejection. That's how I felt when I had to pass her test. The problem with typing my responses is that they lack all affect. I can't warm up my words with tone.

"If you were redesigning AvaStar, what would you change?"

She rocks slowly, "Well, hun, that's not hard at all. I'd start with the dressing rooms."

"More specific?"

She stops rocking and sits up straight. "The first time I went into that women's dressing room and saw my choices, it just broke my heart. I thought to myself, if I have to go out into this game as Barbie, instead of a strong, complex femme, who am I going to attract, except Ken or another Barbie?"

She looks out at the forest. I think for a moment the program has frozen, but I can still hear birds tweet and twitter. Femmeangel turns toward me. "And I wondered how the ones I wanted to meet were going to get through that dressing room. And once they did, how would I recognize them?"

I wait a moment, to see if she has more to say. She looks at me.

"May I come in?" I ask.

She raises her arm toward the empty rocker next to her. "Please do."

We sit in silence, the floorboards squeaking as we rock. "It's beautiful up here. It's peaceful." I'm typing small talk, but it's true. "What's on that tree there?" I type with one hand, while I use my mouse to point my avatar arm toward a nearby tree.

"You've got good eyes!" Femmeangel picks up a pair of binoculars from the porch railing.

"Where'd you get those?" I ask.

"Drag it off your tool bar," she replies.

As I search through the tools, I make a mental note to come back later and check out the coiled rope icon marked "rappel."

I scan a strange variation just inside a hollow in the trunk, clicking upward in magnification until I can see it more clearly. "What is it?" I type. "I still can't tell."

"It's a bat," she tells me. "There's lots of them up here." She points toward the mountain range. "You see that stand of trees? That one on the right? There's a big, big nest up near the top that's home to a pair of golden eagles."

I click up the magnification as far as it goes until I can see every twig and leaf in the nest—but there's no one home.

"What would you change about this game?" Femmeangel asks me.

"Mmm, I'd make the dressing room multisex! And there'd be so many choices. Multiple ethnicities. Different bodies with different abilities. Smooth bodies, hilly bodies. You could be an animal or a shape or a symbol. And you could find boas and old ties, all sorts of quirky clothing hanging up in the closets to mix or match, or you could sit down at the design board and sew your own."

"Footwear!" Femmeangel says. "Very important."

"If," I type, "you have feet."

"And please," she implores, "create some better ways to flirt. All I can do is place my hand on someone's arm. Make it so I can drop my glance or cut my eyes, or something. This cyber face only smiles one way. I've got a thousand different smiles."

I wish I could see each one. I type: "Right now they only give you a dozen words to describe yourself. What if you could really describe yourself—audiotape or video or written or imagery. Add up all that and send people out to talk and play and then you got yourself a game!"

"I'd play!" she says. "I'm very good at that game in real life." She looks at the scenery. "There aren't many ambiguities here. You have to play the game to find them. Your name didn't go with your avatar. I was interested in your paradox."

"My 'dox' is more than 'para.'"

Femmeangel sits catercorner on her rocker and studies me. "I couldn't really tell what you were."

"I'm not a what, I'm a who."

"I'm sorry." Her apology is soft. "I'm not a 'what' either." Her tone perks up. "And then I saw that you'd added these descriptions to your bio. And that's who I was hoping you were. That's who I was looking for."

"I'm flattered."

"I noticed none of these descriptions say 'lesbian.' I don't want to assume. Are you a lesbian?"

"Yes, I am. A butch and a lesbian. There's a lot of words I didn't use to explain who I am. I just picked a couple that place me in the period I came out into and that maybe still have some meaning now." I lean back and touch the bark between the wicker latticework of the back porch wall. "Like a slice of this old tree, they're the rings of my life."

I pause, thinking about her bio. "You didn't say you were a lesbian, either."

She laughs. "Well, I am."

"I get sick of people thinking I have to be one thing or the other, instead of all of the above," I type, without any explanation.

"Me too," she sighs. "Me too."

She changes the subject abruptly: "Earliest television memory?"

"*Milton Berle*. You?"

"*Our Miss Brooks*."

"Ah," I sigh as I type. "Elders in their rockers." I add a smiley face.

Femmeangel places her hand on my arm. "I do feel like I've known you for a long time." The leaves rustle as the wind passes through them. "We're birds of a feather," she says.

I hesitate before I type. I don't know what to say. Ruby and I are birds of a feather, too. And so are Thor and I. But I know what Femmeangel means and I don't want to distance myself from her. So I type, "We've shared a lot of history. We've been through a lot together."

Femmeangel stops rocking. "I wish I could talk to you more," she sighs. "But it's really late."

"This is early for me. I work third shift. This is my night off."

"It's too bad. I've been traipsing across this planet all evening looking for someone interesting to talk to. And now you're here. But I've got to get some sleep. I have something important to do in the morning."

"Yes," I agree, "it is too bad."

"Do you want to make a date for tomorrow night, here in this tree house? We could talk some more."

"Sure!" I wonder if the exclamation point was too enthusiastic.

"Would you bring me some pictures?"

"Of what? Of me? I don't have any."

"You don't have any pictures of yourself?"

"Not really."

"Well, then bring me pictures that mean something to you. If you load them before you come up we can look out of the tree house at your world." She smiles: "If you show me yours, I'll show you mine."

I'm sitting alone in my office smiling, too.

"Ok," I type. "I'll try to get my sound repaired by tomorrow night."

"If you can," she says. "Same place. What time?"

"What coast are you on?"

"Left."

"Is two AM your time too late?"

"Wow, hun, you are a night owl. Ok, I'll take a nap first."

"Wait," I type frantically. "How will I find the right tree?"

"Well, you found it this time, right?" her voice is teasing. "Good night, Pollygender. Don't miss the forest for the tree!"

A now-familiar message appears on my screen. "Femmeangel has left this planet."

I'm afraid I won't be able to find Jasmine at the corner of Canal Street and Broadway. The sidewalks are thronged with people, like the summers of my childhood when the neighborhoods teemed with life lived outside. I go with the flow, past people weighing decisions about fish or crabs displayed on beaches of crushed ice, appraising vegetables, clustered in groups to smoke and argue and laugh.

But something's strange about the automobile traffic on Canal Street. There're so few cars. And as far as I see down the thoroughfare, the moons of the traffic lights are all eclipsed.

The sun is high, its white shadow burning my skin. The heat is sweltering, making my T-shirt stick to my body. I wish I smelled sweet for the moment I kiss Jasmine on the cheek, but I'm afraid I stink of sweat. I'm hungry, but I'm in too much of a rush to stop for food or to buy deodorant and a fresh T-shirt. Maybe if I hurry, Jasmine will have time to eat lunch with me.

I see her on the corner up ahead, looking around impatiently. She spots me, waving her hand like a flag.

"That's what I needed. Thank you!" She takes the two boxed reams of leaflets that I picked up from the copy shop from my hands.

She opens one box and pulls out a leaflet. I peer over her shoulder. The leaflet is in Chinese, I assume. But as I look more closely, the characters are in blocks that don't look similar.

I can recognize the Korean and the accents of the Vietnamese. There's Tagalog on the bottom. I don't know what the other languages are.

She scans the leaflet. "Looks great," she says, bending down to stuff the boxes in her backpack.

I look up, above the crowds, and everywhere around me on the faces of buildings are signs that I can't read. I point to one of the characters: a box with a vertical line through it. "Can I ask you, what does that mean?"

She follows the direction of my finger. "It means: middle."

The moment I hear its meaning, the ideograph takes on life for me. "What about that trident?" I point.

"Mountain."

"And that one that looks like a person walking?"

"Yes, that's a person."

"And that?" I point to a triangle of little squares above an eatery. "Taste."

This is thrilling! I could stand here all day asking her about each character I see. But from a glance I can tell that Jasmine doesn't want to stand on this corner much longer teaching me to read Chinese.

"I have to go by Happy Cheng's and drop these off to some of the girls there," she says. She looks around. "I'm thirsty."

"Me, too."

Nearby, a small circle of people gathers around two men playing a board game with wooden disks. "What game are they playing?" I ask Jasmine.

"Like chess."

"What's the Chinese name of it?" I want to google it and see if it's played online.

Jasmine checks her watch, puts her hand on my shoulder, and maneuvers me a little faster through the crowd. "Come on," Jasmine turns the corner. "Go this way." I can tell her schedule is pulling her like a riptide.

As we turn down the narrow side street, the signs above me call out for me to read them. I see a now-familiar character, the little pyramid of squares, but this one is above a store with bolts of fine silk in the window.

"Taste," I point to the sign. "Is that like 'good taste'?"

"What?" I've pulled Jasmine out of her thoughts into mine. She looks at the sign and then at the store and then at me. "Yes," a small smile grows. "Yes."

A group of people near us are huddled around a radio turned up loud. "What's up?" I ask.

"The power is out," Jasmine says. "All over the island."

"No work tonight!" I say, with relief. Although come to think of it, Rick probably won't pay us.

She points to a restaurant just down the block and we continue to walk in silence. As we pass each shop, I see small statuettes in the windows. A dragon holding a ball in its talons. A mustached figure, red and ferocious.

Jasmine directs me toward the restaurant. It's crowded and noisy. I can't understand the language I hear surrounding me, but now that I'm immersed in it, I can hear the patterns of inflection, the accents: flat, up, down, dipped from down to up. I searched on the Internet last night for how to say a couple of things in Mandarin. But maybe Jasmine speaks Cantonese, instead.

Jasmine speaks to the waiter, ordering us cold drinks I hope, and then continues a conversation with him about something. She doesn't seem in so much of a hurry now. The no-business-as-usual reality of the power outage seems to be short-circuiting her schedule.

The waiter hands us each a plastic cup of milky tea, a little ice floating on the top, purple tapioca pearls on the bottom. With one sip, the taste of jasmine and sweet milk relaxes me. The day feels like an adventure.

"*Xiè xiè*," I timidly thank the waiter as we pay. I'm not sure I said it right, but he beams at me, so maybe I did.

Jasmine doesn't hear us. She is worrying. "This is very hard for Chinatown. We did not get electricity restored here for too long after 9/11.

Then the SARS scare." She points to a sign across the street with the trident symbol of the mountain on it. "My people came here to find the Golden Mountain." Her words are acrid.

My tone is bitter, too. "Yeah, so did mine. They thought it was the *goldene medina*. The golden country."

"My family ended up laundering clothes."

"Mine stitched them."

Jasmine changes subject abruptly. "I have to go to Cheng's."

I want to go with her.

"Which way are you walking," she asks.

"I don't know. I'll walk you a ways."

As we amble back to the corner of Canal Street I can see that the street is almost empty of cars and taxis. But the sidewalks are more crowded than ever. People are gathered around battery-operated radios, mopping their brows, talking excitedly.

"Someday," I ask gingerly as we make our way through the throng, "will you tell me your real name?"

Jasmine looks at me over her shoulder, her smile guarded. "I've had many names," she says, closing the subject. Jasmine points us toward another side street.

She stops at a table, outside a shop, filled with figurines and fans, bracelets and old coins, and little statues of five-toed dragons.

As she picks each one up to study, I remember the first character she translated on the sign—"middle."

"I've seen that character before!" I tell her excitedly.

"What character?" She looks around and then back at me.

I draw a box with a vertical line through it, leaving a hiss, a whiff of smoke, in the air. "It's Chung, the Red Dragon!"

The smile that spreads across her lips is relaxed and playful. "Yes," she says. "How do you know that?"

"Mah-jongg. I grew up with the game, with the tiles."

"Remember *Fa*?" As she invokes the name of the Green Dragon, she draws the ideograph in the space between us—a flash of fire. "The arrow about to be fired."

This moment feels like that particular ivory tile to me: a start, a beginning.

"The one that frightened me the most as a child," I remember out loud, "was the White Dragon."

"*Pai*," she voices the name. "Why were you afraid?"

"Because it was the powerful thing I could not see."

Jasmine nods, still looking at the little dragons displayed on the table. "I am trying to decide which of these *Lung* to get for Thor. I am trying to figure out," she explains, "what kind of *Lung* is right for him."

I feel a little deflated that she is thinking of Thor at this moment. I pick up a gilded picture of a dragon descending from the sky.

"Not that one," she says. "That's female."

I discreetly examine the dragon's body. How on earth does she know that? "You know that Thor was the god of thunder?"

She purses her lips and nods in a way that doesn't tell me whether she knew that or not. Jasmine picks up a figurine of a black lacquered dragon holding a little polished sphere in its talons and hands her money to the man standing quietly beside us. He wraps it in brown paper and gives it back to her with her change. Jasmine slips the little gift into her backpack. I want to ask her about the *Lung* she picked for Thor, but right now I don't want to hear her talk about the qualities that make him a dragon.

"I think of you like a dragon," I say to Jasmine.

She smiles. "My people are descendents of dragons. There are many types of dragons, with different personalities."

"What kind of a dragon are you?"

She doesn't answer. Instead she asks, out of the blue, "You are not afraid of me, are you, Max?"

Only her judgments, I think, but do not say out loud. "Why would I be afraid of you?"

"I have a lot of anger."

"So do I. So do most of the people I know. Whether or not I like a person depends on what makes them angry."

Jasmine laughs. "Do you like me?"

"I'm starting to." I grin. That's not true. I like her a lot. "I taught myself something on the Internet last night, to say for you. You want to hear it?"

She clasps her hands in front of her. "I'm ready. Yes."

"*Hin baow-chyenn, ligh-wan-la.*"

She wrinkles her brow, "What did you say?"

"*Hin baow-chyenn, ligh-wan-la.* I'm sorry I'm late."

Jasmine looks at my face, my hair, and then my eyes. "You surprise me sometimes, Max."

I laugh out loud. "Sometimes I surprise myself."

She looks at her watch and makes an apologetic face. "I want to see if the girls at Happy Cheng's are still at work."

"Go," I say.

"How will you get home to New Jersey?"

I look toward the west. "A boat, probably."

"The ATMs won't work—no electricity. Do you need money to get home?"

"I don't have bank accounts," I say. "But I have enough cash to get home, thank you."

"It is very hard to function without a bank account," she muses. "Well, if you can't get home, you can call me—if the cell phones are working."

I thank her. But I will not call her.

She kisses me lightly on the cheek and she is off. I feel diminished by her departure. I walk up Broadway, looking around. Helicopters hang in the air, apparently motionless, like dragonflies in the late afternoon sky. Heat shimmers up from the asphalt street. The temperature must be hovering in the high 90s, maybe even triple digits.

The diagonal avenue has taken me out of Chinatown now. Without electricity, merchants are closing. Some are nailing wood up over windows or securing their metal gates, remembering with dread the blackout of 1977. That night in the darkness people went into the stores and took the things they needed but couldn't afford.

Now the city is already shuttered. Commerce is almost shut down. But the streets are swarming with people. Many are still gathered around radios, listening intently as newscasters reassure that there has been no attack on the city. I stop and look at the images on a battery-operated portable television: tens of thousands milling around in Grand Central and Port Authority. A sea of humanity flowing over the bridges, on foot, to outer boroughs.

It will be twilight soon. I'll walk around a little while longer, until the crowds waiting for the ferries to Jersey have thinned out.

I stop at a deli in Greenwich Village that's open and ask through the little window if they've got any bottled water left. "We're out of five-dollar water," the person behind the counter smiles slyly. "We've only got ten-dollar water left."

I make my way west across the island, until the sun is red and low in the sky ahead of me. Neighbors and friends are forming little circles on the sidewalks and steps in front of their buildings: talking, laughing, playing music, drinking wine, smoking weed. Others are making little nestlike beds on their fire escapes.

As the sun sets below the horizon, darkness spreads quickly over us all. Virtually no cars on the streets. No lamplight. I stop and look up at the night sky, strewn with stars. I forget in the neon universe of Manhattan that I am turning in the darkness of space.

It is hard to walk, though, and difficult to navigate. I step off a curb, unexpectedly, and twist my ankle. As I walk carefully in the night toward the ferry, I can only tell if someone is coming by the soft scuff of footsteps or the firefly glow of a cigarette between their lips.

On Christopher Street I pass a gay bar, almost unrecognizable without its sign lit. Inside, dozens of candles flicker. I ask to use the toilet. The bartender waves me toward the back without a word.

I stumble around in the darkened back room, until I find two bathroom doors, both marked "Gents." Inside, rose petals and two candles in aluminum shells float inside a water-filled ceramic bowl on top of the toilet tank.

When I leave, I take one of the candles with me to help guide me through the back room. My little flame casts the shadows of writhing bodies onto the walls.

I remember reading once that when streetlights were first introduced in Europe, people protested and smashed them. They were afraid the artificial light would help the police control them in the night.

Tonight, as darkness blankets the city, it is the police who are fearful.

I'm lucky to have caught the last ferry to intersect the strong currents of the Hudson River. It's almost midnight now—it has been a long walk home from the pier.

The electricity appears to be on in my neighborhood in Jersey City. The traffic lights are glowing, and so are a few homes. That means I'll be home in time to log on to my computer and keep the date to talk to Femmeangel about my day.

As I pass under the low-hanging tree branches near my building I look up and stop in my tracks. The overhead lights are on in my living room. Shadows move across the window.

Someone is in my apartment.

I run to the sidewalk across from the front of the building and look up at my bedroom window. It's broken—a jagged jack-o'-lantern mouth. I cross the street and stand under Alma's window to see if she's up, but her lights are off.

Mohammad's store lights are on, unusual at this time of night. I cross the street and try his door. I'm not surprised that it's locked. Maybe the electricity came on after he closed up.

I walk back slowly across the street and pace back and forth in front of my building. Slivers of glass that had rained down are crunching under my sneakers.

I'm not going to call the police; that would just bring trouble down on me. And for all I know, that is the police up there.

On impulse, I call out, really loud, "Who's up there? Hey! Who's in my apartment?"

I'm shocked that a person leans halfway out my window to answer. Mohammad calls down, "Max? You better come up here, my friend."

I sprint up the stairs, two at a time. But when I get to my landing, I slow down, reluctant to go inside. My door has been bludgeoned open. Splinters of the wooden door and the door frame are underfoot.

Mohammad greets me in my doorway. "Max," he puts one hand over his heart. I gently push past him. I stand, stock-still, in the living room. The huge symbol crudely painted over my Yiddish is not the ancient swastika rendered in marigolds but the modern profane threat of blood-shed dripping down the wall.

My body bag, still hanging from the ceiling, has been slit open with a knife. I bend down and touch the mound of granules that has spilled from it. The gritty feel of reality. Cardboard boxes are neatly stacked on the floor, marked on the outside in Arabic. The Palestinian flag is neatly folded, placed on top of the boxes. I pick it up; the familiar colors almost warm in my palm, and tuck it into the pocket of my chinos.

"I did not know if you would be home tonight," he explains. "The window is broken, and the door. I was afraid to leave your books and clothes in here. I was going to take them down to my store. I hope you don't mind."

"Thank you," I say, in a daze. I have been here before—come home other times in my life to find my apartment broken into, gutted, trashed. Those other times I just turned around and walked away with only the clothes on my back.

I stand up slowly and stare around at the room that used to be a refuge.

"My friend, I had nothing to do with this." I'm surprised that Mohammad says this to me. It never occurred to me. He would never do anything like this.

"I know that," I say. I see how worried he looks, but I can't do much to reassure him. I need reassurance myself. "How did you know?" I ask.

"When I closed up the store, I saw your lights on. I saw your window was broken. So I waited till someone went into the building and I came up here. I stayed here. Anyone could take your things if someone wasn't watching your home." He pauses. "I'm so sorry, my friend. Who would do this?"

As our eyes meet, we both know the question is rhetorical. Maybe the same person or persons who painted the racist slur on the metal gate of his store.

I remember the car following me. And finding one of my posters stuck to my front door. It could be the cops. A warning to stay out of the disappearances? But there are people much more involved than I am who aren't getting threats like this, at least not as far as I know.

Could it be connected to our organizing for the upcoming Sheridan Square protest? But there are antiwar activists leading huge demonstrations. And I'm not that central an organizer for our protest.

"Maybe the guy across the street, and his son," I say out loud, their hateful faces vividly conjured up by the thought.

Mohammad sighs heavily, his face settling into anger. "This man is very bad."

I suddenly feel so tired.

"You can stay in my home tonight," Mohammad offers generously.

"Thank you," I shake my head. "But I'll call a friend and try to get set up somewhere tonight that I can stay until I find another place."

Ruby doesn't need to deal with me on her couch and my boxes in her living room. Neither does Thor right now. And I don't feel comfortable asking Jasmine or Deacon. I pick up the phone and dial up Heshie. He's wide awake. As I tell him what's happened, he responds with one word—inflected not as a question, but with resignation. "Again."

He adds. "You can sleep on my cot here at the factory if you want. Until you find a place. I'll be there soon. I'll bring the truck."

"Thank you, Heshie." There's gratitude in my voice, but he's already hung up.

"My friend is coming to pick me up," I tell Mohammad. And then I amend that: "Another friend."

I wander into my bedroom. The word "faggot" is scrawled in paint on the wall. A few pieces of clothing have been thrown around the room.

I turn around and go to my office. The world maps are torn, half hanging from the plaster walls, the brightly colored pins scattered on the floor—resistance no longer marked, but unerasable. My monitor is smashed. My computer—my spaceship to the universe. I feel a pang of pain as I envision Femmeangel, rocking in her chair, alone, thinking she's been stood up.

Mohammad has been giving me privacy, but now he follows me to the kitchen. "Come, my friend. You must be hungry, yes? We can wait for your friend in my store. I will fix you something to eat. Something to take with you."

"Thank you," I say in a dreamlike state. "Thank you."

We find Alma in the living room, staring at the mess. "The landlord is coming," she says. "Someone called him." She looks around. "You better get your stuff and go. He's gonna be mad."

My voice begins to rise. "He's going to be mad?"

She looks around. "You painted on the walls. You ruined the place. He's not gonna give you back your security deposit."

"Alma," my voice is quiet now. "You think the Yiddish ruined the wall or the swastika over it?"

"The owner," she doesn't finish her thought. "Are there more boxes? I'll help you take them down. We should hurry. I don't want him to call the cops on you."

"You want more? I have more food!" Mohammad opens his arms wide to take in his whole store. An empty plate sits in front of me on the counter; a few olive pits, a smear of hummus, and the mint-green oil from the grape leaves are all that's left. I use the last piece of warm pita bread to absorb the fragrant remains on the plate and pop it into my mouth. I can smell the coffee Mohammad is brewing.

We are sitting on my boxes of books, our feet flat on the floor. Mohammad offers me a cigarette. "Thank you, no." I wave it away. So much damage has been done to me tonight that at this moment I don't want to do any destruction to myself. Instead I want to savor the sharp bite of garlic on my tongue.

"Thank you, Mohammad." I'm frustrated that I can't put as much appreciation as I am feeling into my words, my voice. "You are a *mentsh*. You are a wonderful human being."

He turns his face from deserved praise. "Please," he holds up both hands. "It is nothing."

I've left Thor's phone number, scribbled on a brown bag, on the counter. "You'll call me if there're any protests for Hatem? I could hand out leaflets or post them up. Whatever is needed."

"Of course!" he assures me. "I will call you right away when I hear anything."

I look at the photos on the wall behind the counter. He smiles at the memories they hold for him. "Have you ever been to Egypt?" he asks.

"No. Someday, I wish."

"Oh, you must go!" He stands up. "You must, my friend. Oh, you must go to Alexandria. Very beautiful. The beaches?" He kisses his fingertips to answer the question. "Cairo is a wonderful city. My mother and sisters and brothers are there. You will tell me if you are going. And then I will call them and they will take you everywhere. They will show you everything. They will treat you like family."

Heshie pulls up across the street with his truck. "Excuse me," I interrupt at this inopportune moment. I go to the door and call out for Heshie.

I turn around and look at my boxes. Mohammad thrusts a piece of paper in my hand. "This is my phone number. You will call me when you go to Cairo, yes?" He points to the paper. "You will not forget."

"No," I say, sadness clutching my throat. "I will not forget you. Thank you for everything. Everything."

He reaches out and takes my hand in both his hands. "You are a very good person," he says, his eyes brimming with tears. "This should not have happened to you."

I groan my agreement. "This should not be happening to any of us."

"Yes," he says. "That is true."

The bell above the door jingles as Heshie walks in. Mohammad greets him like an old friend. "Come in," he says. "Would you like some coffee? Are you hungry?"

Heshie waves away the offers with his hand and a quick, "No, I'm fine.

Thanks." I can see how guarded Heshie is. I wonder if that's the way I look from the outside.

Heshie points to the few boxes on the store floor. "Is that your stuff? Is that everything?"

I don't answer. I just look at the boxes.

Heshie goes out and brings the truck around. Mohammad and I carry out the boxes and put them in the back. Once they're in, Mohammad fiddles with them, adjusting each one so that they fit tightly in the back. "You don't want anything to break," he says over his shoulder.

I wish I had something to give Mohammad. Something as precious as all he has done for me. My hand reaches into my pocket. I feel the flag, a gift I've long treasured from a Lebanese friend. For a moment my heart aches—I don't want to let it go. But an instant later, I am ready. This little flag is continuing on its journey, and I am just a part of its travels.

I reach out my hand to Mohammad. "I have something for you." I turn my palm over and open my hand, the colors visible under the streetlamp light.

He draws back, "No, my friend. I can't take that. It is too much. You must keep it. It is important for you to have it."

"No," I shake my head. "Please do me this favor. This is part of my heart, of what my life is about. Please take it."

His hand extends reluctantly. "Are you sure?"

"Please."

He takes the flag in his hand and wraps one arm briefly around my neck. "Thank you, Max," he says, emotion growling in his voice.

We stand facing each other, awkwardly. "Wait!" Mohammad says. He hurries inside the shop and comes back out with a large brown bag. "I made you a sandwich, and there's some other food for later, when you are hungry."

He reaches into his pocket. "I have something else for you."

"No," I hold up my hand. "You have already given me so much."

He shakes his head. "Hatem gave me this." He places a key ring in my palm. It's an embossed red triangle uniting black, white, and green bars of lacquered color on a piece of copper hammered into the shape of Palestine. "I believe this is for you. You see, my friend, everything you give will come back to you."

Heshie leans forward in the driver's seat to see what's going on. I extend the key ring in my open palm for him to see. Heshie gives it a long look and nods imperceptibly.

I close my hand around the little piece of Palestine. "Thank you. This is very precious to me." I shake Mohammad's hand again; this time our bodies move closer in a little hug. As I get inside the truck and roll down the window, Mohammad leans forward and says to Heshie, "You are always welcome at my store. Anytime. Your friend here, she . . . he is like my own family."

Mohammad looks chagrined at having stumbled on my pronoun. I am taken aback. What am I surprised about? That he knows I'm queer? Who doesn't? Of course Hatem knew, too.

Mohammad places his hand on my elbow, which is angled out the window. "We are cousins." These are the last words he says as Heshie slowly pulls away.

I look back and see him wave. I settle into the front seat of Heshie's truck. I don't know where I'm headed. But I feel a strange sense of calm and of longing. I wish I could tell Raisa, "I will never be a stranger in Egypt."

26

"Shut the fuck up, Weasel." I throw my towel on the bar. "Not another word, do you hear me? I'm dead serious."

"It's just a joke. You haven't even heard the punch line."

I point my index finger. "Not one more word."

Weasel appears to be unbothered but leans back away from me, hands held up in surrender. "S'all good, dawg."

I can feel the arteries throbbing in my neck. Ruby saunters over. "Weasel, you are one sorry, stale slice of white bread."

"Wolf! My name is Wolf." Weasel turns away from Ruby toward me. "I don't know why you have it in for me, bro. What'd I ever do to you? We're all in this together. We're all up against The Man."

I lean forward. "You're a trust fund baby from Connecticut. Your family owns half this island. You *are* The Man. Now I'm telling you one time and one time only: I'm not your brother, I don't want to hear your racist 'jokes,' and I'm done serving you at this bar. Last call is over, Weasel. Get the hell out of my sight."

Weasel sulks away from the bar. "You got no right, Rabinowitz!"

I wish I had a cigarette right now. I wish I could smoke in here.

Ruby polishes a glass and holds it up to the light to inspect. "Uh-huh," she says, as though that explains everything she's thinking.

I'm still seething.

"Things goin' okay for you, stayin' at Heshie's?"

"Yeah, sure. It's a little weird, but it's okay for now."

Ruby puts the glass down. "I hope you don't mind me sayin' this, sugar, but you are strung tight as a bow right now. You are stressed."

I turn around, anger ready to fire in any direction, but she holds me off with one hand.

"I'm not sayin' you did anything different from what you should of done. And I hate it when Weasel goes all Wonder Bread on me, too. But you're goin' off all Bruce Lee lately. I'm just sayin'."

"What?"

She shrugs her shoulders. "Maybe you need a little stress reduction."

My own laughter surprises me. "Stress reduction?" I look at the row of liquor bottles.

"Lord no." Ruby makes a face at me and the bottles. "I'm talking about somethin' soothing."

"Like what?"

"Thor told me he offered you a back rub."

"Yeah, body work. That's how he's going back to making a living. It was a nice offer."

"So?" Her hands are on her hips now. "Why didn't you take him up on it? People pay him to do that to them."

"Yeah, I know," I demur. "I'm just not ready to get naked with anybody. You know what I mean?"

I'm certain that Ruby does. But instead of answering my question, she says, "I got an idea. I gotta call my friend Leroy. He'll get us in to where he works the night shift as janitor. And besides, I wouldn't mind hookin' up with him again. He's one sweet, sweet man."

Weasel is back, sneaking halfway down the stairs, shouting at me, "Fuck you, Rabinowitz. You'll be sorry, you Jew bastard!" As soon as the words are out of his mouth, Weasel bolts back up the steps. I'm ready to jump over the bar, my fists clenched like sledgehammers.

But Ruby is already around the bar and racing after Weasel. "I'm gonna smash that little rat!" she shouts.

Leroy is tall and skinny, all elbows and knees, shaved head, stubbly cheeks. But the moment he smiles, well, no wonder Ruby cares for him. It's like a moonbeam. And he seems to be directing all that sweetness, wordlessly, at Ruby.

I can see they want to be left alone. The three of us stand awkwardly together near the indoor swimming pool until I speak.

"Can I have less light?"

Leroy nods and dims the artificial suns overhead from noon to dusk.

Ruby speaks for Leroy. "It's all yours," she says with a sweep of her arm. "You can have the whole health club to yourself. You have privacy here, if you get my drift. Leroy turned up the heat in the sauna. When you're ready, just come upstairs. Just give us a little time." Leroy drops his gaze to the tile floor and smiles, that amazing smile. Off they go out the door, night-watch keys jingling.

Wisps of mist rise from the pool, which is radiating with light like a phosphorescent turquoise pond. The only sound in the dim room is water lapping—trapped liquid slapping the poolside, bobbing like Jell-O. The little waves cast ever-shifting patterns of light and shadow around the room.

I take off my shoes and socks. I'm not ready to take my clothes off. I sit down and dangle my toes in the water. I'm never, ever, in a room like this—space for bodies to just be bodies. The doors of dressing rooms—the stripping rooms—are marked with symbols that bar my entry.

Even though I know I'm alone, I look around first before I take off my jeans. It's chilly in the room. No wonder the water is steaming, it's warmer than the air.

I step gingerly into the pool, still dressed in boxers and a T-shirt, and slip down into the water.

With a deep breath I duck under the surface, no sound except for the bubbles of my own breath. My body and this water are one as I swim underneath the surface, feeling my muscles tense with effort and relax in the currents of warm liquid.

I come up for breath, wiping the streaming water out of my eyes, already irritated by the chlorine, coughing a little, almost laughing with a sudden wave of joy. I paddle to the deepest water, lean my head back on the hard edge of the pool and see my body, as though it is not connected to me in any way, float effortlessly.

I float. I float.

I drag myself up and out of the deep end of the pool, suddenly weighted down by wet underwear. Rivers of water run from my body, puddling near me. The air feels even chillier than it did before. I stand up carefully on the slippery tiles, leaving a trail of water across the floor as I check out the sauna.

It's a little wooden hut in the corner. Inside, the mound of glowing embers is fake, but the heat is real and intense—a new element. The walls are smooth redwood, bone dry. It feels primordial and protected, like the cave of my bedroom.

I peel off my T-shirt and my sopping wet shorts, twist and squeeze them over the pile of faux charcoal. The searing hot metal pops and sizzles and a cloud of burning steam envelops me.

I climb up to the highest level, near the ceiling. Here I sit, elbows on knees, water dripping from my chin, sliding down my belly and back in rivulets, puddling beneath the fur between my legs.

I feel calm and strangely hopeful. Clean, relaxed, safe. I can't remember the last time I felt this good. I wish I could hold on to this feeling.

I'm sorry I agreed to go to Thor's apartment for a massage today. That's the last thing in the world I want. I've been crying on and off for hours and I don't even know why. Memories are bubbling up in me like a pot of hot water about to boil over.

A fragment of song my mother used to sing to me woke me up midday. Just one line of a song she sang to me as a child as I lay in the dark, wondering if she was going to die soon. How long? *Vi lang?*

"Vi lang vet ir glentsnde raykhtimer shafn far dem? *How long will you produce riches for those who rob you of your bread?*"

I can't remember the rest of the song. I can hardly hear the resonance of her voice any longer. All but a few bits of wisdom she pressed into me are slipping away. Even her face is blurring in my memory. When I try to picture her, I see the photo of her and Raisa, kept on our mantel, when they were both very young.

I wish she was here right now. I suddenly feel like I don't know how to live my life. I want somebody to tell me what to do.

So here I am on a street corner on Seventh Avenue, hiding my red-rimmed eyes behind sunglasses, looking for the building where my mother took me to work with her on the days my school was closed. I think she worked in that building right across the street, but I can't be sure, and there's no one left to ask.

Two little shards of recollection glitter in my memory.

Sleeping against her rough wool coat as we rumbled on the subway before dawn to get to her job on time.

And her scream when the sewing machine needle pierced her index finger. The other women rushed to her side, some comforting her in languages I couldn't understand. The foreman came with a bottle of alcohol to pour on the wound and barked at the women to get back to work, as though they were children. The song the Jewish women sang as they worked, to soothe my mother's pain, that *I can remember:* "Nodln vern tsebrokhn—*needles get broken, fifteen a minute. Fingers get stuck and blood runs from them.*"

Later, still humiliated by how he'd talked to her, I asked my mother how the foreman could treat his own people that way. "He is not your people." She seemed so angry at my question. She held up her wounded finger, a spot of red blood seeping through the white bandage. "The ones at work whose fingers look like this, they are your people."

I close my eyes, trying to conjure her, but it's Raisa I recall. She stood with me, on this corner I think, holding my hand after the memorial the union held for my mother. We had to press our backs against a building to keep out of the way of men pushing racks of shirts and dresses and coats across pedestrian traffic.

Those who streamed into these buildings before first light, those who sewed and trimmed and pressed, were immigrants who had fled shores of repression. Now there's a Starbucks in the downstairs of this building. And needles are stabbing other women's fingers as they sew, night and day, in sweatshops far from here.

"Raisa," I whisper. *"I'm not working in a factory anymore. There's no union. There're no strikes. I'm alone—just me and a few friends. Maybe I'll get separated from them soon, too. We have no power. You didn't live to see this. We're so small and they're so big."*

I remember how she'd lick her fingers and then smooth my hair with her hand as she'd ask me, again and again. "Who does all the work of the world everyday, tayere?"

"*We do.*"

"*Who built it all?*"

"*We did.*"

"*Who owns it all?*"

"*They do.*"

"*So that's what has to change.*" She smiles. "*Can you turn back the clock and make me a teenager?*"

"*What?*" I ask, *not understanding what she's talking about.*

"*Nothing goes back in time,* leybele. *Only forward.*"

"*What does that mean?*"

She shrugs, "*You are so big and they are so small, mayne tayere. It's time to take it over.*"

"*But how?*"

"*Ven ale mentshn zoln tseyn oyf eyn zayt—if everyone pulled in one direction. . . .*"

I already know what she's going to say: "*Volt zikh di velt ibergekern— the whole world would turn over.*"

But how?

Raisa won't give me a simple answer. She kneels down in front of me: "*Remember,* leybele, *the rich get richer and the poor get poorer. How long can that go on? Not forever,* mayne tayere. *Not forever.*"

How long? Vi lang?

She answers her own question. "*Until it becomes unbearable.*"

How long? Vi lang?

She takes my small hand in hers. "*When it comes, it comes fast. It all snaps forward like a rubber band. All of us who raised you, we are working for that day.*

"*Don't worry,* leybele, *just as you will awaken, our sleeping giant will wake to its power and rise.*"

* * *

"Are you okay, buddy?" Thor examines my face closely.

I turn slightly from his scrutiny, but rather than lie I just say, "I don't know."

Thor waits a moment and then quietly instructs me to lie facedown on the table, under the towel or the sheet, wearing whatever I want to keep on. He goes out of the room and leaves me alone.

I stand ill at ease in his bedroom, facing the table. I take off my clothing, one layer at a time, fold each piece, and place it in a neat little heap on a nearby chair. I get down to my briefs. I pull off my T-shirt, but leave my BVDs on. That feels kind of silly to me though, so I take them off, quickly. I put the sheet on top of my clothing on the chair and I scramble onto the table, lie face down, and cover myself as best as I can with the towel.

Thor graciously delays returning to the room, so I nervously reposition the towel before settling down, my face resting in a round pad, covered with a ring of clean tissue paper.

My breath is quick and shallow as Thor steps back into the room. He stands at the head of the table. Through the ring I can see his bare feet. "You comfortable?" he asks.

I readjust myself without answering.

Thor's feet disappear. I hear him pad back, rubbing his hands briskly, building up heat between his palms. And when he touches my shoulders, his hands slide across muscles that haven't been kneaded in such a long time. The oil is fragrant—essence of lavender.

This is Thor's gift to me.

At first I give in to the massage, and then, as he presses deeper into tissue, into neurons still reeling from the impact of trauma, an old memory comes up, hard as concrete against my face.

The fight in front of the bar. The pain of a sucker punch blinds me with my own blood. I see Shayna—the first love of my life—flailing at the circle of men around us. More of our friends come out from the bar, beer bottles wielded as weapons of self-defense, but they're trapped in the doorway by the skirmish. The police car pulls up. We're surrounded now. Then the guys with chains and bats melt away. The police are arresting Shayna. Others are being cuffed and dragged to the police cars. I already know they're going to drive us to a lawn in Central Park to carry out the sentence. I see an opening in the cordon around us and I run. I run away. I run away.

Thor has stopped massaging; he's stroking my hair, saying something to me, but I can't hear him.

"I never saw her again," I say out loud.

"Who?" he asks. "Who, buddy?"

I shake my head. Those are the only words inside me, and now they are out.

Thor's hands explore deep tissue. "This is the place to heal your wounds," Thor whispers. "Where a warrior comes after a battle. Let go of it now."

My tissue pushes back: I'm not a warrior. I don't deserve to heal.

Thor responds: "Hold on to the lessons, let go of the pain."

And, somehow, every nerve ending hears him and understands on some level. I'm hurtling through space at warp speed, the stars bending into streaks around me. The lesson seems so clear.

"If you don't fight the war, leybele," *Raisa whispers, "the war still comes to find you."*

27

I stumble out of one of Heshie's big metal pods, slightly dazed. Heshie is already under the sphere with a wrench. I pull my helmet off, careful not to disconnect the wires that run from it like arteries.

"You okay?" he calls up to me. He's on his back, working near a hydraulic line.

"Sure, it was a great ride. We done?"

"No, no." he says. "I've got to have this ready by next week. You'll do a little more, yes? I'm sorry, I know it's your night off."

"Sure," I agree. "Why not? It's fun."

Heshie looks up at me from his work. "You're a great test driver. Your focus is incredible."

I have no idea what he's talking about—after all, it's a game. But I'm flattered. And I am sleeping here. It's the least I can do after all he's done for me.

We're both startled by a loud buzzer. "That's the sandwiches," Heshie announces like a clairvoyant. "Can you get the door? There's money on my desk."

I grab the cash and open the series of bolts and locks on the metal door. A young delivery person, without looking directly at me, thrusts forward a cardboard box stuffed with sandwiches wrapped in butcher paper, pickles floating in their own brine in clear plastic bags, packets of mustard, and cans of warm cream soda wedged in between. I scrounge around in my pocket for a decent tip and nod in thanks, but the delivery person has already taken the tip with a lowered gaze and turned away.

"Hesh, you expecting company to come eat all this food?"

I watch him pull himself to his feet using the machines around him to help. "We may have to work all night. I have to feed you."

Heshie uses his arm to push aside some power tools and curled-up rolls of mechanical drawings, clearing off half a work table for us to eat. "What do you think of the changes I made in the speed of the game?"

"Great." I'm digging around in the box for napkins. "But the maneuverability in motion still lags."

"Sure, I know that." Heshie waves his hand. "But now you can turn full circle."

"The roll bars are good and the safety belts held tight. But maybe if you're planning any crash landings I need an airbag?"

Heshie rolls his eyes.

I lean forward, elbows on the table. "There's just one thing. I know this sounds crazy. But sometimes I can do things that trick the computer. Then later, I try the same thing, and it seems like the computer knows what I'm gonna do before I do it."

Heshie smiles. "That's the beauty of this program, Rabinowitz. It learns."

"What?" I sit back against the back of the chair. "That's not fair! The computer is smarter than me. And now you're telling me it's learning my patterns?"

"Yes," he says. "Exactly."

"But what's the incentive for me if the computer is always one step ahead of me?"

Heshie looks genuinely bemused, as if the answer is so elementary. "To grow, Rabinowitz. To develop. That's the incentive. Isn't that what you want? Otherwise it's just an arcade game."

Suddenly this game feels hard, like life. "Is that why you gave me AvaStar?"

Heshie chews and swallows. "I gave you that game because I don't want you to be lonely in life, Rabinowitz. It's a door I could open for you that leads to other people."

"Not enough doors, though. Only two to enter."

"So, you made your own way in the game. You found your way in, yes?"

"Yes, I guess." I smile wistfully, thinking of Femmeangel rocking high above the treetops.

"Before my mama died," Heshie sighs, looking at his sandwich as though it is an unfamiliar object, "the last thing she said to me was, 'I don't want that you should ever be lonely.' "

"Rivka loved you, Hesh. So did your father."

"Ach." Heshie puts his sandwich down. "In his way." He takes off his glasses and squeezes his eyes shut with his fingertips. "It still pains me that I couldn't say *Kaddish* for him."

Heshie polishes his bifocals with the edge of his Linux penguin T-shirt and places them back securely on his nose. He examines his sandwich closely, picks it up, and resumes his meal.

We eat in silence. I look around the loft at the machines that resemble half-split dinosaur eggs and metal chrysalides.

Heshie says quietly: "Why not two flags?"

"What?"

He repeats his question slowly. "On your wall in your office at home. Why not two flags together? Why just the Palestinian flag?"

"Oh, Heshie," I put down my sandwich. "Again with this? We've been arguing about this our whole lives. You know why I wouldn't put an Israeli flag on my wall. It's the Zionist flag. It's a colonial flag: a Jewish state from the river to the sea."

Heshie's smile is fragile. "At least we talk to each other about it. Our parents didn't. I just don't understand why there can't be two states that live in peace."

"Yes, you do, Hesh. You just can't deal with the solution yet, that's all. You're not a Zionist. We couldn't be friends if you were."

Raisa's voice, from long ago: "If we don't stand up and speak out, they will carry out this terrible crime in all our names."

"Don't you ever want to feel at home someplace on this planet?" he asks quietly.

"Heshie, I was born in the Bronx! How can I go pick the olives when the people who planted the trees can't go home?"

"There's enough room for Arabs and Jews," he argues.

"There'll be enough room in Palestine, Hesh. The Jews who fought apartheid in South Africa still live there; they're respected."

"I'm just afraid," he says. "Afraid without a homeland the anti-Semitism will just get worse."

"Heshie." I lean across the table, stomach acid burning my tongue. "How can it be worse than seeing what the soldiers and tanks and fighter jets are doing under the Star of David? You think Bush and Nixon and Reagan give a damn about Jewish lives? They want us to do their dirty work for them, Heshie. They don't care how much hatred it whips up against Jews." My stomach feels clenched and sour. "I won't fight for their empire, no matter what flag the occupation flies."

Heshie sighs and shakes his head. "You think there's ever gonna be peace?"

"Yes," I tell him, settling back and calming down. "I do. How can it stay this way?"

Heshie carefully wraps up the last bite of his sandwich. "Anyway, the reason I asked is," his voice trails off.

"Is what?" I hear suspicion in my tone.

"I got an e-mail from a friend of mine in Israel, after they killed Rachel Corrie. He was in the military, but he's going to jail soon—he's a refusenik. He wrote to me: 'When does a Jewish life not matter so much in Israel? When we defend a Palestinian.' "

I open my mouth to speak, but he holds me off with one hand. His other hand covers his face. I don't remember ever seeing Heshie cry before.

"I'm sorry," he says. "I can't talk about this right now." His chin is trembling. "Are you ready to finish the tests?"

"Yeah, sure," I say, but now I'm exhausted and really ready for sleep.

I roll over on the creaking cot in the back corner of the factory. The sound of Heshie's dot-matrix printer pulls me out of sleep, droning and chirring and clacking endlessly.

I think I've been snoring, but Heshie couldn't possibly hear me over the noise in the loft. He was thoughtful enough to put up a wicker screen around the corner of the factory in which I'm sleeping. My clothes are stacked on an overturned cardboard carton and my books are still packed in boxes.

I sit up, stretch, and stand up slowly. I change into clean underwear, a pair of beat-up jeans, and a sweatshirt that doesn't smell too bad. I have to get an apartment soon. I've been working so hard in my free time on preparations for the rally this weekend that I haven't been apartment hunting.

I need some privacy. I want a place to go where I can paint what I'm feeling on the walls. I want a computer so I can go look for Femmeangel and apologize.

I stagger out into the loft in bare feet, toothbrush and toothpaste in hand. "Rabinowitz," Heshie says without looking up from his monitor—he's absorbed in something. "I'm glad you're up. I've got something to show you."

"Can I pee and brush my teeth first?"

"Yeah, sure." He seems disappointed but resigned to waiting.

When I come back, I feel a little more human, but not ready for company—not ready to be company.

"You want a bagel?" He points to a plate on the work table, which is strewn with papers. I have no idea if the flat silver moon outside the dirty factory window is rising or setting.

"Thor called here looking for you earlier," Heshie recalls. "He wanted to know if you were okay. Are you okay?"

"Yeah, sure," I say, spreading a shmear of cream cheese on half of a stale raisin bagel.

"What kind of name is that, anyway?" Heshie asks.

"What?" I frown.

"Thor? That's a name?"

I'm not in the mood. "You think that's a funny name?"

"Sure," he says, with half a smile. "Don't you?"

"You think Moishe is a funny name? Or Shlomo?"

"I'm not saying it's funny. I'm just saying your friends have strange names. They sound like they should be comic-book characters."

That makes me angry, and he sees it. I can tell he didn't mean to make me mad, he's just being testy. But it's too late. "Don't talk like that about them, Hesh."

"I know," he waves me away, "they're your friends."

I'm adamant. "They're more than friends. More than family. They're warriors, Heshie. They're fighting to change the way things are. We're doing it together."

He does a double take. "Since when are your people Scandinavian gods? A name should sound like a name, that's all. Like a real life, not like a myth."

My mood shifts again. Now I just feel far away from Heshie. "Don't make fun of their names. They chose them because they fit their lives, Hesh, just like you did."

He studies a poppy bagel, up real close. Without looking up, he says something I never recall having heard him say to me: "I'm sorry." He takes a deep breath. "I didn't mean anything by it. It's just," he leans back, turning the bagel in his hand like the discovery of the wheel, "I want to mean that much to you."

"Heshie, you've been a friend to me my whole life!"

Heshie pushes his plate with the half-eaten bagel aside. "Am I your people?"

I look at his hands. There's a spot of blood seeping through the Band-Aid on his index finger. I think about the hands of my mother and the women she worked with. He lets me look into the depths of his eyes, and I see a good and decent human being. "Yes, Heshie." I lean forward toward him. "Of course you are. And thank you for this home when I need it."

He glances around at the brightly lit factory. "Not much of a home, is it?"

I look around at the same scene. "It's been a haven."

"Solace in a storm." He laughs sadly. "You're leaving soon, aren't you." It's a statement, not a question.

"Yes," I say. "After the rally this weekend. Are you coming to the protest?"

"To march around in the street?" He makes a face. "Find me some activism where I don't have to run around catching up with you all, then call me."

"I'm sorry," even my voice sounds embarrassed. "I didn't think about that."

He chews in silence.

"I'll look for a place in Jersey City," I say out loud.

He nods. "It's been nice to have you here. You were good company."

"I'm not dying, Hesh. I'm moving."

"I know. I know. You need to find your home."

"I need an apartment."

"You need a home."

"Yeah," I mutter. "We all do." I stare at the little piece of bagel left in my hand, grateful for this bread. "Don't you think it's strange that fishes and eels and all kinds of critters can travel halfway around the world and find the exact place that's home, and I can't even figure out what that means?"

Heshie says. "*Mishpokhe.*"

"Family." I turn the word over in my mouth. "Chosen family, maybe. You are my family, Hesh."

He wants to hear that, but he can't listen. His hand flutters in front of his face like he's shooing away a fly. "Maybe you just need to find your niche, like I did here. That's what organisms do. Maybe that's what home is—just a niche."

"I don't know," I look around at Heshie's world of mechanical animals. "I don't think organisms find ready-made niches. I think they also have to work to develop them."

Heshie nods his head, very solemnly. "Organisms aren't just the object of evolution, they're the subject of evolution." He is drawing designs on the side of a cardboard coffee container with his pen. He looks up. "You see? I'm gonna miss you, Rabinowitz," he says with finality. "And now, I've got a present for you."

"No," I say with irrevocability. "No more presents!"

"This is a different kind of present." He smiles off at a corner of his loft. "This is an experience I want to share with you. You'll be the first."

I need coffee first, but the pot is empty, frying on the glowing coils of the nearby hot plate. I turn it off. I realize I haven't had a cigarette since the break-in. I don't actually want to smoke, but the idea gnaws at my innards.

"Come with me," Heshie rises, grabbing only one cane. "I want to show you."

He leads me to a part of the loft that's closed off by boxes of parts and supplies, stacked high as a wall. "Look," he says, as though a revelation is at hand.

All I see in the dim corner are giant silver rings of metal, crisscrossed with cables and belts. At the center is a kind of pod, a soft shell. "It looks like a gyroscope."

"Climb up," he urges me. "Get in."

I look around. "Get in where?"

"Into the harness." He hurries me with his hands. Heshie turns and boots up the computer. His creation whirs and purrs with life. The rays from blue lights, spaced out around the diameter of the steel circles, crisscross my body as I climb up the contraption.

"Stand on the platform, that's right," his voice is alarmingly urgent. "Like that. Cinch yourself in—snug, not too tight."

I am standing on a metal platform, patterned with light, corseted in a girth of leather.

"Now put on the safety straps, the white ones, there. They buckle like a seat belt, you see?"

I am more and more enmeshed in this machine.

Heshie takes a helmet, connected to ropes of cables, and hands it to me. He stretches up. I bend over as far as I can within my constraints and grasp it.

"Now put on the helmet," he directs me. "You see there's a chin strap? You have to fasten that. Good. Now step into the ankle belts and tighten them up. Now you see those sleeves hanging there? Connected to those belts? Slip your arms in there."

I can't see now. I feel like his science project. Like he's Dr. Frankenstein waiting for a bolt of lightning to power up this mechanism. Heshie clickety-clacks on his keyboard. "Now don't be afraid," he advises me.

Instantly, I am. "What do you mean?" Even as I speak, the cables begin to pull my arms and I lurch a little as the cables attached to the ankle sleeves pull taut.

"Don't worry, the machine is going to pull the sleeves and the ankles tight, but cables have elasticity."

"This is a lot of work for S&M, Hesh."

"Funny," he says dryly.

"I don't know, Hesh. The last time a Jewish revolutionary was in this position, it didn't turn out so well."

He doesn't make a sound. I think I've hurt his feelings. But this is too weird.

A light flashes in front of my eyes, flickering to life like an old tube television screen. Pixels scramble into place. I am standing on a snowy mountain top. The world is spread out beneath me, blues and browns, far below. My wings are outspread at my sides, feathers as silver as mercury. Wind is blustering in my face.

"Wow!" I say out loud.

"Cool, huh?" There's an "I told you so" in his tone. "Are you ready?"

"Ready for what?"

"To fly, Rabinowitz. You think I got you up on that mountaintop just for the view?"

Awe in my voice. "This is your dream, Heshie! You made it come true!"

"What?" He sounds momentarily confused. "This isn't my dream.

This is my father's dream. I couldn't say *Kaddish* for him. So this is what I'm doing for him. Are you ready?" he asks again.

"How do I fly?"

His ironic tone is as sour as a pickle. "I'm sure you can figure it out."

"I don't know. This is a little scary. I am very high up here, Hesh."

The last words I hear Heshie say to me are gentle: "Just lean forward, Rabinowitz. Trust me. Just lean forward into the wind."

And I do. I do.

We're surrounded by the police in a little vest pocket park in Sheridan Square. On every corner, I see people trying to cross the streets to get to the protest, but the cops have penned us off with metal barricades and won't let anyone through.

"Dammit to hell." Ruby snaps shut Thor's cell phone. "There's hundreds of young ones on the piers and the cops won't let them march to hook up with us. We got to get a chant going. We got to hold this together. Get the spirit up. In fact," she looks at the crowds on the nearby corners, "if we could get everybody chanting the same thing at the same time, that'd put the fear of the bejeezus into these cops. Make 'em think twice."

I'm being pushed further to the curb by the crowd in this little park. I'm nose to nose with police. I see how many plastic handcuffs are looped in their belts.

I don't recognize most of the people at this protest—there's a few Asian and Black trans women I know from the clubs, and some drag kings. It's the faces of the people whose photos are on the posters that look so familiar: Sakia Gunn. Shani Baraka. Rayshon Holmes. Gwen Araujo. Rita Hester. Tyra Hunter. Amanda Milan. Venus Xtravaganza. Matthew Shepard. Brandon Teena.

Fallen warriors are with us here, carried on our shields into the battle for the living. The hair rises on my forearms. Everywhere I look I see

Netaji's face on placards we made at the Fightback Network that demand: "Stop the racist roundups!"

I hear Ruby on the bullhorn: "One, two, three, four—we don't want your racist war! Five, six, seven, eight—stop the violence, stop the hate!"

The moment her words become amplified, a phalanx of cops moves toward her, roughly pushing their way through the crowd. Ruby passes off the bullhorn and ducks down, disappearing. The cops, standing where Ruby stood a moment ago, appear perplexed. Ruby reappears on top of a park bench, raising her voice above the cheer that greets her from all the nearby corners. "We made our own history, right here at Stonewall. We didn't need a permit to riot here in nineteen sixty-nine did we?"

"No!" The roar reverberates.

The cops are trying to shove their way into the park, but the crowd is densest there and disinclined to yield.

Ruby climbs up the wrought-iron fence to be heard. "We got a right to march in the streets and that's what we're going to do. Whose streets?"

"Our streets!" we all thunder back.

She vanishes again. The cops are visibly angry and restive. Orders pass down their lines, from mouth to mouth. Helmet visors snap down into place. Fists clench around nightsticks.

I feel the subway rumbling under the concrete sidewalk beneath my feet. Moments later, more people emerge from the subway entrance—a little delta across the street—but they are trapped on that concrete island across from ours. I see Estelle with people I recognize from Vickie's memorial—Jorge and Moishe—carrying placards with side-by-side photos of Vic and Vickie. Estelle and I wave at each other, separated by the cordon of police between us.

Deacon tugs on my sleeve. "We need to put our heads together." He points to a spot on the curb facing the Christopher Street entrance to the park. We work our way around people packed together almost too tightly to yield. I can see Jasmine and Ruby and Thor waving their arms to get our attention.

Thor is looking around, assessing the situation. "We need more people who know tactics. We don't have any communications network set up. We don't have people trained to do security."

We just look at Thor. We already know that. We are victims of our own success. We never expected so many people to turn out.

Ruby and Jasmine talk fast, rapid-fire, finishing each other's sentences.

"Ruby's got an idea."

"It's Jasmine's really."

"The cops are just going to wait for the support around us to dwindle."

"Then they'll move in on us anyway."

"So we try to break out of this isolation now."

"While we've got all this support."

"We could try to march."

"Try to link up."

"From there." They both point in unison at the tip of the triangular park that points like an arrowhead west toward the piers.

"The young ones are there."

"For Takeesha's memorial."

"We try to hook up with them."

"It's legal to march on the sidewalk."

"The four of us get on a lead banner."

"Not you, Thor. You already got enough police trouble."

"We try to lead this group across the street."

"Maybe we can pick up all these other people around us if we stay on the sidewalk."

"If we get big enough, we can take the street."

They both pause, for a moment. We all take one deep breath. Wordlessly, we each grab an edge of a hand-stenciled banner that reads: "Stop the war at home and abroad" and slowly work our way along the edge of the crowd, walking the curb like a tightrope, to the western tip of the park.

Some of the police move with us, following our path, grouping in front of us when we stop.

The bullhorn magically appears in Ruby's hand. "It's legal to cross the street, right people?"

Everyone grows quiet.

"The police got us all fenced in here. And they got you all fenced in over there and over there. They don't want us to get together. But we know you want to get with us. And you know we want to get with you. So people, here's what we're gonna do. We're gonna wait for the light to change from red to green, and we're gonna walk across this street, all nice and orderly and such, and we're gonna walk down that sidewalk over there to the piers.

"Who wants to come with us to the piers?"

Cheers greet us from every direction, even from corners filled with what I thought were just onlookers.

"Say: Whose streets?" Ruby shouts.

"Our streets!"

The cops are conferring, bent toward each other. Cops on motor scooters line up in front of us.

The light changes to green, but we're not going anywhere, not yet.

A cool wind gusts, autumn in its scent.

A few feet away from me, Thor is standing on a fire hydrant, pointing in the same direction. "Look!" He's agitated.

"What is it, Thor?" I shout over the crowd noise. "What do you see?"

"Weasel," he yells. "Weasel, no!"

I lean forward in time to see that hateful Weasel, a few feet away from us in the crowd, drop a burning pack of matches into a trash can filled with garbage. For a moment, nothing happens. But when the paper ignites and the flames blaze, the police charge forward, as if on cue.

"Thor! Get down!" I shout.

Thor climbs down quickly. "Link arms!" he shouts up and down to those who can hear him. "Don't let the cops through. Link arms!"

But before we can interlock arms, a cop who looks like Darth Vader collars Thor and drags him into the street.

"Let him go!" I start the chant.

Others who see what's happening pick up the demand "Let him go!" while hundreds behind us are still chanting, "Whose streets? Our streets!"

"Let him go!" Our voices rise with greater urgency and anger, and the crowd surges forward toward the police. A higher-ranking cop in dress uniform whispers to Darth Vader, who loosens his grip on Thor. I lean forward and pull Thor back behind our ranks and we all link arms. We cheer our own small victory.

"Thanks, buddy," Thor pats my shoulder.

"Now or never!" Ruby commands.

"Let's go!" Jasmine concurs.

The traffic light has changed from red to green.

"Whose streets?" Ruby asks the crowd, letting the police hear how many voices are raised along with ours. We move slowly as a group, off the curb, onto the asphalt. The police, like a blue sea, part to let us pass. I crane my head back to see if anyone is behind us—everyone from the park is lined up behind us.

Slowly we move across the street, and at every corner people strain against their barricades, wanting to join us. I see that some are melting away, hurrying west down the sidewalks to join up with us down the street.

As we approach the opposite corner, we are facing old-style wooden police barricades. We are stuck in the street.

"Dammit to hell," Ruby cusses again. "They're gonna say we're in the street."

Jasmine urges us all, "Reach out to the people on the other side of the barricades."

"What?" I ask.

She reaches her hand over the barricade and a hand from that side reaches out to grab it. "Hold hands across the barricades!" she shouts out, holding up already linked hands. Many hands extend in search of ours.

The police push roughly in between the two groups and begin disassembling the wooden barriers, throwing them noisily along the curb. With a cheer and lots of hugs, our group links up with those who have been trapped in a pocket on the northwest corner.

There's no room on the sidewalk for all of us. Deacon shouts out: "Keep movin', sisters and brothers, keep on movin' to the piers."

Slowly the motion on the sidewalk begins westward. Our little group on the banner is not at the front of it anymore. Now we're in the middle of a slow-moving mass. People on the other sidewalk are also moving west toward the piers.

Thor catches up to our banner. He opens his mouth to speak. But over his head, across the street I see Def, who has shinnied up a lamppost. Def is signaling frantically.

I hear motorcycle engines rev, throttles open, before I see them coming up over the curb. The police steer their motorcycles into the crowd, knocking people down, forcing us off the sidewalk. And the moment Thor and my feet hit the asphalt, the cops grab us.

People try to crowd around the police, but the cops push them back.

"You're mine!" Darth Vader says to Thor as he cinches his wrists.

I feel my arms pulled roughly behind me and the slice of plastic cuffs into my skin. The cops are pulling Thor and me toward a different police wagon, parked nearby. Could the crowd break through and free us? I'm scared they won't. I'm scared.

Thor tries to duck as he's pushed into the van and stumbles onto the floor. I try not to step on him as I get propelled in behind him. The door of the vehicle slams behind us, muting the sounds of the protest. "Let them go! Let them go!" We can hear the chant, but they're too far away to help us.

"Oh, shit," I say.

"Listen." Thor lifts his head. "Listen!"

I can hear a new chant: "Stop the bashings, stop the roundups! Bring the troops home now!"

"That's the Fightback contingent. They're here!" he says.

"You think they can get us out of here?" I ask, hopefully.

Thor just looks at me, blankly.

The door opens again. This time it's Jasmine who's pushed into the van. She settles on the bench across from us. "Well, we got out of the park," she laughs, without mirth.

Thor says sardonically, "Let's see if Weasel gets arrested tonight." He shakes his head from side to side. "We should have invited more groups to work with us, people who could've helped us with security. We need to organize this differently next time."

"Whose streets?" We hear a great cheer go up nearby. And then the sound of the boisterous response—"Our streets!"—begins to recede.

Jasmine smiles. "They're marching!"

"Wouldn't you think that after decades of going to demonstrations," I sigh, "I would have learned not to drink coffee beforehand?" I rub my wrists—the red welt imprints of the cuffs still visible—and look around at the cell. The police have converted this little cell into a multigender "Queer tank," isolating us from others arrested at the protest.

Jasmine laughs a little. By now we all have to pee. But there's no toilet. We've already been informed by the male cops who put us in here that if we want a toilet they'll take us out one at a time to use one, supervised, in an open cell. Who knows what would happen then. So I'm trying to ignore my aching bladder.

Somehow the cops didn't find Thor's phone when they patted him down. Now he's under the bench we're sitting on, trying to contact people at the demo to let them know where we are and to find out what happened on the march.

"Gives new meaning to the term 'cell phone,' doesn't it," I say to Jasmine. She smiles wearily and leans her head against the wall.

Thor rolls out from under the bench, whispering excitedly, "Ginger and Estelle say there are hundreds of people waiting for us outside here. And Jorge and the Fightback Network put out a call for more."

Thor thrusts the phone at me. I lift it to my ear, like a conch shell, and hear the ocean's roar: "We want them out without a scratch. Let them go now!"

Ginger's voice shouts over the others. "Do you like it? That's my chant! Hang on. Miriam—the lawyer—she wants to talk to you."

I recognize Miriam's voice. But now it sounds different to me—warmer. Miriam is my lawyer now.

"The cops are anxious to get rid of you all," she shouts into the phone. "There're so many people across the street out front. And the media's taken some notice, too. But Max, you have a particular problem. You didn't have any form of identification when they booked you. So we have to wait for your roommate Heshie to bring down your ID."

There's information in that last statement that doesn't make sense to me. "What ID?"

Miriam speaks very slowly and loudly, articulating each word carefully: "I said, your roommate has offered to bring down your identification papers, okay?"

If Heshie's that good a counterfeiter, I hope he prints up some bail money for me, too.

Miriam reads my worries. It must come with the job. "Let everyone in there know that the offer of bail has already been made."

"Who?" I interrupt.

"Some of the folks at the Immigrant Workers' Alliance and the People's Fightback Network put out a call for funds. But I think at this point the cops just want you all out of their hair. They're willing to let you walk out of here with a court date down the road if somebody will show them some ID. By now they'd probably be satisfied with your library card." She chortles.

"Max?" Miriam raises her voice. "Can you still hear me?"

I cup my hand over the mouthpiece, trying to be heard by Miriam, not the jail guards. "Yes."

"We're going to get you all out of there. Don't worry. We're not leaving till each one of you is out the door, safe and sound. I know it's hard to remember that, but listen to this crowd behind me."

I press the phone to my ear, but a little series of beeps declares the death of the battery.

"Oh, no," we groan in unison, as I hand the now-dead contraband back to Thor.

Jasmine and Thor lean forward to hear any news. "She says they aren't leaving till they get all of us out. She said don't worry. And that folks have offered to put up our bail but she doesn't think we'll need it."

Our spirits are visibly buoyed, but each of us chews over the information in silence.

Two familiar faces appear in front of the bars of our cell. "Hey, children!" Ruby sounds chipper. "I just dropped in to see if y'all need anything."

Her hands are cuffed behind her back. Deacon is standing next to her, also cuffed, standing ramrod-straight and tall.

A cop pulls out his knife, cuts the plastic binding their wrists. "In you go," he says.

We applaud them as they enter the cell. "What happened?" We are hungry for every detail.

Ruby is still bubbling with excitement. "Well, after y'all got busted we kept the march goin'. Y'all know that, right?"

We're eager for more.

"Well the word got down to the piers that we were comin' down, so the young ones at the piers marched up to meet us. By that time there were people everyplace—sidewalks, streets, comin' this way, goin' that way. And the traffic got all messed up. The cops were losin' it. All of a sudden, we hear something up ahead of us and we look up and there they are, we can see 'em. We made it to each other.

"Here they come, down Christopher Street toward us, all these young ones, a lot of them from Newark—AGs and femmes. Some of 'em were like thirteen, fourteen years old. I'm tellin' you, they were hundreds strong."

The smile grows on Ruby's face. "You should'a seen the cops when they saw all those powerful young ones marchin' down the street so determined—it threw the police for a loop. They pulled back a little. Who knows? Maybe they didn't want another Stonewall on their hands.

"And once we joined up, we were big. I mean big."

We all lean forward. "Then what?"

Ruby looks at Deacon and sighs. "Then we got snatched up."

Deacon smiles sadly. "The cops were lookin' for Miz Ruby all blessed day."

"But that was hours ago, wasn't it?" Jasmine looks at her watch.

Deacon shakes his head. "Lord, Lord. They had us in a city bus, parked for a long, long time."

"Just the two of you?" I ask.

"No," Ruby shakes her head. "They took a few others that they arrested and put 'em in other cells."

Thor is listening, but he's leaning against the cell bars, alone. I'm afraid he's reliving his last arrest. "Hey, Thor," I call out to him. "Call us in sick to work tonight, okay?"

He smiles, wanly.

Deacon sits down next to me.

I look around at the cell. People have scratched little messages into the dirty walls: "Help me." "Giuliani is a fascist." "No justice, no peace."

"Well," Ruby picks up the tempo. "What should we organize next? What's next on the agenda?"

It's not funny, but we all break into laughter. It's a relief to laugh.

Thor frowns in concentration. "Maybe we should have had a leaflet ready at the march for the next action to build for a bigger protest."

Jasmine assures him. "We can use our court dates to organize some publicity and build another event."

Ruby laughs. "I'll tell you one thing. We sure as hell are gonna need a fund-raiser for all the legal fees!"

"A drag show!" I suggest.

Everyone perks up a bit at the suggestion. I embellish: "Maybe it could be the old generation of drag queens and kings together with the new generation. Ruby, maybe you and I could even brush up our old act together."

Ruby's hands go right to her hips. "Who you callin' old?"

"I think it's a great idea," Jasmine says. "But not just drag kings and queens. All the trannie performers we know, all together on one stage."

"Live music!" Deacon adds, emphatically.

Jasmine raises her index finger. "You all know about this new show they're trying to open at one of the downtown clubs? The 'Rice Bowl'?" She glowers. "They've putting together a show with white men performing as Asian women. They put out these palm cards with the most racist image you can imagine." She leans back. "We're meeting to form a coalition to stop them. It would be great if we could get some support."

"Sure," we all confer with a glance and agree.

"We might have to meet right here," I say. Nobody laughs.

Thor interjects, "I'm speaking at the antiwar rally coming up in D.C. Can we get a Queer contingent together? Like a 'Spirit of Stonewall' kind of thing?"

Ruby nods. "I like that. Get me out of here and give me a phone and some leaflets. I know plenty of folks who'll want to be there. We got to get that '60s liberation spirit up again. We've got to be wherever people are struggling."

I say more softly, "What about a union? Has anybody ever thought about us organizing night-shift workers at the clubs? Maybe we could get some health care benefits?"

Jasmine leans her head back against the wall. "Well, that's a tall order. We could talk about it. We could at least organize a 'sick-out' around some demands."

The little uptick in our collective mood descends into silence.

I close my eyes, trying to conjure up Raisa—what a comfort if she would appear to me here. But when I open my eyes, I see two cops standing at the door of the cell with a roster. "Ronald Jackson." They unlock the cell door.

Deacon stands up, slowly, and faces them.

I stand behind him, my hand on his shoulder, as others hug him. I whisper to him, "You told me to try to get over my fear of this place. To try to see it as just a building."

He nods, almost imperceptibly. "Well sir," he says, over his shoulder, "someone taught me that many years ago—that you can't change the world if you're scared to go to jail. Now it's my time to walk my talk."

"Step out of the cell," one of the cops commands. When Deacon does, they chain his hands behind his backs. No plastic now.

"Where are they taking him?" I ask out loud, as though anyone else in this cell knows more than I do.

Jasmine and I sit back down, a little more heavily. Ruby is gripping the bars, straining to look down the corridor. Thor is pacing, lost in thought.

Jasmine rolls her head close to mine. "Can I ask you something?" she asks in a low voice, out of the blue.

"Sure."

She stops and thinks. "I don't know if it's right to ask you this. Never mind." Jasmine at a loss for words? What does she want to ask me? "It's just that, I was wondering." Her pauses are maddening. "Do you know if Ruby, well, if she only dates guys?"

I struggle to keep the same expression on my face that was there a moment ago. My whole body aches like I'm coming down with the flu. I wish it was me she was yearning to be close to, longing to know better.

I chew my lip, the only betrayal of my feelings, but try to pass it off as concentration. "Well." I speak slowly. "I'm not sure if Ruby has a single either-or in her life. But, of course, you'd have to talk to her."

My words actually seem to please Jasmine.

"Tuh-su-ee," a cop at the cell door is sounding out a name.

Jasmine stands up, quickly, and presses her lips together. Ruby opens her arms and hugs Jasmine, long and hard, rocking back and forth. My heart actually hurts, even though all I want for either of them is joy.

Thor wraps his arms around Jasmine.

One of the cops pulls Jasmine away, chains her hands, and roughly drags her away.

Thor and I stay at the cell door. He leans against the bars. "I've gotta call my sponsor as soon as I get out of here." He sounds agitated. "I've got to get to a meeting. A lot of meetings."

I lean against him. "Maybe I'll go to one with you."

Thor looks at me, surprised delight.

"I'm scared," I whisper.

He closes his eyes and rests his face against the cold steel. "This is just the beginning of a new movement. A new era of struggle," he says. "Just the beginning."

As two different cops walk down the corridor toward us, we back away from the bars.

"Finster," a cop reads the name. "Carol Finster."

Thor takes a long, deep breath and turns to face Ruby and me. Ruby and I reach out for him, but he lifts his arms to ward us off.

As the cop cuffs his wrists, Ruby calls out to him, "What's next, Thor?"

He lifts his head high as they pull him out of the cell: "Seize the day— we're gonna give those words new meaning!"

Ruby and I sit on the bench farthest away from the bars. She slides close to me and we hold each other's hands.

"There's a lot of people waiting out there for us." She tries to strengthen us both. "We just gotta hang on. Lord knows a lot of folks had to go through this. Stay strong now, sugar, you hear? Keep your pride in here," she pats my heart.

"Lanier," I hear a voice say loudly. "Tyrone Lanier."

I close my eyes and squeeze Ruby's hands tightly to hold back my tears. I won't let the cops see me cry.

"It'll be okay," she whispers. "You'll see. They can't stop the struggle." Ruby stands up and smoothes her wrinkled clothing.

"C'mon," one cop says. "We ain't got all day."

I move toward Ruby as the cops handcuff her, but the other cop holds me back with his outstretched club. I can hear one of the cops whisper in her ear, "C'mon, sweetie."

I shout out, "You too, Ruby! Stay strong! Stay proud!"

"Don't I always?" she yells back before I hear the sound of metal clanging on metal.

I grip the bars with both hands and pull hard on them as though I could bend them.

"This is just the beginning," I hear Thor whisper.

I sit down on the bench and fold my arms across my body.

"They can't stop the struggle," Ruby says.

I close my eyes.

I see myself walking through the tunnel of this jail out into the light of day. Miriam will be at my side. I'll blink in the sunshine like a mole, my breath sour, my clothes sweaty. Voices shouting, "We want Max out without a scratch! Let! Max! Go!"

My friends, their faces flush with relief and caring, bound up the steps toward me—Ruby, Thor, Jasmine, Deacon. Their arms tangle around me in a group hug; their energy surges through my body.

At the base of the steps, a photographer shouts, "Let's get a photo!"

"Look at the camera!" the photographer urges us. But I can't. I'm seeing the faces of people I love in the crowd. Estelle and Ginger with their arms wrapped tightly around each other's waists. Moishe squeezing Estelle's hand.

Jorge pumping his fist in the air, nodding toward me, leading many voices to raise up this truth: "Obreros unidos jamás serán vencidos!"

Nearby, Heshie is leaning on the barricade, waving shyly. His silver cane glints in the sun as though he's leaning on a beam of light.

Def and John D. Arc stand facing me, holding hands. John slowly takes off his fedora and bows to me. Def places hir fingertips over hir heart, draws hir fingers back, and with a gentle toss sends the precious gift to me.

As I look at them, each one, they are so beautiful and so strong they seem larger than life to me. But they're not. They are real people. Flawed, like me. No heroic proportions. Just human. Who knows? Maybe this is what legends are made of—real lives lifted up in retrospect to mythic proportions.

"All right, look here," the photographer appeals. "That's it."

"No wait!" I call out. I reach out for placards with the faces of Netaji and Hatem. I hoist the photo of Hatem; Ruby holds the placard with Netaji's photo against her body.

The photographer's frustration is apparent and audible. "All right people, let's take this picture, shall we?"

We raise our fists and the lens captures us in the light of this moment.

As the photographer puts the camera down, I see her face—it's Vickie. With us still. I look around for Raisa but I don't see her anywhere. Instead, I hear my mother's voice, singing in my ear: "Es togt shoyn, vakht oyf—It's daybreak, awake, open your eyes, and see your own strength!"

I open my eyes. I have slept for many years. I am awake now.

Like a starling murmuring before daybreak, I have made the snippets of a lifetime of songs my own. I hear footsteps in the hallway grow closer. The cell door swings open. "Rah-been-oh-witz." The cops sound out my name, mocking me.

"Maxine Rabinowitz."

About the Author

Leslie Feinberg is a managing editor of *Workers World* newspaper and a political journalist whose weekly articles can be read at www.workers.org. *Ze* is a steering committee member of the national LGBT Caucus of the National Writers Union/UAW; a member of Pride at Work, AFL-CIO; an associate member of the Steelworkers Union; a founder of Rainbow Flags for Mumia; and a national organizer for the International Action Center. Feinberg's homepage in cyberspace is www.transgenderwarrior.org.